WELLSPRING OF EVIL

Stacy — More tall tales & crazy characters — hope you enjoy!

2/29/20

Copyright © 2019 by Todd Parnell

All rights reserved. No part of this book may be used or reproduced in any manner, including electronic storage and retrieval systems, except by explicit written permission from the publisher. Brief passages excerpted for review purposes are excepted.

This novel is a work of fiction. Names, characters, places, and incidents are either the product of the author's imagination or are used fictitiously.

ISBN: 978-1-68313-203-5
LCCN: 2018961297

First Edition
Printed and bound in the USA

Pen-L Publishing
Fayetteville, Arkansas
www.Pen-L.com

Cover and interior design by Kelsey Rice

WELLSPRING OF EVIL

— The Children of the Creek Series —
Book One

by Todd Parnell

Books by Todd Parnell:

The Ozarkian Folk Tales Trilogy
Skunk Creek
Swine Branch
Donny Brook

The Buffalo, Ben, and Me
Mom at War
Postcards from Branson

DEDICATION

This second trilogy of Ozarkian folk tales is also dedicated to my wife, Betty P.

You see, it was she who challenged me to write fiction. When I asked how, she advised ". . . start with something you know and understand— the Ozarks, small towns, creeks and rivers, float trips, make it a mystery, then add a little violence, corruption, sex, humor, exaggeration, and even a hint of the supernatural . . . and let it rip." I am grateful for her recipe and can only hope that this celebration of life amidst chaos and confusion entertains as well as frames a fictional village and its colorful citizens as heroic, resilient, and deeply rooted. It has been fun to try!

Todd Parnell
SUMMER, 2017

AUTHOR'S NOTE

A spring is a ring in nature's nose.

I began writing this second trilogy of Ozarkian folk tales before the dust had settled on the last draft of the first one. The sense of continuity that is the history of the Ozarks filled my head and heart with new characters and tall tales to relate to contemporary issues and challenges in that rich and colorful context.

The Children of the Creek series is set in the Ozarks, that vague notion of geography and culture tucked into southwest Missouri and northwest Arkansas. I was privileged to grow up here and I treasure the history, the beauty, the humor, the toughness, the kindness, the independence, the gentleness, the lore and the legend, the bonds that bind us.

Wellspring of Evil, the first book of Children of the Creek, again features the village of Hardlyville as hero, beautiful Skunk Creek as backdrop, and a large support cast of "next generation" Hardlyvillains facing grave natural, unnatural, and environmental threats to their way of life. It is a mystery grounded in Ozarks waters, culture, and history, and set in tragedy, love, lust, and resilience. Crafted in the long tradition of Ozarks storytelling, *Wellspring of Evil* is bawdy, irascible, and irreverent, and extends its reach far beyond city limits to centers of government, distant foreign cultures, and ancient roots of terror and evil.

I was raised in a giving and extended family and community, short of perfection, but long on love. Characters and locales featured within are fictional, but grounded in the imagination and tall tales of my youth. At the same time, jabs at prevailing political and moral hypocrisies play out every bit as well alongside a beautiful Ozark stream as in a teeming metropolis. Earthy and ribald moments are meant to soften body blows and bring a chuckle, not to offend. Beyond all, I smile at my homeland, its rugged elegance, its many special characters both real and imagined, fond memories, and huge hopes.

LIST OF PLACES AND CHARACTERS

Hardlyville — Fictional Town
Hardlyvillains — Residents of Hardlyville
Skunk Creek — Fictional Creek

— HISTORICAL CHARACTERS —

Thomas and Petunia Hardly — Hardlyville founders
Octavia Rosebeam — Granddaughter of founders

— INSTITUTIONS —

The Daily Hellbender
Skunk Creek Church of Christ
First National Bank of Hardlyville
Hardlyville Chamber of Commerce
The Homer Society

— CURRENT CHARACTERS —

CHILDREN OF THE CREEK

Otis Hendricks
Lucas Jones Junior
Vixen Jones

Girl Jones
Mona Arrow
Lucas Jones Junior II
Abi Abdul
Pres Bloom
Peli Arrow
Flambeau Adonis Jones

HARDLY VILLAINS

Lettie Jones — Village Heroine

Lucas Jones — The Spirit of Hardlyville

Jimmy and Sally Jones — Entrepreneur and wife

Jamin and Mabel Bennell — Banker and wife

Wendell Bennell — Artist and Lover

Captain Happy — Banker Jamin's best friend

Tiny Taylor — Greasy Spoons Grill and Bar

Booray and Lil' Shooter Abdul — Country Lebanese Restaurant

Pomp and Uvi Peters — Donny Brook Inn and Hardly Yoga

Pastor Pat — Preacher

Billious Bloom — Publisher, the Daily Hellbender

Newton Diddle — Sheriff

Rifleman and Steele — rifleman.com, Chair of Hardlyville Chamber

Feral Fister — Bi-Polar Man

Anel Feckle — Bi-Polar Man's lover

✕

GOOD GUYS

Pinky and Rosetta Flawed — Rock Star and wife

The Former President of the United States of America

Uno thru Seis (Rosie, Doseta, Ethel, Opal, Walli, Urma)— Rescued sex slaves and Mexican Caps, LLC

Naught — Native American Rock Art Guide, Bluff, UT

Clavical Autry — Ozarks Tracker

April — rescued victim

BAD GUYS

Beauford "Bo" Bevel — Really Bad Guy

Sandy Smith — Really Bad Guy's Girlfriend

Johnny Protem — Really Bad Guy's assistant

CONTENTS

Prelude / xvii

Chapter 1: Carnage / 1

Chapter 2: Evil V. Evil / 6

Chapter 3: Children of the Creek / 8

Chapter 4: The Usual Suspects / 11

Chapter 5: Another Child / 15

Chapter 6: Bi-Polar Man and Mr. Fister / 19

Chapter 7: Saying Goodbye / 24

Chapter 8: Clues / 29

Chapter 9: The Not So Great Beyond / 34

Chapter 10: Rock Art in the Ozarks / 41

Chapter 11: Spring Field / 45

Chapter 12: A Focal Group / 48

Chapter 13: Haute Hardlyville / 54

Chapter 14: Comings and Goings at Puke / 59

Chapter 15: Canoe Nymph / 66

Chapter 16: I Pres, Take Thee Vixen / 68

Chapter 17: Moon Child / 75

Chapter 18: Entrepreneurial Instincts / 80

Chapter 19: In Search of . . . / 85

Chapter 20: A Dream Within A Dream / 88

Chapter 21: Fatal Attraction / 95

Chapter 22: A Suspect / 98
Chapter 23: Neck-Ed / 107
Chapter 24: Catatonic Contentment / 110
Chapter 25: Pinky / 112
Chapter 26: Full Moon / 120
Chapter 27: Roots / 125
Chapter 28: Neck-Ed, Again / 128
Chapter 29: Justice Served? / 134
Chapter 30: Rock On / 138
Chapter 31: Sign of The Times / 143
Chapter 32: Re-Search and Destroy / 147
Chapter 33: All for Naught / 158
Chapter 34: Back to the Garden / 172
Chapter 35: A More Perfect Union / 179
Chapter 36: The Loss of a Child / 185
Chapter 37: Reporting Back / 189
Chapter 38: Evil V. Evil, for Real / 198
Chapter 39: Serendipity / 213
Chapter 40: Into the Garden, Finally / 217
Chapter 41: Loose Ends / 221
Chapter 42: Free at Last / 228
Chapter 43: Rules / 231
Chapter 44: Big Apple / 239
Chapter 45: Double Down / 255

"A man is judged by his love, and his offspring."
Lucas Jones

"Evil against evil, breathed the curator..."
The Exorcist
William Peter Blatty

"The beauty of life is that it just keeps on going."
Wellspring of Evil
Lettie Jones

PRELUDE

The shaman stared intently into the wood-fired kiln. The piece that baked was meticulously sculpted and polychromed in sky blue with light reddish bands and zigs on gray. It was shaped as an oblong oval, base slightly wider than mouth to provide stability. The mouth would be sealed by the thick clay plug roasting next to it. The final product must be impenetrable and inescapable. The shaman would see to that with his craftsmanship, and a final blessing. The essence of those ashes that lay next to him in a tightly cinched leather pouch must never again see the light of day or darkness of night. They must remain bound in the nether world, from which they came, for all eternity. It was the shaman's solemn oath to his people.

As his receptacle and plug cooled in the chilled night, he urged the people to take up a chant that purged the presence of the yellow-eyed evil one.

His remains would be embedded behind rock that no human could roll away.

The shaman carefully emptied the ash-filled leather pouch into the oblong oval. He then plugged and sealed the opening, firing the edges to overlap the seal for good measure, and muttered in the language of the ancients who had gone before him a prayer of good riddance and eternal exile.

He interred the vessel in a small fissure in the contiguous sandstone rock face, and ordered four of his strongest warriors to wedge a large boulder into the gap, chiseling it to assure a tight fit. He sealed that with a prayer as well.

He then led his people in a joyous and riotous celebration of their triumph, of the victory of good over evil, of closing the portal to those in the darkness, of returning the evil leader to his own dank world forever. The ancient ones had prevailed again despite their loss of many. As with Urraca Mesa, Chaco Canyon, and other sacred battlefields, they had dispatched the evil ones back to their source.

The mesa was restored to order and logic. The entire bloody episode was commemorated in a memorable and beautiful petroglyphic panel painstakingly chiseled by the shaman's stunning daughter and overseen each step of the way by the shaman himself.

Late that night, the earth trembled violently as the shaman and his people slept within stone walls beneath the sturdy rock outcropping that provided them shelter from the elements. When it collapsed all were killed except the shaman's daughter who had slipped away, to join a warrior from a rival tribe in lust, without permission from her father.

As the tremors subsided they raced to her village, beyond fear of the discovery of their coupling. They found only death, ruins, and her petroglyphic panel which had been spared the general destruction by its location high beneath the collapsed frontage. They pulled her father, the shaman, from the wreckage of his dirt-floored room and heard him mutter one word.

"*Evil.*"

One word, only once.

They ran to the sandstone-boulder-packed entombment site and found the clay pot, spit forth and shattered on the ground, colorful sherds* all around. Had it caused the quaking or just been freed by it, they wondered? But not for long. Each grabbed a fragment and backed away slowly before racing to the young man's village.

Both were found dead a day later, strangled in love's repose.

In archaeology, a sherd, or more precisely, potsherd, is commonly an historic or prehistoric fragment of pottery. (Wikipedia)

CHAPTER 1: CARNAGE

The relatively new sheriff of Hardlyville went by Newt. He didn't like Newton Diddle, and in fact got downright hostile when a stranger called him that. No one who knew him ever would. Relatively new remained part of his persona, as time moved slowly for most Hardlyvillains, despite his three years in the job. His beloved predecessor, Sheriff Sephus Adonis, had long since passed on, but Sheriff Newt always seemed to be viewed in his imposing shadow.

Sheriff Newt was perplexed by the body. She was stripped naked, with her slender throat sliced clear through her spine. Dried blood was splattered all around. He couldn't tell whether she had been sexually assaulted but he would lean toward a yes. A good looking, tall, slender, young blonde, draped over a bale of hay with what appeared to be her clothes—and there weren't very many of them—strewn about the barn floor and her head dangling by a swath of pale skin, had probably been raped. Young doctor Abi Abdul would have to verify. At this point in his career, it was better to have her poking around down there than him.

There had not been a murder during his three years as sheriff of Hardlyville. He was, in fact, told when applying for the job that there hadn't been one since olden days, when a crazed woman evidently terrorized the village for several decades. Funny thing was, she reportedly cut most of her victims' throats clean through as well.

He didn't know what to make of it all, but the young boys who had led him to the murder scene were gawking and obviously waiting for him to say or do something.

"Ain't you boys never seen no naked lady's body before?" was about the best he could come up with.

One of the younger ones raised his hand to confirm he had, before adding that his mamma's sure didn't look like this one. This set the other ones to giggling and sheriff sent them scrambling by firing a round over their heads and admonishing them to run home and say nothing.

Sheriff Newt's cell phone began to emit a piercing emergency signal. This was a national alert signal and he immediately picked up a text message addressed to all law enforcement agencies and their leaders in the United States of America. It advised each recipient to report immediately to the Police Department closest in proximity to any community named Spring Field in response to a national terrorist threat. It listed and provided GPS coordinates for the thirty-eight cities, towns, and townships so named in the United States. It quoted from an intercepted and decoded secret text message that "this Independence Day in Spring Fields across America will make 9/11 of years past look like a church fireworks show." It was sourced from a new and self-proclaimed terrorist agency, The Homer Society.

"Wow!" was about all Sheriff Newt could muster. His predecessor, Sheriff Sephus Adonis, would have surely spat out his signature "shit, brothers," to add color and gravitas to a perplexing situation, but Sheriff Newt was no Sephus Adonis.

WELLSPRING OF EVIL

In that both Missouri and Arkansas had "Spring Fields," Sheriff Newt had a decision to make. He remembered once reading that Spring Field, Missouri had been named the "most similar to *The Simpsons* Spring Field" and quickly hopped into his police car, set the siren to wailing, and roared out of Hardlyville in a northwesterly direction. The dead body of the beautiful blonde would have to wait. What a Fourth of July this had been and stood to become.

The young boys, of course, did nothing Sheriff Newt had asked them to do. They ran straight to the *Daily Hellbender* to report the facts and hopefully get their photo taken standing next to the nude body in a subsequent edition. This would confirm them as heroes plus establish impeccable credentials for prurient behavior. At least that was the word Sheriff Newt had used in shooing them off. They knew the former would sell well with local lassies and assumed the latter, though they had no idea what it meant, would simply reinforce the community's gratitude for their manliness.

The publisher of the *Hellbender*, Ms. Billious Bloom, initially scoffed at their story but soon sensed that the panic in their voices carried more than a shred of truth. As she followed them on foot through the woods to the old barn, she couldn't help but wonder where Sheriff Newt was.

Ms. Billious Bloom, mother of Pres Bloom, courtesy of dalliances with a previous president of the United States, had remained unwed all of these years. She was proud of her son, who served as Hardlyville's youngest ever mayor and editor of the *Daily Hellbender*. She was also unashamed of her perch in history as the only known Hardlyvillain mistress of a sitting president. As executive director of the prestigious Rosebeam Foundation, repository for one of the largest collections of original Latin texts in the world, history was important to her. This notch in the Hardlyville book of time was both historical and remained pleasurable.

Octavia Rosebeam, granddaughter of town founder Thomas Hardly and long time Latin teacher at Hardlyville High School, had dreamed of a Hardlyville with international repute for Latin studies. Ms. Bloom had boldly pursued that vision, leveraging Ms. Rosebeam's founding bequest with an uncanny knack for fundraising and a skillful application of personal attributes to build a priceless collection of Latin antiquities. And, oh, what a grand time she had doing so.

Ms. Bloom remained close to her presidential lover far beyond his retirement, but chose never to share their son's identity with him. She was protective and yet ambitious for young Pres, who showed great political instincts and a potential for politics far beyond Hardlyville. Bloodlines aside, she did not want to encumber him with the steamy baggage of her past liaisons.

As her thoughts wandered to Sheriff Newt, while she tromped with the young men through the woods to what would likely be a very gruesome scene, a smile crossed her face. Despite their age difference, she was attracted to the new young sheriff who was so shy that he couldn't even mumble out the most basic greeting to her without blushing bright red and starring at his shoes. She found this extremely sexy and began to go out of her way to prompt chance encounters all over town. She knew it would go nowhere but found great sport in posing as a sheriff tease.

Back to the carnage at hand. Billious Bloom had never seen anything so gruesome in all of her life. As she entered the barn, she was unable to stifle her urge to vomit. This caused some of the boys to titter until her withering gaze brought back the gravity of the situation. She questioned each with authority and firmness. She wanted to know all of the details of their process to discovery and what the sheriff's reaction had been. There would be no photos out of respect to the victim, but the boys would be given due credit for their role in seeking help quickly.

She sent them running home for the second time in an hour, covered the body with a saddle blanket she found in the corner, and returned to town to gather Dr. Abi, undertaker Bob, and Pastor Pat of the Hardlyville Church of Christ to minister to the body. She tried Sheriff Newt's cell phone and could raise only an automated message that he was engaged for the foreseeable future in dealing with a national emergency. This too piqued her interest as a journalist but, given all that was going on in her own back yard, it would have to wait.

Dr. Abi could find no evidence of sexual assault, undertaker Bob confirmed the cause of death as almost having her head cut off, and pastor Pat prayed for mercy on her soul. None of it made any sense. No one knew who the poor lady was, a previously and obviously very sexy lady had not been sexed, and the damn sheriff who had already visited the crime scene was nowhere to be found. "What the hell is going on?" they asked each other.

CHAPTER 2: EVIL VS. EVIL

Evil in all of its forms is evil. And yet Evil manifests itself in many iterations.

Some evil is normal, a natural part of the human condition. Along that human spectrum, some evils are more horrible than others. Murder is murder, but is killing an innocent child worse than shooting an enemy combatant with innocent children of his own? Rape is forcing sex on another. Should a perpetrator differentiate a victim who leads someone on and then says no from one who never has the chance to say no? Infliction of unbearable pain can be called torture or it can derive from loss. Are both evil? Surely evil in the context of humanity is part of the macro cycle of life—unpleasantness or even tragedy to be faced and dealt with, scars to scab over or bleed to the death, wounds to heal or ooze.

Some evil is supernatural, grounded in myth or superstition. Are forms or shapes or acts that don't fit within the human context real or imagined? Does this evil lurk in the shadows of a mind or heart, next door, or beyond the next veil? Does this evil rain down pain and misery by selection or by chance? Does this evil derive from or prey on fear? Is evil beyond life?

Is supernatural evil worse than its human counterpart? Is one evil stronger than the other? Is existence a battle between good and evil, or evil and evil? What happens when evil gets pissed off at itself? When does evil become Evil?

CHAPTER 3:
CHILDREN OF THE CREEK

The children were all born in Hardlyville. Each grew up on the banks of Skunk Creek, which had returned to its near-pristine state as a premier Ozarks stream under the federal protection of National Refuge status. Several shared the same father and mother, some one or the other. Inbred? No. Crossbred? Maybe. Hybrid? Definitely. Genetically honed and reflectively refined through and through in a Hardlyvillain kind of way. Beyond that, they were as different as individual fleas on a coon dog.

Few alive could remember the Big Pig Flood which had devastated both the village and the creek, or the brutal antics the yellow-eyed Demon Lady and her followers directed toward the extermination of all Hardlyvillains. The children of the creek had only heard the stories and had written them off as dementia-induced meanderings among a select set of antique Hardlyvillains. The tales were simply too tall to be true.

A tidal wave of squealing pigs, bloated carcasses, and pig farm lagoon water and solids coursing through the streets of Hardlyville? Impossible.

A lady so evil that she could only find pleasure in killing, sexing, or hitting her own daughter? No way.

WELLSPRING OF EVIL

A town jester named Dinky Doodle who often appeared naked or cross-dressed to provide comic relief for a village stretched to its emotional limits? Got to be kidding.

A convoluted love triangle involving sexual sleight of hand and the seduction of the president of the United States for the preservation and protection of beautiful Skunk Creek and other environmentally sustainable ends? Laugh out loud.

A French bombshell who contributed more love and affection to more Hardlyvillain males in just two weeks than some Hardlyvillain wives did over the course of their marriages? Well, maybe.

An overweight, overwrought, often bumbling sheriff reputed to be the most exquisite lover in all of the Ozarks? Say what?

An old maid Latin teacher who stole from a corrupt banker on his death bed to seed an internationally acclaimed collection of Latin antiquities? A town hero named Lucas who loved floating, fishing, and Bud Lite more than life itself, excepting wife Lettie of course? A fallen pastor, a crusading newspaper editor, a nationally renowned gourmet chef named Tiny, a Bedouin shivaree, a Hardly Yoga Studio?

You must be kidding. The tales and tellers go on forever. And before them, murder, seduction, and carnage all the way back to founding daddies and mothers. What a wacky tale, this history of Hardlyville. At least most Hardlyvillains had a sense of humor, no matter how bizarre and distorted, that fed their resiliency.

The children of the creek humored their elders' misplaced memories and cared for them deeply. After all, they were from, and now part of, this colorful history.

"They" would be, in birth order, and with birth parents in parenthesis:

Otis Hendricks (Sabrina Hendricks, unknown); Lucas Jones Junior (Lettie and Lucas Jones), Vixen Jones (The Demon Lady and Lucas Jones), Girl Jones (Sally and Jimmy Jones), Mona Arrow (Lettie Jones and Pierce Arrow), Lucas Jones Junior II (Sally and Jimmy Jones), Abi Abdul (Lil' Shooter and Booray Abdul), Pres Bloom (Billious Bloom and the former president of the US), Peli Arrow (Lettie Jones and Pierce Arrow), and Flambeau Adonis (Airreal and Sheriff Sephus Adonis).

Count them. Ten in all. The current repository of four generations. Much of the good, bad, irrelevant, and humorous DNA of a resilient and persistent peoples, all wrapped up in the future tenants of tiny Hardlyville.

CHAPTER 4:
THE USUAL SUSPECTS

Sheriff Newt pulled the cardboard box from deep in the closet corner. It was covered with dust and spider webs. Hand written in the upper right hand corner were the words "Hardlyville's Worst." Former sheriff Sephus Adonis's signature below confirmed the official nature of the files enclosed, dated decades earlier.

Sheriff Newt had been released from Spring Field duty at 10AM on July 5th, as had all Spring Field guardians around the country. Evidently it had been a total hoax. Not one single act of terror was reported, not one trace of The Homer Society observed, not one single sign of either intent or action uncovered. The FBI was flummoxed, the CIA embarrassed, and the White House was scrambling for cover. Late night talk show hosts were already honing their ridicule for public consumption. Odd, thought Sheriff Newt, that the prevailing emotion trumpeted by the national press was indignation as to whom to blame, as opposed to relief that there had been no national disaster. Such a shift in perspective from the horror of previous terrorist attacks.

Blame the press? Blame the people? Lay it all on this new phenom generally grouped as social media? Sheriff Newt didn't much care, but he was pissed that between a bloody murder and a faux national emergency he had not been able to go fishing over the Fourth of July holiday.

Sheriff Newt's spirits drooped further as he pulled up to his office. There was that damn Billious Bloom again, wearing a sly smile and a very revealing dress, with the top two buttons undone, for one of her generation. She usually freaked him out and appeared to be prepared to do so again.

He had heard tell of her voracious sexual appetite. And while Sheriff Newt was not necessarily against sex, it had gotten him in trouble before. And since that would surely cost him his job if even a whisper of such emerged, he had taken a private vow of celibacy. Besides, she was a good bit older.

Ms. Bloom was friendly in kind of a flirtatious manner. After shaking hands with Sheriff Newt and clinging to his grip longer than required, she coyly unbuttoned the third on her blouse to reveal a little more skin and winked. Sheriff Newt hated this and could only stare at his shoes.

Ms. Bloom was most anxious to discuss the murder of the young blonde and wanted to know what the sheriff was doing about it. She also wanted to know where he had been for the past twenty-four hours. Just trying to do his job or something like that he thought, unable to put it into words beyond a stuttered stammer. Ms. Bloom took his hand in hers and urged him to calm down, which only set him back further. He excused himself to the men's room and stayed there until she went away, promising to return later in the afternoon and hoping he was not having a serious bowel problem. He assured her all was well and he couldn't wait for her return, before falling asleep on the toilet seat. After all, he had been up the entire night.

When he awoke he placed the "Sheriff Out" sign on the door and turned out all lights, to buy time and privacy. He pulled out a tiny flashlight, popped open the top of the box, and found a chronological handwritten summary inventory, again signed by Sheriff Sephus Adonis. Listed therein were a handful of names under the title "The Worst Scoundrels in Hardlyville history." A taped folder dedicated to each lay stacked beneath. If any of them were still alive, they, of course, would leap to the top of his suspect list.

The Demon Lady file lay on top. The terror she had inflicted on not only Hardlyville but random others, like floaters on Skunk Creek, innocent victims of Anorchia (testes deficient), and presidential SWAT team commandos trying to track her down, was unparalleled in Hardlyville history. And of course there was her brutal murder of town hero Lucas Jones. Long knives were her preferred weapons, and a severed throat to the point of decapitation was her signature act of cruelty. But of course she was dead. Or was she?

Aimless Bevel was next. He had been an Agenda 21'er whose passion for property rights was matched only by his racist rage. His attempts to lynch Hardlyvillain Booray Abdul had led to a full scale shootout in which Sheriff Sephus Adonis was seriously wounded. He later turned to robbing banks with his blonde accomplice who had led attempts by the investment banking firm Lolly, Gag, and Maggot, LLC, PC to syndicate the village of Hardlyville for sale to private investors. Her specialties had been coercion, seduction, and bribery, all in the name of closing the deal. They both were still apparently alive and living in a remote commune in the heart of the Ozarks, existing in a state of blissful drug use, doing harm to none.

Banker Bud had been the scoundrel who sold out to Big Pork and bore great responsibility for the Big Pig Flood that decimated Skunk Creek and Hardlyville. He was dead for sure. Heart attack. His running mate, a former chairman of the State Clean Water Commission, was equally guilty of that travesty but didn't seem the violent type. He might even still be in jail.

And then there were the Freeload Twins, and they were violent. Their victims of choice were generally innocent animals, and while details were sketchy they evidently had shot and killed endangered species on several occasions. They had forever been exiled to Texas from Hardlyville according to the previous sheriff. They deserved further investigation, reasoned Sheriff Newt.

There were files on Anny Qingdoa and a man named Garth that were tied to the brutal murder of town founder Thomas Hardly. Both had been dead for generations.

There was not much to draw from here, beyond the shady and sordid side of Hardlyville's history, deduced Sheriff Newt.

Ms. Billious Bloom began banging on his office door so he reluctantly let her in.

Ms. Bloom was all business now. She had seen the brutal murder scene and attended to the poor deceased's needs in the sheriff's absence. She was aware of the national emergency over Spring Field terror threats that had drawn the sheriff away from the brutal murder scene. She probably knew more about both than the sheriff himself, she guessed.

"What next," she demanded?

Sheriff Newt just wanted to go fishing.

CHAPTER 5: ANOTHER CHILD

There was another child of the creek. A different creek. Stinking Creek. It is so named because it totally disappears in numerous places along its journey to the big waters below, leaving behind odiferous traces of dried mud and algae. It runs parallel to Skunk Creek, but its children do not run parallel to the others.

Beauford (Bo) Bevel hated just about everything. He hated his name, and the parents who had bestowed it on him.

Aimless Bevel had been an outlaw who hooked up with a crooked investment banker to levy chaos on first Hardlyville, then small banks around the Ozarks, before establishing a hippie commune in a cave along remote Stinking Creek far away from law enforcement and authority of any kind.

Aimless Bevel had been the poster child for property rights folks, Agenda 21er's, Ayn Rander's, though none would have ever heard or read of John Galt. One day Aimless got tired of creating mayhem and retreated into a haze of drugs, sex, and sleep. He had never gotten caught, had only briefly seen the inside of a jail cell, and had always secured a misbegotten alibi to set himself free. His busty partner in crime and bed had just been happy not to serve ten to fifteen years for her financial chicanery in trying to package clueless Hardlyville for syndication and sale to unsuspecting investors. Aimless had snatched her from that charade and made her his own.

Aimless Bevel's decline into harmlessness spared him criminal prosecution for prior misdeeds. What court would convict a worthless pervert who couldn't remember a thing in his drug-fogged brain, surrounded by others of a similar bent? Why bother?

Members of his commune came and went as their drug and sexual proclivities dictated, while Aimless and his lady drifted into a state of self fulfilling semi-consciousness, birthing Beauford along the way. He was raised without direction, without rules, without a sense of conscience and morphed over time into the logical solution to that equation.

Bo also hated colors, particularly anyone of color. He was not picky. Black, brown, yellow, red, or any combination thereof. Bo was lily white and proud of it. There was no place for rainbows in his world.

He targeted his harshest, most vitriolic feelings toward authority of any kind. In that his stoned parents exerted none, he grew up in a world where he, and only he, was boss. His personal whims and fancies provided his only context for action and reaction, from the earliest memories he could conjure up.

As such he became de facto leader of whatever other worthless spawn emerged from the random couplings of other communal souls, coming and going. Most were drawn to his sense of preservation and self serving instincts. Most preyed on each other within the context of his assumed authority and few ever questioned his judgment, which became more onerous and demanding with each year of their subservience. This was a bad and dangerous grouping of lost souls seeking little beyond immediate gratification. These anarchists posed a threat to anyone whose way they crossed.

Finally, Bo hated Homer Simpson because his stoned parents made him sit in front of their Dish Network TV and watch, while they cavorted in bed or passed out. He must have been made to watch every episode two or three times over the years, as they did cavort and sleep a lot.

All of which had spawned Bo's Fourth of July joke on the nation. Among his few gifts was an unnatural understanding of social media and its power to disrupt. To even try to delve into the depth of his cyber-depravity would stretch any storyteller's words so this one will simply relate the results rather than the means to those ends.

Beauford "Bo" Bevel cracked national-security-apparatus codes to an extent that allowed him to catapult over other legitimate threats to the good ol' US of A on this particular Fourth of July and bring an entire nation to its knees in fear. That he could do so in the name of hated Homer Simpson and his beloved Spring Field only heightened Bo's sense of accomplishment.

After all, there were close to forty Spring Fields spread across the country whose birthday most idiots were celebrating with barbecued ribs and beer. What better than to strike terror into the heart of every Spring Fieldian, most of whom showed a particular affection for both barbecue and beer, for twenty-four hours without harming a soul? That Bo Bevel, and his mysterious Homer Society, had done so with excruciating precision, and then just dropped out of sight, left authorities of all levels of security clearance scrambling.

What was this Homer Society? The ties to Spring Fields across the country were obvious from the beginning. Homer Simpson? Spring Field? Ha! Why had it taken so long for the best and brightest of America's secret side to figure that out?

What was the purpose of bringing the nation to high alert and then harming no one. Who was the prankster who had dreamed this one up? How had he or she snuck in the back door and fanned the flames of fear so fully? Blame a hacker instead of a cracker? Their questions were endless, the finger pointing ceaseless, and the results almost humorous. To some.

Bo Bevel smiled. What would he do next for fun? His following waited in their creekside cavern with fetid breath. They called it Puke, Ozarks, and didn't know or much care whether it was in Arkansas or Missouri.

CHAPTER 6:
BI-POLAR MAN AND MR. FISTER

The village of Hardlyville had a new superhero. Bi-Polar Man.

His legend was born the day he zipped out of his refrigerator repair shop, stripped to purple boxers, and leapt into frigid Skunk Creek to rescue Girl Jones' baby puppy.

Girl, whose given name evolved from the fact that her parents forgot to give her a proper one in the celebratory chaos of her birth, had thrown the puppy into the creek, thinking all dogs could swim, to help him mature into dog adulthood. Her screams as the puppy had bobbed up and down in the current squealing like a piglet brought Feral Fister running to the rescue.

As he handed the shivering puppy to Girl Jones, all she could mutter was something about how brave Feral was, and how Hardlyville needed a new hero.

Girl Jones also observed that every hero needed a name and she bestowed one on the blushing Feral Fister on the spot. Bi-Polar Man. He owned a refrigerator repair shop and seemed to have the ability to be in two places at once. Yes, Bi-Polar Man it would be. Superhero.

Feral was deeply moved at this tribute. He had received few in his life beyond the usual "Thanks for getting my refrigerator going. Now I won't have to throw out the fresh carp."

Feral went home that evening and embroidered the initials BPM in red on his purple boxers. He also began to dream of other heroic acts he could perform. He would always have his superhero uniform on under his daily work clothes. This would require a lot of laundering until he could add additional purple boxers to his wardrobe, but he was on the hunt and up to the task.

Feral Fister had come to Hardlyville by way of Colorado and at the urging of banker Jamin Bennell a number of years back. Banker Jamin was a legend in himself.

He had arrived in Hardlyville with his entourage in the wake of disaster, everything from the Big Pig Flood to dissolution of the Evil Coven to corrupt banker Bud's demise. He had assumed ownership of the failed Bank of Hardlyville, had restored community banking to its rightful role in the growth and development of any small village, and played a key role in assuring the financial sustainability of Hardlyville, including clandestine service as chairman of the Hardlyville branch office of the Federal Reserve Bank. So secret was his service that, in fact, not even the Board of Governors of the national Fed had a clue as to its existence.

Funded by a secret stash of antique silver dollars housed in an underground rock vault guarded by a nest of copperhead snakes and the spirit of Lucas Jones, The Hardlyville Fed would introduce liquidity into the village economy in times of contraction and withdraw it as inflationary pressures began to build. Banker Jamin was the Hardlyville Fed's chief economist as well as chair, a fact shared only with now deceased Pierce

Arrow and Sheriff Sephus Adonis, rendering the quiet banker as a true financial wizard and czar.

Quiet was probably an understatement. Most residents had never heard banker Jamin utter a single word and as such considered him a mute. That his entourage included interpreter and best friend Captain Happy, in addition to wife Mabel and one child for each year of their marriage, which happened to be ten at time of relocation, spoke to his shy and quiet side. It was even rumored that banker Jamin was too shy to have sex more than once a year, but that he made the most of each occasion in terms of propagating his line.

Most of Hardlyville also knew him to be a brilliant thinker, capable of reducing perplexing problems to simple solutions and analyzing complex numbers and dollar signs to Hardlyville's best interests. The past saga of Hardlyville to Donny Brook and back, which involved the sale of the village to syndicated investors and ultimate reversal of the transaction to the benefit of both, stood as testimony to his brilliance and love of place.

Some thought banker Jamin's name a bit odd, but as Captain Happy had explained, he had been the tenth generation of his family to enter banking with the birth name of Benjamin, stretching back to rural England, a country banker by lineage. His mother had big dreams for her boy. She thought him to be quite special and beyond the Benjamins who had preceded him. So instead of Benjamin or Ben, she split the difference and called him Jamin the moment he popped from her loins. The nickname had stuck and her forecasts of "special" did as well.

Back to Feral Fister.

Banker Jamin knew him to be an honest and knowledgeable businessman when it came to the art of keeping cooling systems running, everything from refrigerators to air conditioners. He also had his eye on him as prospective husband to his oldest daughter Uvella, despite their age difference. Jamin was a firm believer in older gents wedding younger girls in pre-arranged marriages. It had worked pretty well in his case.

Unfortunately, or fortunately as time had since proven, a young Uvella got pregnant from a one night tryst with Lucas Jones Junior II under the Hardlyville Bridge. Lucas Junior II had stepped up to the plate to take responsibility, and the two had been happily married ever since. The "unfortunate" related to Feral Fister not finding another and assuming the mantle of a confirmed bachelor.

Perhaps this was why his new role as Bi-Polar Man was so exhilarating for him. Who knew what good he could bring to Hardlyville beyond cool houses and refrigerators in his later years!

In the meantime Banker Jamin had begun grooming Uvella to take over leadership duties of the bank and the Hardlyville Fed. She had inherited his grasp of numbers and, beyond having babies, enjoyed nothing more than dealing with financial challenges, be they personal banking issues or economic policy in tiny Hardlyville. And, again fortunately, she resembled her mother Mabel in appearance.

Feral's dreams were troubled that first night as Hardlyville's new superhero. They centered on a beautiful young lady trying to scream as her life hissed away with a silent sigh through a severed throat. He could almost feel her shock and pain as he grasped his own, tightening his fingers around his own windpipe until they left marks.

WELLSPRING OF EVIL

He awoke gasping for breath and biting his hand to break its death grip. What in the world was going on he screamed to no one in particular. It was as if he had been momentarily possessed by a dream within his own dream and might even still be in it. Two dimensional dreaming was not something Feral Fister wanted to know more about. He shuddered at the thought, and then dreamed it again.

After all, he was Bi-Polar Man, with the supernatural ability to be in two places at once.

CHAPTER 7: SAYING GOODBYE

Pastor Pat slipped slowly into his white ministerial robe. He had performed many acts so clad—some inspirational, some heretical—but none of more significance than today. Laying tiny Lettie Jones' remains to rest between first-husband-and-town-hero Lucas Jones and long-time-partner-and-father-to-her-youngest-children Pierce Arrow bridged their shared stories but severed a vital living connection to Hardlyville's past. Lettie had been one of the final links between the heirs of the village and their colorful past. She had seen it all in her more than seventy years of making Hardlyville history.

Lettie had left Hardlyville only four times in her long life, each on a heroic mission, generally impossible, but ultimately accomplished. Two involved a sitting president of the United States in the nation's capital and resulted in the resurrection and preservation of precious Skunk Creek as well as the return of her precious little girl with the big yellow eyes, Vixen, from the clutches of evil. One solved a murder mystery. Another reclaimed her second love, Pierce Arrow, to his fragile Hardlyville roots from flirtations with the romantic red rock country of southern Utah and a former lover. Each was a tall tale in itself that, ironically, was generally true—though the stories themselves remained barely believable. Each changed the course of Hardlyville history in ways Lettie could never have envisioned. Pastor Pat mused on what little Lettie might have accomplished on the world stage had she travelled more.

His dilemma today was how to pay tribute to a fiery, fearless, passionate mother and lover of life and without giving away all of the details. Memorial services were not the place for tales of seduction and sex, dead men with no balls, presidential lust, or naked romps beneath red rock arches. No, somehow, Pastor Pat needed to keep the focus on outcomes, not means, today. But it was all so bland without the selfless, colorful, corollaries to the end results. And who would believe the ones without the others?

Maybe he could present in long convoluted sentences, one to each historic occasion, which would pay proper homage to magnitude as well as confound the listener with enormity of scale? Pastor Pat knew from decades of experience that if he went on for more than twenty minutes his flock would either succumb to sleep or wander aimlessly away, shorting Lettie of her due. No, Pastor Pat would have to be at the top of his game today, despite his own age and frailty. He owed it to tiny Lettie and her gargantuan footprint on Hardlyvillains past, present, and future. He tumbled it all over in his mind.

"How about something like this?" he murmured to himself.

"Did you hear the one about the naked president of the United States armed with only a pittance of a penis chasing a similarly clad young lady around the oval office in heated search of a quid pro quo for an executive order establishing the Skunk Creek Watershed National Refuge, interrupted by an international nuclear missile crisis which was his potential prey's saving grace?"

Yes, that is exactly what he needed. Brief, crisp, poignantly spoken, mind boggling in its depth, discernible to only those who could comprehend, vast, and true. Yes, that would honor Lettie.

"Or, the one about Anorchia Anonymous meetings in far off Denver, Colorado, in search of an evil perpetrator of murder and intimidation, designed to rid the world of men born without gonads and intimidate a small Ozarkian village into abject submission, until a brave detective figured it all out to the salvation of Hardlyville and that poor minority of steer-like men?"

Yes, yes, he had it going now.

"Or, the one about the tiny baby discovered on deceased Lucas Jones' grave by prior and future lovers Sheriff Sephus Adonis and Pierce Arrow, the baby with the yellow eyes of her evil she-devil mother and the heart and soul of dear Lucas, conceived at his moment of self-sacrificial death, nursed and raised by a surrogate mother into one of Hardlyville's finest?"

Maybe better not name any names in this case, Pastor Pat reasoned.

"Or even the one about a lithe lover and partner, Pierce Arrow, dashing and dancing beneath a moonlit natural arch, rolling in red dust, consumed with ancients spirits of lust and procreation in the red rock country of distant Utah, spawning fresh love and Peli Arrow, the youngest of her offspring, named for the flute playing, humped back Hopi Indian imp of impregnation?"

He had heard that one in confession.

So much to be crammed into so few words and so little time, the legacy of a life well and fully lived. Lettie's four trips abroad, namely beyond the Hardlyville city limits, would succinctly frame her life of giving and loving to all within her reach. *We owe her a lot*, mused Pastor Pat. He would do justice to the legend of Lettie Jones. And he wouldn't even need to use her name.

Pastor Pat wondered if this would be his final rite. He was old and tired. This fallen, but much beloved, man of the cloth had presided over everything from Bullrush Festivals in honor of baby Moses, to a Bedouin shivaree, to the defrocking of a beloved virginal village icon, to memorializing Hardlyville's finest of the past half century, to sharing his religious philosophy with a French porn star, to spiritual purging of pig feces, to half-hearted pledges of celibacy.

Pastor Pat had simply seen and done it all, sometimes with pride and honor, occasionally with guilt, but always with a solid belief in the power of forgiveness, for others and for himself. He certainly hoped that he was right.

Vixen sat in the front row of Skunk Creek Church of Christ with tears leaking from her big yellow eyes. She was surrounded by her half-brothers Lucas Jones Junior and Peli Arrow and sister-soulmate Mona. Mona, Peli's sister, sat beside her and held her hand. Her brothers had an arm around her. Each child from different blood lines but bound in love by Lettie. Vixen had always been the center of their world.

Lucas Jones Junior was conceived just before father Lucas's fateful encounter with the Demon Lady priestess that resulted in the former's death and Vixen's conception. It was a strange and convoluted encounter, yet one that left Lucas Jones a town hero for giving his life in a final and painful act of sex to buy minutes for authorities to raid and disburse the Demon Lady's evil coven before she could kidnap three of Hardlyville's youngest in revenge for the loss of three of her minions.

She had escaped, but not unscathed, for she carried the daughter of the man she murdered in cold blood at moment of consumption. Hating the concept of motherhood as she hated most things, She had returned the baby to Hardlyville on Lucas's grave, where Lettie picked up the little girl, nursed her to good health, and raised her as her own, the final link to her Lucas. Lucas Junior and little Vixen came into Lettie's world nearly as one, despite their circumstantial differences, and were inseparable thereafter.

Mona and Peli were birthed from Lettie's unofficial post-Lucas union with Pierce Arrow, now deceased owner and editor of the Hardlyville *Daily Hellbender*, one term congressman, and recipient of a Pulitzer for his coverage of the evil coven and Lucas's brutal death. It was a strange but romantic circle of love that spanned decades and adventures too strange to even be labeled fiction.

Nestled behind Lettie's brood was Pres Bloom who was engaged to be married to Vixen. Pres was Billious Bloom's illegitimate son by way of a former president of the United States and current mayor of Hardlyville, the youngest and brightest in a long line of ineffectual hacks.

"Dearly beloved," Pastor Pat began, "we are gathered here today—"

Whoops, he thought, *that's the "getting married ritual," better begin again.* Pastor Pat had always been good at covering his tracks, be it with needy female parishioners or inane religious meanderings. He barely missed a beat before sharing his tribute to Lettie's life framed in the results of her four trips "abroad."

Twenty minutes later, most were confused but grateful for this life Lettie had lead. They proceeded to Hardlyville Cemetery to lay her box between the two men she loved as no others.

CHAPTER 8: CLUES

Jimmy Jones hadn't descended into the garden for over a year. It was physically more difficult for him now.

Back then, when he and Sally were young, freshly minted in marriage and lust, and following clues from town founder Thomas Hardly's hand-drawn map to a hidden opening, it had been easy to descend on a rope into an ancient but fresh subterranean world, untouched by the excesses of mankind. It had been inspiring to see the species which had once flourished in the Ozarks, hellbenders, niangua darters, grotto sculpin, blind cave fish, and even Ozark Hellbenders living in beauty and grace. It had been fun to fling off clothes, make love quietly and reverently in honor of the inhabitants, wander aimlessly through silent passageways dimly lit from unknown sources, then make love again before rising hand over hand up the rope to real life again. That Girl Jones was conceived during their first encounter with paradise lost only punctuated the moment in his memory.

He had been back several times since, finding solace and counsel with the spirit of cousin Lucas Jones, who claimed the garden as final resting place for his soul. Jimmy wanted to spend eternity here as well when his time came, but cousin

Lucas said the laws of life beyond, as he understood them, dictated finding a special space of one's own. Who was Jimmy to argue with one who had settled in such a precious place.

The garden held clues for his future beyond, but the answers rested with someone or something beyond him. He only knew he wanted the spirit of his beloved Sally somewhere near, if at all possible. When his time came, he had his impassioned speech ready.

Sheriff Newt visited the barn again and again. The scene of the vicious murder had been scrubbed and scavenged thoroughly with little to show. He was still looking for clues.

No one knew the pretty lady who had been murdered. There had been no missing person reports from surrounding law officials. He had circulated a head shot, facial expressions massaged to eliminate the terror of her final moments, blood spatters wiped from her brow, to no avail. He had sent DNA samples to a national data bank and still not heard a word back. That was nearly a month ago. The unsolved murder had garnered some attention locally after *Daily Hellbender* publisher Billious Bloom's front page piece, complete with photo. But she had been respectful in her coverage, airbrushing the gaping wound and placing Band-Aids over the young lady's private parts. Unless you saw it in person, you simply couldn't grasp the raw brutality and cruelty of the pretty victim's last moments.

He still couldn't figure out the sex part, specifically the lack thereof. Dr. Abi had gone over the young lady's privates with a fine-tooth comb found nothing. No signs of forced entry, no evidence of foreign DNA, no lingering indications of sexual activity. Dr. Abi even went so far to say that while not a virgin, this sexy young lady might not have had sex for months.

Say what? Sheriff Newt just didn't get it.

Her blood had been spread far and wide around the scene of the crime, but he guessed that could have come from spurting rather than some ritualistic patterning.

There had been no fingerprints. No gloves. No fingernail scrapings. No evidence of trauma beyond a jagged slice across and through her neck.

In fact, that was the only sure clue Sheriff Newt could produce. The young lady's throat had not been slit with a scalpel, or even a sharp knife. It had been severed with a more blunt instrument of some sort. All the way through her spine. Sawed or hacked or carved. And what kind of clue was that? Sheriff Newt had seen cold cases with no leads only rarely in his career. This was one.

He saw to it that the young lady was given a proper burial in a far corner of Skunk Creek Cemetery with an unmarked gravestone. He even paid for a small bouquet of plastic flowers out of his own salary.

And then Sheriff Newt decided he would try something new in pursuit of answers, something he had never done before in his career. He would organize a focal group in search of clues.

Jimmy rolled away the large boulder that covered the garden entrance. He knotted a fraying rope around the base of a large tree nearby, tested it with a strong tug, intertwined his feet below, grabbed the rope above with arthritic hands, and began his descent into paradise. He didn't tell Sally where he was going as she would worry about him making it in and out without a fifty-foot fall. Jimmy was also looking for clues, these of a weightier nature. He needed to communicate with cousin Lucas about his future, about what lay beyond for him, Sally, Girl, and Lucas Junior II.

Cousin Lucas Jones had always been Jimmy Jones' hero. From floating and fishing Skunk Creek with Lucas in his earliest years, to sharing his first Bud Lite and a toke on a funny cigarette as they drifted aimlessly through a stretch of rapids, to seeing Lucas once scoop a hellbender from behind a boulder, to landing a twenty-inch smallmouth, cousin Lucas had always been there for Jimmy's big firsts.

It was Lucas who taught Jimmy about sex and love, the similarities and differences between the two, and the rollicking good times that occurred at the intersection of both.

It was Jimmy who provided cousin Lucas, Sheriff Sephus Adonis, and Pierce Arrow the horses, borrowed from another cousin, that they mounted and rode back into the hills in search of the murderous coven of evil and their "Demon Lady leader," as Pierce Arrow called her.

It was cousin Lucas who waved goodbye that day to Jimmy with a broad swath of bravado and conviction. It was the last time Jimmy would see him alive before he gave his life for the children of Hardlyville.

Jimmy Jones had come a long way from his early dope-dealing days to respected entrepreneur and village elder. Apart from almost losing all of the "children of the creek" on a dangerous Skunk Creek float trip flood due to his insistence on keeping the beer cold, he had made few mistakes or taken few ill-conceived risks in his later years. He had retired in comfort and love, and had watched with pride as his children had grown in the same.

Jimmy was seeking clues from cousin Lucas about how to, post-life, age gracefully. He had tried Pastor Pat, but found him lacking, beyond platitudes.

Lucas was living the post-life dream. Jimmy wanted to know how.

Jimmy was also curious as to how he and Pierce Arrow were going to share their affections with Lettie Jones now that she had passed. Who got to sleep with whom, so to speak. He had raised that question with Pastor Pat and gotten some inane passage from old testament Solomon about dividing babies in half.

CHAPTER 9:
THE NOT SO GREAT BEYOND

A word needs be shared about what was going on outside the relatively naive environs of the Hardlyvillain sphere of activity.

Sure, Hardlyville youth still got high, drank cheap beer, and reveled in pre-marital coital activities, with an occasional unintended pregnancy which was generally owned up to and remedied with an act of marriage. In that way, Hardlyville had hardly changed in its couple of hundred years of existence.

Life outside the Hardlyville bubble was another matter.

The once-popular and crowded paradise of California was becoming home to a burgeoning population of lizards, jackrabbits, and rattle snakes. They didn't require much fresh water to survive, and California had little to offer. Old swimming pools filled with debris and blowing silt provided first class accommodation for reptiles and other desert critters. Once-pristine beaches were now seared with heat. Rusty desalination plants sat idle in partial states of installation, introduced too late in the game to stem the new eastern migration. Wild fires finally died out from lack of combustible fuel. California had partially withered and died in front of a nation's disbelieving eyes.

When the water left California, many Californians began to leave as well, in search of moisture. The same was true to a lesser extent of Arizonians, New Mexicans, Utahans, Nevadans, West Texans, Eastern Coloradans, Kansans, and Nebraskans. Only the hearty, the foolhardy, and the severely stoned stuck around to dance naked in the next thunderstorm, whenever that might come.

The Colorado River system drained to nearly dry and the Ogallala Aquifer thinned to inches, not feet. Climate change led the assault on fresh water supplies. Human greed filled the void. Use far outpaced recharge, demand trumped supply, and agricultural contamination soured what was left.

With fewer crops in the ground, the national economy benefitted in the short term from a reduction in expenditures to artificially prop up agricultural prices and hold land fallow. That soon changed as basic commodity supplies declined and prices surged. Five dollars for a loaf of bread or two ears of corn? Corporate farmers sure couldn't afford to feed pigs or cows grain or produce at those prices. Again, in the short term, consumers smiled as confined animal feeding operations dumped their half fed swine, beef cattle, and pullets at bargain prices and shut their doors. However, over time, resultant shortfalls drove meat prices beyond the reach of only the wealthiest, whose numbers also began to recede. The $20 pork chop found its way onto fewer and fewer plates across the country. The United States of America could no longer afford to feed its own, let alone the world.

As refugees from the west and the high plains descended on wetter climes, the price of real estate soared. Small family farms were sold for far more than generations of farmers had eked out over decades.

Hardlyvillains by plan or chance had insulated their future.

First of all, they had plenty of pure, fresh water. Skunk Creek flowed fuller and cleaner than ever before, and Hardlyvillains—

stung earlier by the Big Pig Flood—were committed to keeping it that way. Thank you, US of A federal government, Lettie Jones, Billious Bloom, and Mr. President for the Skunk Creek Watershed National Refuge.

More importantly, they didn't sell out. Oh yes, there was the Donny Brook fiasco when an investment banking firm syndicated a private placement of Hardlyville, its assets, its name, and its history with a respectable rate of return to investors (buyers) and a lifetime of financial security to villagers (sellers). But this had occurred years earlier and had been quickly unwound to reflect disappointing results to all parties along with reinstitution of assets, name, and history to rightful Hardlyvillain owners, past, present, and to come. It had been an embarrassing and painful lesson in greed and avarice for a generally unsuspecting populace.

And they had learned well.

Upon dissolution of "The Deal," as most called it, the citizens of Hardlyville immediately took steps to protect their village and its colorful history from any similar debacle far into the future. They didn't need outside money. They didn't want outside money. They had heard about speculators and fabricators and manipulators seeking a fast buck, generally at the expense of the rest, namely innocents like themselves.

Town Ordinance 113, the number representing the total sum of village laws that had or still existed over the centuries, was simple but far reaching in its impact on future generations of Hardlyvillains.

It simply stipulated that "No current piece of residential real estate within the Hardlyville city limits or directly abutting thereto, including land and structure(s), may be sold." Period. Ever. It continued that "Said land and structure(s) may only be gifted, preferably to family or heirs, but in the absence of either, to other Hardlyvillains only." Rent, population, and price controls all rolled into one.

This brilliant piece of legislation was drafted by Pierce Arrow, editor of the Hardlyville *Daily Hellbender*, banker Jamin Bennell, president of First National Bank of Hardlyville (as communicated by Captain Happy), and Steele, chairman of the Hardlyville Chamber of Commerce to preserve forever the birthright and history of all Hardlyvillains past, present, future. And in a corollary law of unintended consequences, to protect all Hardlyvillains from real estate speculation, runaway inflation, and bubbles in asset valuation.

TO113 passed by a 70%–30% margin with most opponents spouting a property rights agenda. That it might be unconstitutional bothered few, as few in Hardlyville had ever read the constitution or spent their days stewing about how to comply with it. Most Hardlyvillains welcomed tax revenues generated from tourist purchases at local businesses like Greasy Spoons Grill and Bar, Hardly Yoga, Country Lebanese, rifleman.com, The Donny Brook Inn, and Jimmy Jones Enterprises, Legal and Not. But beyond that, "you can't spend what you don't make" became something of a local mantra.

The immediate impact of TO113 was negligible because most Hardlyvillains didn't sell property anyway. Nor did they need much in the way of infrastructure beyond water (wells), sewer (required by the National Watershed designation) and a sheriff. Most other public services were provided by volunteers (i.e., volunteer fire department, volunteer road maintenance) or supplied by private entrepreneurs. K–12 education was tended to by those who enjoyed teaching, not administering. Parents tipped the good ones well and skimped on the others. Most food and drink was raised, produced, and distributed among themselves. Barter was the law of this land, and when cash was needed, banker Jamin and First National Bank of Hardlyville stood at the ready.

While a few cried communism and others anarchy or even free market socialism, the breadth of complaint was dwarfed by the depth of contentment. Most of Hardlyville was very, very, very happy.

The village of Hardlyville was simple and cheap to govern, and most residents thrived with a smile in their happy cocoon of provincialism, stable prices, and a healthy equilibrium between supply and demand, deaths and births, comings and goings. In many ways, life in Hardlyville simply stood still for a long while.

The long term implications of TO113 were substantially more consequential. Fast forward to current time and place, and the chaos of an outside world turning upside down.

No one will forget when the first refugee from California showed up at banker Jamin's office, waving a money order with lots of zeros on it. He wanted to open an account and acquire or option any property(ies) in the village currently for sale. When informed by Captain Happy that he was not allowed to do so because of TO113, he pulled wads of $100 bills from his pockets, waving them furiously in the air and demanding to see the mayor. When advised that the mayor had retired several years before and that the village hadn't gotten around to electing another, he sputtered in confusion and asked who was in charge of this two bit, second-century-BC excuse for a town. When advised by Captain Happy that it was a village, not a town, with no one particularly in charge, he flung his Franklins into the air and fled in his black Mercedes for a saner place to invest the remains of his California fortune.

Funny thing, it happened again and again and again, to the frustration of immigrants from the west eyeing supple Skunk

Creek, which pulsed life through the village and for the entertainment of locals. Some visitors screamed "discrimination" while others settled for "stupid rubes, don't you want to be rich?" Genuine entrepreneurs like Jimmy Jones flinched when he heard six-figure offers for his garage but knew in his heart that it was more important to have good neighbors, a healthy place to raise his family, and clean water than a bank account so full he could never spend it all. And without the escalation of real estate prices his children and theirs would not need to build large net worths to prosper and live comfortably in tiny Hardlyville, which was by definition not going to become much larger as long as die off approximated birth rate.

It was all so simple, and apart from normal squabbles, illicit affairs, petty theft, and drunken stupors, life in the village of Hardlyville hummed along like a finely tuned F-150 engine. Clean water, minimal inflation, supply and price equilibrium led to lives well and happily lived, and generally unchanged.

Amidst the outside agitation and churning, village elders concluded that it probably was time to restore some sense of local governance. None of them wanted the responsibility, so all eyes turned to young Pres Bloom, who had in many ways been serving as de-facto mayor for several years.

When squabbles among citizens arose, they generally ended up on Pres's desk at the *Daily Hellbender* for resolution. He had a keen sense of fairness and was not afraid to think or act. Sure, he was short on age and experience, but few doubted his sincerity or integrity.

When Pres Bloom declared for mayor, most of Hardlyville flocked to his campaign. His political roots, which extended to a retired president of the United States, were the stuff of rumor, not acknowledged fact, as mother Billious Bloom had revealed her meanderings with a former sitting president to only a few, most of whom were dead or senile on election day.

When the final vote was tallied, the 233 to 35 margin of victory signaled a mandate for enlightened leadership in increasingly troubling times. That the total votes cast far exceeded the number of eligible voters caused a few eyebrows to arch but no one begged a recount in that the 35 were generally citizens voting for themselves.

And, after all, Hardlyville had never been able to agree on exactly how many Hardlyvillains existed from time to time, as evidenced by the population counts recorded on signs at opposite ends of town. If one entered Hardlyville from the east, he or she was greeted by a small green sign declaring 285 residents. When exiting city limits to the west he or she was bid goodbye by 314 hardly souls, with a hopeful message that they would come back some day. Surely 268 votes fit comfortably somewhere on that spectrum.

In essence, Big Money was kind of like Big Pork. Both distorted the local economy, played to greed and manipulation, and discounted root values. Hardlyville sought none of either.

All's well that continues well seemed to be the mood of the day, even these times, in Hardlyville.

Which is precisely why this brutal, unsolved murder felt so out of place.

CHAPTER 10:
ROCK ART IN THE OZARKS

Jimmy Jones slipped down the rope hand over hand into the eerily lit cavern, feet touching down lightly in the cold spring water, before carefully picking his way to the mud bank where he and Sally had co-mingled so many times. He smiled at their return on that investment of love-making, namely Girl and Lucas Junior II, the latter so named because Lettie had already named one of hers Lucas Junior, and Jimmy felt a compulsion, with her permission, to further honor and memorialize her deceased husband. Pierce Arrow, Lettie's partner, thought it sounded a bit too much like royalty, but Lettie teased him for being a snob and granted her concurrence.

Jimmy followed a branch spring through a tight bend to the rock where the spirit of Lucas generally hung out. It wasn't there. Because they communicated in thought, not voice, he sought out Lucas in his mind without reception. This had happened on occasion, so he was not concerned. He would pass some time checking out another branch he had recently discovered and then return.

As he wandered down the alternative cave branch, a mark on the rock wall caught his attention. And, then another. Jimmy had never passed this way before and knew not what to expect. He pulled a tiny flashlight from his pocket, shielded the light with his hand so as not to disturb others in the garden, and entered yet another world beneath the surface.

When he and Sally had first discovered this subterranean Garden of Eden decades ago, he had been amazed to travel back in time to what an Ozarks environment from centuries past had resembled. They had no idea of how or why this sliver of back then had survived, but they reveled in its natural beauty and the special creatures that could no longer survive mankind's footprint above ground.

He now found evidence of man himself as he had once lived with them.

Starring back at Jimmy Jones in the dim light was a full panel of etchings into rock, mostly anthropomorphs. Some figures were of stick men, some of stick women. Some men were bedecked with crazy headdresses. Several sported what appeared to be duck heads. Some women were hunched over as if bearing a child or a burden. Some stick figures were joined together, doing the dirty deed in some form or fashion, Jimmy guessed with a smile. There were also quadrupeds with horns, with long tails. Some were missing limbs. He had stumbled onto a treasure trove of rock art from ancient times, and felt the presence of its creators.

Jimmy sat on a rock close by and sought to soak it all up. What had they been like, he wondered, those who had so carefully carved out their story into rock? How long ago had it been? What were they telling him?

Most obvious was the fact that they had been here, that humankind, pristine water, and now nearly extinct animal life could once have existed together, taking and giving no more than was needed, from each to the other, to survive. There was a shadow of guilt that crossed Jimmy's mind with that conclusion.

He sensed that all could not have been perfect. Several of the petroglyphs were flat-out nasty. What could that be extending from the backside of a fat, horned animal but a long snake baring its fangs?

One dog-like creature appeared to have a spear embedded in the same orifice. These were not kind and gentle representations of life in olden days. There were others that Jimmy just couldn't make out, exaggerated shapes, forms, appendages.

Then one set of stick figures particularly caught his eye. Their shared image was imbued with violence. A jagged edge extended from just below the circular head of one, the second looking on, with spots of what must be blood splattered all about. This was bad stuff and spoke to murder, war, or worse. Jimmy couldn't look at that one for long.

Jimmy fingered several sherds of what appeared to be clay pottery in the dirt below. They felt strange to him, even clandestine, but he quickly pocketed one.

Jimmy sat for a while and wondered what it all meant. There was a chill in the air that he hadn't noticed before. He would read up on the rock art of the ancients in the Ozarks and come back one day. Today he needed cousin Lucas for grounding in the delicate topic of life beyond.

Jimmy Jones returned to the rock where he often found Cousin Lucas meditating, or whatever one did with time on their hands in the life beyond. Still no sign of Lucas, so Jimmy sat a spell longer. As he drifted off he began to dream about a dream which troubled him deeply, a dream of violence, a dream of flesh tearing, blood gushing, strangulation and mutilation, a dream of death, a dream that shook him to his core.

He awoke with a start, short on specifics, but full of fear. He didn't understand his shortness of breath or why his hands were clutching his own throat.

He only knew at that moment that he needed Lucas and hoped he was okay.

And then it was Sally, Girl, and Lucas Junior II he transitioned to. He'd better get home and check on them. He would return to discuss weighty matters with cousin Lucas another day.

Jimmy scrambled up the rope, oblivious to the aches and pains of age, rolled the concealing rock back in place, untied and carried the rope to his pickup, and returned to Hardlyville with his heart in his throat. The dream, which he could not exactly remember but still sat like a vague burning ember of jalapeño pepper in his stomach, was unlike any he had ever experienced. And to have it in his special garden, his own safe place, cousin Lucas's back yard, birthed an intense sense of dread and foreboding.

Jimmy roared up the gravel driveway, leapt from the truck before it stopped rolling, and flung open the door to his house screaming their names. Sally. Girl. Lucas Junior II.

CHAPTER 11: SPRING FIELD

Being a lesbian in this town had never been easy. But then again, neither had been being the illegitimate daughter of Newton Diddle. Thankfully, she had escaped him long ago. As she had gotten away, her bitterness had turned to relief, until he had showed up as sheriff in a small town uncomfortably close to her new choice of residence. She was thankful that he probably hadn't a clue as to her whereabouts. She simply never wanted to see him again.

Yet she also had an innate longing to get even for the violence and abuse he had inflicted on her mother and herself while they had lived together. He was always drunk when it happened, and generally apologized after the fact, but neither fact diluted the damage.

Sandy Smith simply hated her father and, at times, she still wanted to hurt him.

She occasionally wondered whether his antics had been what turned her against men in general, but concluded it was not a factor, as she was comfortable in her skin and in the arms of her female lovers. No, Sandy Smith had found where her heart belonged and had come out to embrace her sense of belonging long before her relocation to Spring Field. She felt at home here, at least until she read of Newton Diddle's appointment as sheriff in tiny Hardlyville.

Spring Field, the one of thirty-eight so named closest to Hardlyville, had been a nice mid-sized town before the speculators from out west began to circle.

This Spring Field had a colorful past, from founding in the early 1830s next to a natural spring, to basic agricultural economy, to railroad line in 1868, to its development as a regional and diverse economic center. Its location near major rivers birthed the city symbol, a johnboat, sturdy and yet agile enough to run their perilous rapids. Spring Field had lots of water and California immigrants thought they had died and been resurrected in paradise. Property values were on the rise.

This Spring Field was also 90% Caucasian and conservative to the bone, though local attitudes had softened to the point that many, like Sandy Smith, were finding comfortable respite within its boundaries.

Sandy had never had a steady partner but hoped to one day. She was happy with her lot as a marketing consultant by day and a steady player on the local social scene at night, at least for now. She didn't exactly consider herself hedonistic but she did generally enjoy a good time.

That is, until the old memories of sheriff and father Newton Diddle stirred beneath her casual exterior, as they occasionally did. The things he had done to her mother and Sandy herself should have landed him in jail, not running one. She had blamed her mother for not standing up to him or turning him in. But her mother's single goal in life had been to protect Sandy, and when she finally fled with her one very cold night back east, and hitchhiked across the country, offering herself up as compensation on occasion for a safe ride, Sandy had been freed.

She ought to be a little more grateful to mom. And very hateful toward Newton Diddle.

Another very dark thought crossed her mind. What could she do to hurt the man, to get even for her and her mother?

CHAPTER 12: A FOCAL GROUP

Sheriff Newton Diddle was obsessed with the brutal murder of a beautiful young lady on his watch. He couldn't sleep at night without at least one awakening to the vision of her demise, or the stench of death and blood. He had even thought seriously about taking a drink of something stronger than diet coke for the first time in decades. He knew that was a loser, and probably worse. He was a hard-core alcoholic and did very nasty things under the influence. He had hurt people before. If he hadn't been married to such a pansy during his drinking days he would probably have been in jail today.

After she had escaped the cycle with his only child, a snot-nosed, sassy little daughter, he bottomed out. At least until he had raped once more and gotten away with it. This victim had strangely taken pity on his besotted ass and accompanied him to a shrink she knew well. Why, he would never understand, but between the two of them he found hope that he could start over. Surely he could trust someone he had raped in a drunken rage and yet who cared enough about him to get him help? From confessional therapy to twelve steps, she had held his hand along the way. His recovery had been wrenching and she finally had no more to give. She died suddenly and without reason. She just didn't wake up next to him as she had every morning since his journey had begun. He shunned an autopsy for fear of what he might discover, maybe a sign he had missed that could have saved her life.

It was going to be hard enough to live without her. Additional guilt would bury him. He simply said goodbye, considered a drink, decided against it in honor of her, and carried on.

She had helped him find solid footing on slippery ground and he continued the climb out of that deep, dark hole on his own. That he ended up toting a revolver and sheriff's badge was testimony to her unconditional kindness and a quiet resolve he finally discovered within. And to the fact that no one ever filed charges against him. He could never let her or himself down. He would rather put that revolver in his mouth than abandon his recovery.

Sheriff Newt had to do something different or he could lose himself again. He had read somewhere about the wisdom of consulting with others on particularly knotty problems or challenges. He seemed to recall one approach called a focal or focus or fecal group, wherein a small cadre of diverse souls set around focaling or fecaling on a matter, exploring all kinds of theories, then converging on a range of logical conclusions. Sheriff Newt decided to employ a focal group to help solve the grisly murder of the young lady.

He would have to select participants carefully. The group would need to be diverse with respect to age and gender, generally respected in the community, and trustworthy when it came to confidentiality. He recalled something about a focal group only working when everyone could speak their piece and not have it end up in the paper. That by definition would eliminate the fearful Billious Bloom, publisher of the *Daily*

Hellbender, and her son, Mayor Press Bloom, editor of same. Thank Goodness. He wanted nothing to do with either.

He decided to take Booray Abdul, owner of Country Lebanese Foods into his confidence for a private discussion of his idea. Sheriff Newt didn't know Booray well, but loved his food. Surely that was a basis for trust?

Booray laughed out loud when Sheriff Newt shared his focal group idea. This confused the sheriff to no end. He had always thought Booray a serious and polite young man?

Booray chuckled that what Sheriff must be contemplating was a focus group, not focal or fecal. Sheriff Newt blushed but took responsibility for his stupidity, offering that he had only scanned the article.

Booray confirmed that utilizing focus groups was a legitimate business tactic to gage receptivity to an idea, a movie, a Lebanese dish or such. He had never heard of such a gathering being employed to kick murder ideas and theories around, but allowed that it probably couldn't hurt, given the desperation of the community to find a solution. He suggested that Sheriff ask Paul Michael (Pomp) Peters, Mona Arrow, Feral Fister, and newcomer to town Anel Feckle to join the sheriff's Murder Focus Group.

Sheriff wondered about Mona Arrow, given her genealogical rooting in the news business through father Pierce and the Hardlyville *Daily Hellbender*. Booray pointed out that Mona had never shown the slightest interest in much of anything beyond her husband Otis Hendricks and helping others, but that if she shared her father's reasoning instincts she could be an invaluable source of logic. Anel Feckle was not well known to anyone which also might be a plus. Sheriff Newt had never even met her. Booray would, of course, participate as well.

Sheriff Newt asked if Booray could gather the nominees for a brainstorming session as soon as possible since he knew them all. He also asked Booray to facilitate the initial meeting, him knowing all about focal groups. Booray agreed and redirected Sheriff to focus on a focus group. Both agreed this was a weighty undertaking worthy of immediate action.

Booray hosted the first official meeting of the sheriff's Murder Focus Group in his restaurant the next afternoon, wowing all with the aromas of his Lebanese special for the evening. In fact, no one paid attention to anything the sheriff provided in his background briefing, as they kept wandering in and out of Booray's kitchen.

Booray finally moved them out on the patio and poured each a glass of Lebanese wine to restore order and focus.

Sheriff Newt summarized all that he knew again:
- scene of the murder – old barn
- victim – young naked blonde lady
- cause of death – severed throat all the way through her spine
- other – no fingerprints
- no weapon
- no sexual abuse
- no motive
- no nothing

So what did everyone think, he wondered aloud?

Anel Feckle was the first to raise her hand. This was surprising in that she was brand new to town and generally an unknown quantity. Her analysis was crisp, relevant, and laced with profanity and sexual innuendo. The young lady had been murdered by her jealous lesbian lover, who had caught her messing around with another effing tart. She had drugged her, driven her to the barn, and cut off her effing head short of one thin layer of skin about the thickness of a effing sack.

Feral Fister was bowled over and immediately attracted to Ms. Feckle in a way he hadn't felt in years. She was matronly without flaunting it, daring in a forthcoming manner, confident, slyly dressed, insightful in her reasoning, and not afraid to drop an occasional f-bomb. *Talk dirty to me,* he smiled. She also reminded him of the Granny that he had laughed at in his pappy's Playboy Magazine years past, gray hair rolled into a bun, sagging breasts over tummy bulge, foul mouth and twinkling eyes. She might be fun to become better acquainted with.

Feral was next with a slightly different twist. He suggested it was a gay man who had attempted to pick up the deceased lady's date and was rebuffed when the date chose her instead of him. Only a man would have been strong enough to cut through a neck all the way.

Anel nodded her respect for his theory. There was clearly something going on between these two, thought Booray.

Sheriff Newt was shocked to see everyone attack gays in the absence of rape. Couldn't it have just been some pervert smart enough to know that DNA is evidence?

Mona reasoned that it might be a political hit job, that perhaps this young lady had gotten frisky with an important public figure, and had attempted to blackmail him or her with a photograph or letter. She simply needed to be snuffed out.

What if she was murdered by her regular sexual partner, who found her cheating on him and had no need to have sex with her since he had already been there, guessed Booray Abdul.

Pomp Peters suggested that it might have been an alien from Tralfamadore. He remembered reading about Billy Pilgrim and Montana Wildhack and their trysts under the dome in front of one-eyed Tralfamadorians in Ms. Bloom's class on Sex Ed. Those aliens were obviously sex-crazed.

Anel Feckle laughed out loud.

Sheriff decided he had better cut things off before Booray poured another round and things got really out of hand. He thanked all for their imaginative deductions and asked each to think about what was wrong with each others' before their next get-together the following week, same time, same place, same wine. He feared that this was going nowhere fast, but was kind of stuck in the middle lane at this point.

He even slept better that night, knowing that they were trying something new and daring.

CHAPTER 13:
HAUTE HARDLYVILLE

Grisly murder aside, cuisine and culture in Hardlyville had never been better.

Tiny Taylor, the 84 pound fry-baby bombardier who had started Greasy Spoons Grill and Bar, so named to emphasize fried food over cheap booze, was still slinging grease. Her commitment to frying every form of food known to man and saucing it with a locally sourced aphrodisiac produced culinary near-miracles and eventually earned her accolades in the New York Times Restaurant Review, four stars in fact.

"This Miss Tiny can truly fry the shit out of anything, then sex it up," the awestruck reviewer raved.

Fried Carp with essence of Absinthe, Snapping Turtle Shell Stew, Fried Skunk Flank, Roadkill Curry, Fried Cottonmouth Tenders marinated in Absinthe, Fried Chocolate Chip Ice Cream with Hot Absinthe Chocolate Syrup, and other apparently loathsome but delicious one-of-a-kind offerings drew epicureans from around the world. With no international airport or train depot within reach, most rented cars, drove in to spend several nights in the Donny Brook Inn, and stood in line for hours to grab one of Tiny's tables and fabled meals.

In line with the general Hardlyvillain philosophy of life, the Spoons didn't take reservations, didn't raise prices, and didn't kowtow to anyone, no matter their station in life or place on the spectrum of the Forbes Wealthiest 150.

The focus on absinthe derived from Tiny's secret but well rumored romance with Ol' Dill Thomas, nearly thirty years her senior, whom she nursed through sex and satisfaction into his nineties, finally giving up the ghost in one final act of pleasure that brought smiles to all who gathered to memorialize him. Ol' Dill was one of those guys whose deafness was forever getting him in trouble, whose claims of paternity and offers of child support to the occasional unwed Hardlyvillain mother far into his eighties earned him laughs, giggles, and respect among his fellow villagers, and whose love affair with tiny Tiny lent the definition of sparkin' new depth.

That Ol' Dill was the third generation owner of the family still and had discovered the secret recipe for homemade absinthe which, when joined with other exotic flavors, tended to replicate the effects of an aphrodisiac, only added to his legend. When he passed on he left it all to Tiny, who launched her own legendary culinary career.

Hardly Yoga, founded and operated by Uvi Peters, was a beneficiary of the Spoons' fame and reputation. Uvi, somewhat of a mail order bride from the middle eastern country of Lebanon, had moved to Hardlyville to wed local hayseed Paul Michael Peters. "Pomp," as Uvi nicknamed him, had been so smitten with young Uvi, whom he had met at her brother's Bedouin shivaree wedding to Lil' Shooter, that he risked life and pride to travel to Beirut and seek her hand in marriage. It was and is a very long story that ended happily with Hardlyville's first and only yoga studio. Uvi's second love catered to the wealthy and snooty clientele from back east that drove in to patronize the Spoons. Uvi practiced a more traditional middle eastern pricing policy for her classes, not only raising prices daily, but bargaining with every customer, a great source of fun and excitement for all involved.

Uvi's older brother, Booray Abdul, had become a civic leader and chef extraordinaire. As such, Tiny Taylor had insisted on bringing him into the ownership circle of the Spoons, despite their frequent competition over the years. His takeout joint, Country Lebanese, had provided Hardlyvillains with culinary choices. Tiny had been so impressed with Booray's deft use of secret Lebanese spices that she had incorporated some in her broad fried offerings. It was only natural that Booray be given the opportunity to join her in melding the traditional from each culture into a new and higher culinary calling. He was successful in doing so, even expanding the Spoons' draw into international markets.

Booray's ascension into the leadership ranks of Hardlyvillain citizens was not a surprise to those who knew him best. He had taken to his new homeland like seed ticks to a groin and earned the respect of all who sought his counsel on anything from the use of cumin in sweet potato pie, to how to shoot a rifle at full gallop on an Arabian stallion, to how to entice one's wife or girlfriend to consume her first dollop of absinthe despite her knowledge of the likely results from such an encounter. His wife remained a willing and eager consumer.

Booray Adbul was simply one Hardlyvillain that no one could find anything to fault. His pride and joy was daughter Dr. Abi Abdul, properly educated at a premier medical school back east who chose to return to the Ozarks and share her extraordinary compassion and diagnostic abilities. Dr. Abi survived a brief but misplaced marriage and bore a son, Star, whom Booray and Lil' Shooter were helping raise. Dr. Abi reveled in her single status, though her list of suitors extended well beyond the Hardlyville city limits. It had also become obvious to her that she preferred the intimacy of female companionship, a fact she had begun to share with those closest to her.

And no cultural survey of Hardlyville could be complete without mention of the Rosebeam Foundation and its world class collection of Latin antiquities, assembled and presided over by executive director Billious Bloom. Founded with a generous bequest from village matron, old maid, and only granddaughter of founder Thomas Hardly, Octavia Rosebeam had given her life to teaching the children of Hardlyville about Romans, toga parties, and Latin syntax. That her gift was burgled from the failing Bank of Hardlyville under bizarre and unusual circumstances could not diminish its impact on the village's greater good. To be sure, Ms. Rosebeam was long gone before her guilt was established, if never acknowledged. Ironically, none considered it an ill-begotten gain, given the immoral shenanigans of the former bank president and owner.

Fortunately for all, Ms. Billious Bloom, town librarian and sex ed teacher at the time, expressed interest in managing and growing the Rosebeam Foundation. She utilized her expertise in both fields to do so. Ms. Bloom was ambitious, driven, attractive in an odd sort of way, and displayed an extraordinary ability to close deals on Latin antiquities around the globe, assembling over the years a world class collection and connections to the best and brightest in the field. She found pleasure in her vocation, and avocation, and put Hardlyville on a classical trajectory that became the envy of all in the field. Ms. Bloom was widely sought out as a lecturer and a lover but remained chaste, in the purest sense, in her devotion to the mission of the Rosebeam Foundation.

Thus between food, drink, yoga, Latin, and Lebanon, tiny Hardlyville had become more than just a dot on the corner of a map. It was not just a time warp or pass through, but an international destination, somewhat of an oasis in a troubled region, country, and world. One that welcomed visitors and hurried them home after sharing with them.

There were no invitations to remain, only warm farewells and "y'all come back soon" salutations.

Could Hardlyville survive "Californication" (as it had been called for decades), internationalization, calcification, inflation? Maybe.

If only she could solve the simple, brutal murder that cast a shadow on her sparkling creek and sunny landscape, as brutal murders occasionally had throughout her history.

CHAPTER 14:
COMINGS AND GOINGS AT PUKE

Bo Bevel had just finished sexing his latest partner. It had been a boring and unfulfilling occasion. He had run out of options for much more in Puke. He needed new partners, new energy, new inspiration if he was to regain his creative impetus to wreak harm and havoc on the world and its creatures of color he so despised.

His mean band of misfits sensed the tension and turmoil building. It excited them, in that these bouts with boredom tended to suddenly erupt in violence and malevolence.

This particular night he roused them at the stroke of midnight and asked for five volunteers to join him in his old nasty Airstream Trailer for a little south of the border fun. They knew of his disgust for any beings of color but were not quite prepared for what greeted them when he flung open the side door.

There squirming on the floor, on the furniture, in the aisles were at least a half-dozen young, Hispanic-looking women, hands tied firmly behind their backs, socks stuffed in each mouth. That each was stripped naked spoke to his intentions.

He announced that he had acquired these beauties from a sex trafficker in Little Rock and that his volunteers were here to do whatever they wished before he killed the women, one by one, thereby reducing the minority population of the world by yet another fraction.

This was too much for even Bevel's most seasoned veterans. No one minded a little sex or physical horsing around, but blatant rape and murder pushed most limits. One by one his minions wandered back toward the home cavern, generally claiming a need to urinate, defecate, or drink a cold beer and promising to return soon.

Bevel was furious at his subjects' acts of insubordination and grabbed trusted aide Pinky Flawed, the last attempting to leave, by an arm, stuck the barrel of a Glock to his temple, and ordered him to have sex with the frightened young lady at his feet. When Pinkie swore that he would love to but was too terrified to get his equipment into serviceable form, Bo Bevel cracked him with the pistol upside his head, threw him the keys to the pickup truck to which the Airstream was attached, and ordered him to take the cheap fleabag whores far into the woods, kill them, bury them in a shallow grave so the critters could feast, and return with proof that he had done so. A lock of bloody hair from each would suffice. Maybe he could even have a little fun along the way once his fear subsided, added Bo. The young, naked women moaned through the dirty socks.

Bo Bevel turned heel and headed toward Stinking Creek to sulk.

Pinky Flawed turned the ignition, and pulled out on the single track dirt road that offered the only exit from their evil abode.

Bevel waved at him in disgust and shouted something about good riddance. And Pinky Flawed was his most trusted lieutenant. What a miserable band of misfits.

About a mile down the track Pinky pulled over and returned to the Airstream. He quickly freed all of the young, Hispanic ladies, removed socks from their trembling mouths. He muttered apologies in his own pidgin Spanish for having no clothing for them to cover up with. He had no idea what Bevel might have done with their clothes. They would just have to stay naked, he observed, covering his eyes in a feeble attempt at modesty. Most had been prepared to die and sobbed their gratitude and relief.

He shared his orders to kill each of them and return with a bloody lock of hair as proof. He would instead drive them to a paved road where they would be on their own. He implored them to get as far away as fast as they could this very night, as his boss might come looking. Pinky then passed a scissors among his captives, advising them to cut hair, draw blood, and put the evidence of their demise on the table while he drove them to pavement. This took over an hour and most of time the young women huddled together for warmth and emotional comfort.

Pinky Flawed dumped his young captives in the middle of State Highway 5, repeating his admonition that they make haste in getting far away. Several muttered gracias, one even hugged Pinky tightly before following the others into the roadside woods, where they resumed their huddle for warmth and protection.

Pinky wasn't sure how they could even begin to express gratitude for being left naked in the middle of nowhere without a clue as to where or what to do next, but he was touched by their gestures. He had given brief thought to giving each of them one article of his own clothing to provide some cover. But he had decided they were better off naked than he would be returning to Puke in a similar state. Maybe they would get lucky and run into a kind soul. They surely deserved it after what they had just gone through and all the abuse and degradation they had likely experienced in their short lives. Sex slaves, Bevel had called them. Maybe even this weird freedom was better than that.

He knew he had done as right for them as he could and just prayed Bevel would never find out. It would surely cost him his life.

As he pulled off of Highway 5 he glimpsed movement along the side of the road. A dog darted across and he floored the pickup to intercept it.

As it lay kicking, he put it out of its misery with a rock and carried it to the Airstream where he spread its blood throughout the interior. Additional evidence that he had completed his assignment well.

Paul Michael Peters and his lovely wife, Uvi, native Lebanese of Hardly Yoga fame, were returning from vacation in Dallas, Texas. They had driven as they always did, owing to Pomp's fear of flying. Uvi had called her husband Pomp from the moment they met, and it kind of fit, in a contradictory sort of way.

There was certainly nothing pompous about Paul Michael, who was the General Manager of the Donny Brook Inn which he had turned from an empty eyesore into a community cash cow. And yet there was a quiet dignity and strength that presented through his hayseed clothes and quiet drawl which particularly appealed to some visitors from the east. Several had even tried to seduce him, but he was so shy and naive he didn't even notice the light touch, a sultry wink, or a blatant flash of bare skin. He only had eyes for Uvi.

As they drove the back roads toward Hardlyville, Pomp announced that he needed to take a leak and pulled his old Chrysler minivan to the side of deserted Highway 5. Uvi nodded through her sleep.

Pomp started to unload next to his vehicle but when he saw a set of headlights in the distance, he moved into the adjoining woods, pants already down and weapon in hand.

Pomp tripped on something and sprawled into a large bush full of naked ladies. He grappled around trying to regain his footing, hands coming to rest on any number of female breasts and buttocks, eliciting screams and shrieks with each touch.

Pomp guessed he was in the middle of a dream about harems and such until he looked up to see Uvi wagging a finger at him and imploring him to get himself and his pants up immediately. The screams subsided and were replaced with sobs and speaking in some dad-gum tongue that Pomp had never heard before. A pair of arms extended from the bush around Uvi's neck with a plea for what was obviously help in any language. Uvi pulled an attractive young lady without any clothes close to her and whispered in her native French which was close enough to Spanish to serve as a favorable response. Slowly five other naked bodies emerged from the bush, all seeking to cling to Uvi. Pomp was now sure he was in a dream and it was turning into a porn show.

Pomp had never seen so many naked bodies in one place and he tried to cover his eyes only to leave a few cracks through which to take it all in. Best as he could tell, all of the young ladies were brown like Uvi, though they certainly spoke differently.

Uvi broke his spell by demanding that he stop leering at the girls and go fetch her suitcase. He did as ordered and watched as Uvi threw it open and offered her clothes to the young ladies for cover and warmth. The girls dressed slowly and with joy. They had never seen or touched such clothing. They giggled like young children.

Uvi and Pomp huddled behind the car. Neither of them had a clue as to who, what, why, or how regarding the young ladies, but they were compelled to help. Uvi had not been able to have children and she immediately felt a motherly bond forming with these girls. She could not understand a single word of their Spanish, but guessed them to be teenagers who had been kidnapped, abandoned, or perhaps even runaways from some awful situation. They were too close in age to all be sisters, but she sensed a connection between them that ran deeper than she could comprehend.

She asked Pomp if they could take them back to the Donny Brook Inn and house them, two to a room, until she could find someone to help translate. They appeared to be exhausted, hungry, thirsty, and penniless.

"Maybe we can help them get back to their home, or stay away, as the occasion warrants," Uvi pleaded.

Pomp nodded his agreement.

Uvi found all the girls in some state of "clothed" when she returned. She explained her idea with hand signals as best she could, indicating eat, drink, sleep, and motioning them toward the minivan. They piled in on top of each other and soon were passed out for the remaining drive back to Hardlyville.

Pomp had left with hope for a week alone with Uvi to recharge their respective personal and entrepreneurial batteries. He was returning with six young ladies that he had fallen into along the side of the road. Naked.

WELLSPRING OF EVIL

His buddies wouldn't believe a word of it.

Puke was quiet and asleep except for Bo Bevel. No one was slumbering more peacefully than Pinky Flawed. He had actually done something good this day. Bevel was disappointed in the minor insurrection of his troops but pleased that he had eliminated a few more citizens of color from the world.

So, what would he come up with for them to do for him next? Should he unleash his anger toward the Spring Fields of the world again? This time for real—no joking around. How about rounding up some Vietnamese or Sudanese from an Ozarks small town settlement, castrating the gents and impregnating the ladies with pure Caucasian sperm? Maybe he would just shoot his worthless parents in their own bed? Perhaps murder a dumb blonde? He smiled at his fertile imagination.

CHAPTER 15: CANOE NYMPH

She glided over the slippery moonlit surface on wings of glow. Her paddle never switched sides as her steady "J" stroke was relentless in its consistency. Skunk Creek was aflame in full moon shine and she was the pilot light.

Peli Arrow glanced sideways through his passionate kiss and froze in observation. Girlfriend Flam Adonis noticed his distraction and followed his gaze. Their lips quickly disengaged, lust giving way to wonder, as in awe, and in confusion as to what and who the heck they were looking at.

Peli and Flam were only the latest children of the creek to find romance beneath the old Hardlyville Bridge alongside Skunk Creek rapid. Both sets of parents, Pierce Arrow and Lettie, Sheriff Sephus and Airreal, had sipped from the same love cup often, slightly hidden from the gravel approach by tall sycamores, nestled between the silver creek and dense woods, one and a half worlds apart from the rest.

There had been more love given and received, more birth control practiced or chanced, more clothing removed and restored in this very spot than any other in the village and environs. Hardlyvillains had come here for lusting, for nesting, for adoration, for restoration since the beginning of Hardlyville time, before the bridge and after, town founders Thomas and Petunia Hardly included.

This magical spot had served the ages well, but never more than this glorious evening.

Peli and Flam could only gaze without moving, their clothes scattered about the coarse blanket, as the tall, slender figure, long dark hair trailing behind, passed their observation point. She scanned both banks simultaneously with radar-like precision. It was as if she was looking for someone or something. Her eyes, large and yellow, locked with theirs in a timeless gaze that lasted only a heartbeat. Her full beauty flashed in and out of the shadows of her movements, silhouetted in moonlit backdrop. She was buck naked. And she wasn't a buck.

And then she was gone, carried by the current and her powerful strokes downstream, backside gleaming in the light, trailing erotic pixie dust in her wake. Peli and Flam quickly fell upon each other with a passion beyond prior encounters, and an urgency to grasp a moment before it slipped away.

When finally quenched they could only gawk, one at the other, and at the creek. "What happened?" was whispered by each to the other simultaneously.

They wondered aloud if what they had seen and felt was real. They were always told of the passion of this place, which is why they had ventured here this night of the full moon. But this? And had her eyes really been yellow? Like Vixen's?

Who in the hell could they tell about this? Who in their right mind would believe them? This would be their secret for a while. Maybe it was a full moon thing. They would definitely come back the next cycle and see. If nothing else, they could have a little more fun.

CHAPTER 16:
I PRES, TAKE THEE VIXEN . . .

Ms. Billious Bloom reached out to her part-time friend and lover, the former president of the United States, and unbeknownst to him, the father of Billious's son, Pres. How that had come to be was a long and twisted tale of sexual intrigue and duplicity that had a happy ending.

In an extremely tight nutshell, Hardlyvillains, as represented by Pierce Arrow and Lettie Jones went to Washington, DC, in the wake of the Big Pig Flood to seek chief executive action to protect Skunk Creek from further ravage forever, namely creation of the Skunk Creek Watershed National Refuge. The president was something of a self-proclaimed ladies man and demanded a quid pro quo in exchange for his support, namely sex with Lettie, whom he found extremely attractive. Lettie reluctantly agreed to take one for the team in the interest of greater Skunk Creek and the Hardlyville good, and over the strenuous objections of Pierce. Fortunately a threatened nuclear exchange between Pakistan and India near the moment of engagement had spared Lettie. In that presidential approval of the National Refuge had already leaked out, the president of the United States demanded a rematch, and Lettie, being a person of her word, agreed. She promised that she would make it worth the president's while if he would visit Hardlyville to formally dedicate the Skunk Creek Watershed National Refuge.

Billious Bloom, being single and consumed with history and sex, offered herself in lieu of Lettie for this historical coupling, pretending to be Lettie in the darkened confines of the community root cellar. The president reveled in her attentions and was so in rut that he paid scant attention to their anatomical differences. Billious was proud to be the only resident in Hardlyville history to have sex a sitting president of the United States and promised him more. Lettie was grateful to both.

Lettie and Billious's sexual shenanigans were finally revealed after the president's second visit to Hardlyville in less than a year for more of the same. It so happened that a photo taken of smiling Lettie while the president was supposedly bedding her, again in the root cellar, surfaced not long after his departure from the village.

The result of that encounter was Pres Bloom. Billious never told either Pres or the president, though she did revel in the president's continued attentions from then to now. Maybe it was time to end the charade and celebrate their son on the eve of his wedding to Lettie's own Vixen and close this unusual circle.

She invited the president to join her in Hardlyville for a long weekend without getting too specific, just that she missed his attentions. He was always more than happy to drop everything and sip from his friend Billious's loving cup. He was in his seventies now but had never lost his lustful enthusiasm for his younger lover, laughing with her often about the great charade that had brought them together. He couldn't wait for their next rendezvous.

Pres Bloom and Vixen Jones had been engaged and in love for over two years. They finally decided it was time to take the plunge after Pres's election as mayor of Hardlyville. Every mayor needed a first lady, even if she had big yellow eyes.

Pres knew about Vixen's roots, the blood of town hero Lucas Jones and the Demon Lady of the Evil Coven coursing through her veins, the preponderance of good she had inherited, with only the big yellow eyes surviving from her mother's gene pool. He also knew of Vixen's unusual strength, having witnessed it only once, as she had saved Girl Jones' life on a recent ill-fated float trip. Vixen also seemed to possess a strange and almost prophetic sense of insight and intuition. Pres couldn't explain it, let alone understand it, so he just shrugged it off as more good fortune. He was simply glad she was on his team.

Pres had heard back-door stories of Vixen's mother's insanely evil ways, her purported liaisons with wild animals, her abuse of her daughter, and her strength and stealth that seemed to border on the supernatural. He chose not to press Vixen on her professed convictions regarding her mother's love, attributing them to her inherent goodness and a dollop of wishful thinking.

Pres had fallen deeply in love with the Vixen he had come to know, not the baggage she bore.

Vixen, on the other hand, didn't have a clue about Pres's little secret. The son of a philandering president of the United States? Billious Bloom was the only one left from those days of conspiracy and duplicity that knew the facts. Nor did either Pres or Vixen sense Billious Bloom's true confession coming.

They just loved each other and wanted to live together in tiny Hardlyville for the remainder of their lives. They did occasionally laugh about Vixen's big yellow eyes. No one knew who, why, or how beyond her mother, though there were occasional rumors that ancient letters implied that long-dead town matron, Octavia Rosebeam, had unwillingly launched the unlikely strain, which would leave Vixen as the longest surviving descendent of village founder Thomas Hardly. Just another strange and discarded historical footnote.

Mr. President Emeritus arrived early the weekend of the wedding that he knew nothing about. It didn't take long for them to catch up on past-due loving, remaining holed up for nearly two days in Billious's comfortable Romanesque log cabin, while Pres wondered where his mother was and why she was so removed from wedding preparations.

Pastor Pat would preside, again in his storied-and-sullied white robe, and worked closely with the bride and groom on their vows. Again, the thought crossed his mind that this indeed might be his last public ministration. He just had to get it right.

When the groom's mother finally appeared, it was with Mr. President on her arm which always occasioned titters and gossip. He had become a familiar face around the village over the years. Billious explained her absence as catching up on affairs of state with a huge smile. Even Pres had a chuckle.

The president congratulated Pres on his nuptials and was honored to be invited by his mother to attend.

The wedding day dawned cool and clear, and most town folk came out to join the celebration. A large tent was set outside the Hardlyville Church of Christ to accommodate the crowd.

Pastor Pat called the crowd to their feet as lovely Vixen, aglow in a yellow wedding dress that complimented her eyes, was escorted through the crowd by her half brothers Lucas Jones Junior and Peli Arrow. Mona led the entourage, tossing honeysuckle blossoms into the smiling crowd. Just as they were to start up the steps toward the sanctuary, Mona caught a glimpse of movement to her right, reached down along the bottom step, and pulled a small garter snake from the untrimmed grass. In one motion she scooped and dropped the harmless and frightened creature into brother Peli Arrow's suit pocket, setting him to screaming and thrashing about in an effort to remove the jacket. She knew of brother Peli's deathly fear of reptiles and thought a little fun could only liven up the celebration.

Lucas Junior, fearing that Peli was having one of his seizures, tackled him and dragged him to the ground, leaving Vixen unattended for the moment. She promptly lost her balance and, to keep from falling on the second stair, grasped the back of Mona's gown, also bright yellow and relatively cheaply constructed. It ripped straight down the back all the way to Mona's buttocks, which were covered with nothing, in that Mona generally didn't like to be encumbered with underwear, setting those closest to gasping. Lucas Junior had finally gotten Peli's suit jacket off him and threw it over Mona's backside in the interest of modesty, in the process of which the tiny garter snake dropped out of the jacket pocket into Peli's open shirt, setting off another round of screams and disrobing. At this point only Vixen was fully clothed, which sent her into gales of giggles. The garter snake finally crawled off slowly into the crowd, which parted quickly for the little scene stealer.

Pastor Pat, with Pres by his side, heard the commotion as the wedding party entered the sanctuary and initially attributed it to joy. When he saw all entering in some state of hysteria or wardrobe malfunction, he signaled time out and hustled them into the vestibule for reclamation. *Oh, these children of the creek and their antics,* he smiled, *what would they do next?* He was sure he didn't want to know.

Fifteen minutes later the wedding procession resumed with Mona adorned in Lucas Junior's suit jacket, Peli wearing one of Pastor Pat's spare communion robes, his jacket and shirt set aside for exorcism of snake spirits, and Vixen, beautiful and aglow in yellow. Pres could only beam.

Pastor Pat began by asking his traditional question of who gives these two in marriage. Only in Hardlyville did the question run both ways, to bride and groom families. It was a novel approach, introduced by Pastor Pat decades earlier to honor both, and on that first occasion to actually clarify if it was the father or the son who was to marry the bride since she had dated both. It worked so well at defusing a potentially embarrassing situation that Pastor Pat made it his norm, and villagers seemed to again enjoy being different.

When Pastor Pat offered the question this special day, Vixen responded on behalf of all of her deceased parents: "Lucas Jones, Pierce Arrow, Lettie Jones, and my mother." The latter caused some to cringe, but Vixen had always been unwavering in standing up for her Mother's instinctual love, though no one else believed it. Most present just accepted it as another outpouring of goodness from a young lady who overflowed with it.

Pastor Pat turned to Billious Bloom who was sitting with her ex-presidential friend, and offered the same. Billious responded: "His father and me." This was a show stopper.

Pastor Pat's first panicked reaction was to do the calendar math in his head as to the last time he and Ms. Bloom had shared sex. *Let's see, had to be thirty years ago, and Pres couldn't be a day older than 25.* "Whew and thank you, Lord," he muttered, cleared of paternity, if not guilt, and then waited with the rest anxiously for her finger to point.

When it settled on the former president himself, there were audible gasps all around. He looked at young Pres, at Billious, and back to the groom with tears leaking from his eyes. In his eight years as the most powerful man in the world, he had met crisis after crisis, world leader after world leader, beautiful woman after beautiful woman, but he had never had a child. He had attained every honor and glory he sought, gotten literally everything in his life he desired, except little Lettie Jones of course, and a son.

Mr. President rose, embraced Billious, took her hand and slid toward Pres and Vixen. He sobbed and enveloped them both in the arms that had held everything from foreign leaders to cheating wives. He had never held something more important to him.

Wedding vows were a second thought.

CHAPTER 17: MOON CHILD

Peli and Flam returned as planned and the moon rose full and bright, temperature slightly cooler. They didn't know what to expect, only that they had thought and talked of little else the past month. Sleep had been fleeting, affection bestowed daily. It was as if the Moon Child, as they called her, had absorbed them in her light. If she showed tonight, they would try to flag her down. They had to understand, or break free of her spell. They also needed to know if her big eyes were really yellow.

They sat sipping a beer as the big moon slipped across the sky. "Maybe we need to be making love for her to float by," offered Flam. Peli was quick to agree. But before they could renew the spark that had last grasped them at this very spot, they heard the light splash of a paddle, and she soon slipped into view, stage left.

Peli quickly pulled his jeans back on and ran to the river's edge, waving gently to the naked young lady basking in moonlight. She quickly back watered, breaking her progress downstream, turning the bow of the canoe toward shore and Peli. Flam had joined him. They waited anxiously.

The canoe touched gravel directly in front of their sandaled feet. She stared from one to the other, smiling, and saying nothing. It was then that they confirmed her bright yellow eyes. They looked just like Vixen's.

Moon Child motioned for them to get into the canoe with her. It was an old one, with ribs of bent wood, long and wide. Peli knew it was from a long-past era, hand—not machine—hewn, rock steady. He had never seen anything like it.

After a quick glance at Peli, Flam took the Moon Child's extended hand and stepped in mid thwart, settling into the bottom of the canoe. Peli slipped into the webbed bow seat, shoving off as he entered.

Not a word was spoken. Neither Peli nor Flam sensed danger.

She spun the canoe around to face upstream. Peli marveled at her strength as she paddled up Skunk Creek rapid. He knew he couldn't have begun to pull against such current while navigating through the rocks.

After about an hour of steady paddling, again without a word, Moon Child pulled into a quiet eddy to a hidden gravel bar and motioned for her guests to step out. She then dragged the monster canoe up a bank and into a stand of woods, totally hiding it from river view. She crooked her finger to say follow and led them to an incredibly beautiful grotto tucked behind a waterfall, which she accessed through a side passage. A freshwater spring slithered down one side of a small, but airy, room. Moon Child lit a kerosene lantern, which cast shadows all around, and then a small wood fire, which added warmth. Peli had never seen a more beautiful spot.

Moon Child motioned for them to sit next to the fire facing a light-colored piece of smooth rock. She retreated to the rear of the room and returned with something in her hand. It was a box of children's crayons wrapped in a piece of rough cloth. She squatted like an animal or small child in front of the rock face, her back to Flam and Peli, and began to draw left to right.

Peli had long since ceased to notice her nudity, in that she wore it so naturally.

She began with a round circle, drew two perpendicular lines from its center, and every couple of inches she branched off stick figures, like a kindergartner might draw, both above and beneath the lines. She likewise drew lines from the stick figures with additional lines protruding. Occasionally she would sketch a rudimentary beast of sorts, mostly antelope-like, with what appeared to be wolves or dogs interspersed throughout. Even a giant birdlike creature would descend periodically, wrapping claws or talons around the neck of a stick figure. Both Flam and Peli agreed that she was trying tell them a story, maybe even a history or a lineage, and she would occasionally glance over her shoulder with a bright smile beneath her blazing yellow eyes.

She stopped abruptly and drew a dotted line with a red crayon straight down from the flow of figures to a round yellow circle, this one encased in a skin of red. Again she drew two lines protruding from the circle. And again, she branched lines and stick figures above and below the central perpendiculars. Most occasional glances over her shoulder now bore frowns or grimaces.

Then one short line extended down toward two tiny figures, unusual in that she placed two yellow dots atop each. One followed a line to a large number of encircling stick figures, large and small, with a crooked blue line running beside. The other small, yellow-topped stick figure was linked to a larger one on the other side of the twisting blue. And then a final yellow line connected the two yellow-topped stick figures. Her smile was back.

Her story took well into the daylight hours to share. She squatted without rising the entire time and finally laid down on her side, motioning for Flam and Peli to join her. She was sound asleep, fully out, within 30 seconds, leaving them to smile at each other and then follow suit.

Peli awoke to Moon Child roasting a whole squirrel on a spit. Her silky skin glowed in the firelight. She stared at him with radiance and calm. He had no idea how long he had slept but dark night outside spoke to at least a full day. *How could that have happened*, he wondered? Maybe it was the peace of the place. He tapped Flam on the shoulder to awaken her to the waiting meal. They ate heartily of squirrel and berries, washing it down with the cold spring water that flowed nearby.

Moon Child pointed to her rock art with a shrug, as if asking whether Flam and Peli understood. When they shook their heads "no" in unison, she retreated to the back of the cavern and began to dig into a slit in the rock. She returned with a single page of tablet paper, covered with the block letters of a semi-literate author.

"To whomever sees this first: This is a child of the moon who is seeking her twin sister. I am the old man who raised her. I found her abandoned in a cave just east of here more than twenty years ago, dehydrated and starving, just several hours old. Signs of motherhood were all around, just no mother. I nourished her as best as I could with milk from my goat, then all things natural and wild, through her youth. We have lived in this peaceful grotto, which I call Ni, or water in the Osage language, along the way. I have tended to all of her needs and sheltered her from the humanity I fled long ago. I love her as my own daughter. I'm very sick as I write this and my time with her is coming to an end. I will take my own life soon so that she will not have to bear the burden of my further decline.

"I have no idea who she is or from whom she came, just that she has unusual yellow eyes, abnormal strength, doesn't speak, and always draws two of herself on the cavern walls. I read that to be that she has a twin sister that she has innately and instinctively come to believe in, and that she longs to find her.

"In my parting words, I will urge her to take my old canoe out the night of every full moon and look for a girl her age with big yellow eyes. I fear her risking more exposure to man, as I have come to know him into my old years, but trust in birth bonds to build bridges, one to the other. If you are reading this, you have found her. Please be gentle and understanding. Please don't harm this innocent and naive soul. Please help her find her sister without leaving her cocoon of safety and security."

The moving and succinct old-style note was signed with an X.

CHAPTER 18: ENTREPRENEURIAL SPIRITS

It hadn't taken long for word to circulate around Hardlyville that Pomp and Uvi Peters had returned from their Texas vacation with a bunch of young Mexican cuties. That's where the stories began to diverge.

Were they illegal immigrants? That sent Sheriff Newt running to ask for passports. He was told that the young ladies had lost them in a fire and that Uvi and Pomp would be adopting them as their own children. This would by definition more than double the diversity rate in tiny Hardlyville, which some would consider a positive.

Were they trading in sex? At least a dozen young Hardlyvillain males were soon sniffing around the Donny Brook Inn for clues and hints.

Was Pomp going to open a new Mexican restaurant? Most discounted this theory as they knew Uvi would never knowingly nurture competition against her brother's Lebanese restaurant.

Where would they live? Since there were currently no available residences in Hardlyville to give away because of TO113, it soon became obvious that The Donny Brook Inn was their only alternative.

Were they suspects in the brutal murder of the naked young lady that Sheriff Newt had failed to solve? This brought Sheriff Newt running again, demanding that they answer questions from his focal group. When Pomp advised him that the ladies spoke no English and—unless he had a Spanish-speaking interrogator in mind—he would gain little knowledge, Sheriff retreated to his office again.

And on and on and around and back they went.

Uvi's first order of business befit her long-dormant mothering instincts. Food, cleanliness, sleep, and clothing, in that order. After the ladies had settled in, eaten heartily, and bathed for the first time in weeks, Uvi loaded them into Pomp's big vehicle and drove them to Spring Field for a shopping spree. She used her yoga savings to outfit them humbly but comfortably.

These young ladies, who had spent most of their lives in various stages of neglect and abuse, were overwhelmed by even the most basic kindnesses. While language remained a barrier, Uvi's knowledge of French and pidgin Spanish allowed her to teach them some basic English words and communication improved.

All settled into a comfortable pattern of existence. The girls began to take over motel housekeeping duties after Pomp showed them in great detail what he expected. They loved his smile and Uvi's kind touches, gained weight, slept well, and adapted quickly and comfortably to their new surroundings.

Names continued to be an issue. Uvi applied Spanish surnames to each. Pomp stuck with "uno" through "seis" applied in order of height.

The only formal Spanish he knew was "dos cervezas, por favor," so he looked up the other numbers online.

Guests at The Donny Brook Inn were captivated by the young ladies, their beauty, their naiveté, their apparent gratefulness for just being alive, and business boomed. Pomp was fiercely protective of his charges, as he would have been of his own daughters. He hovered around them constantly, deflecting advances and unwelcome attention firmly but politely. Occasionally one of the young ladies would be receptive to a handsome young man's smile, which earned a quick lecture from Uvi to just be patient and wait until acclimated to a new culture—quite the opposite of Uvi's own behavior in capturing Pomp.

One day "Tres" was piddling around with balls of yarn and a knitting needle she found in Uvi's yoga studio. She expected to be scolded when Uvi walked in unexpectedly and found her holding a tiny knit cap interlaced with delicate and colorful patterns of the kind her own mother had covered her head with as a baby. The memories brought tears to Uvi's eyes and a broad smile to her face. She rubbed the tiny cap against her cheek and hugged "Tres" warmly.

It was soon apparent that all of the girls knew how to knit beautifully patterned baby caps, probably a skill passed to them by their mothers in their own villages before they were ripped away into slavery.

Uvi placed the colorful baby cap next to her credit card machine in the studio. Her 6:00 PM class was packed with a group of New Yorkers who were in town to sample Tiny Taylor's fare and were spending three days at the Inn. As she collected payments, first one then another picked up the tiny hat. A fight ensued over who had touched it first and had rights to its purchase. Uvi assured the combatants that there were more caps where this one came from. This one was reserved for her first stepgrandbaby, but she would assure a greater selection at the next morning's 9:00 AM class.

At supper, Uvi asked the girls if they could each knit a cap before morning. She covered the kitchen table with yarn and borrowed a couple of needles from friends before leaving the girls to head to bed.

Next morning there were a dozen colorful and unique baby caps where before there had been none. She sold them at her morning class, raising the price on each successive one, to the complaint of none.

That one of the purchasers was a buyer for Macy's in New York City went unnoticed until she checked out later in the week and left a business card. She promised to send Uvi a contract for a large order of the baby caps within twenty-four hours.

Uvi had no idea what large was, but ever the entrepreneur, she had an idea. What if two of the girls could rotate out of housekeeping duties once a week and spend a day knitting these unusual caps to build inventory? She ran the idea by Pomp, who was always looking to boost the Donny Brook Inn's cash flow, and the girls—who seemed genuinely thrilled with the idea—at dinner. All agreed to implement the new schedule immediately.

The promised contract arrived by FAX at 7:00 AM New York time. It called for 5,000 units to be delivered before November first in time for the Christmas season at a price of $50/unit. Uvi was flabbergasted. A quarter million dollars of revenue if they could knock out—she did the math in her head—seven caps per day per girl? She did the math again: 5,000/6 girls/four months/thirty days equals seven. Unbelievable! To hell with cleaning rooms for these talented artists.

The cap she had designated for her first stepgrandbaby was spoken for soon thereafter. "Quatro" showed up pregnant.

When Pomp wanted to know who so he could beat the culprit to a pulp, "Quatro" shyly pulled a small dime store ring from her finger and pointed to her heart.

Uvi intervened with a hug and tears, and a wedding date was scheduled well before the due date. One less mouth to feed, Pomp concluded, and a happy one at that. One less set of hands to knit baby caps was Uvi's response and she set out to recalculate production quotas. All was good in Hardlyville for a moment or two, beyond murders and nightmares.

CHAPTER 19: IN SEARCH OF . . .

Jimmy Jones announced to Sally that they were going on a road trip. The restless stirring in his soul had boiled over. The dream that awakened him often in the past few months pointed toward the desert southwest, toward ancient cultures and symbols, toward life and death. It flashed in rock art panels and blood red images. It sounded like screams. Piercing noises, flashing colors, primitive surges of lust and illusion.

Sally couldn't begin to understand his mumbo jumbo but she had begun to sense a destabilization of her husband's solid core and she didn't much like it.

It had begun the evening he had rushed into the house screaming her name, and that of their children, both of whom were full grown and long gone into lives of their own. Jimmy was convinced that they were in grave danger. After confirming that Sally was okay, Jimmy insisted on driving over to Girl Jones'—now McHaffie, in honor of new husband Cecil—home to certify her well being. She and Cecil were making love, as they often did when he got home from work, and tried to ignore Jimmy. Finally his sense of desperation got the best of them and Girl answered the door in her nightie which caused

Jimmy to ask why she was in bed at supper time? He blushed mightily when he heard those words slip out of his mouth, patted Girl on the head, and said he was just making sure she was okay before stumbling back to his car.

He encountered a similar scenario at son Lucas Junior II's apartment with his girlfriend Sheila something, causing Jimmy to throw his arms into the air in frustration. They could only smile at him and each other before waving goodbye and picking up where they had left off.

Upon returning to Sally and confirming everyone's well-being, Jimmy Jones lamented that no one just ate supper anymore. The twinkle in Sally's eye confirmed that this might not be such a terrible development and that she was game if he was.

Their love games began to deteriorate shortly thereafter.

She was awakened one night with Jimmy atop her, nightgown raised, pushing into her without asking. If it had been a stranger she would have screamed rape. Instead, she just screamed and the stranger became Jimmy again, first confused, then begging for her forgiveness. He claimed to not know what he was doing. He had felt trapped in a dream and powerless to curb the urge to have her. Sally quickly covered herself and hesitantly snuggled next to her trembling man. He sobbed again that he was sorry. She kind of believed him. He certainly had never done anything like that before.

Jimmy said that he had to get away, had to follow a craving for something akin to knowledge and insight. He hoped she would go with him. Her nod of approval brought a sigh of relief from Jimmy. He didn't want to tackle this one alone. They would throw camping gear in the back of the truck and depart the next morning for a locale in southern Utah he had recently read about, for as long as it took to get him grounded again, to snatch him from the clutches of dreams and innuendo. He wouldn't even take time to consult with the spirit of Lucas which spoke to his sudden desperation.

CHAPTER 20:
"A DREAM WITHIN A DREAM"
(EDGAR ALLAN POE)

Their first night out on the road, while they still had internet service, Jimmy looked up a phrase he had been mulling over in his head. A dream within a dream. He didn't know where it came from, but it came closer to describing his confused state of mind than about anything. It was almost as if his life had become a dream that was having a bad dream.

He was shocked to find that horror writer and poet Edgar Allan Poe had already invented the double dream. He had read a little by and about Poe over the years but had never stumbled onto this particular piece.

"A Dream Within a Dream" was published by Poe in 1849 just months before he died and consisted of two stanzas, 12 lines each. Jimmy read it several times before declaring it nothing more than a "big ball of confusion." He even awoke Sally at about 2:00 AM and asked her to read and react. This was consistent with his recent erratic behavior so she complied. It put her back to sleep before Jimmy gently nudged her and asked if she felt like making love. She really didn't but this was his first normal request in weeks and it had been a long time, especially for two who had spent most of their married—and unmarried, for that matter—lives cavorting like rabbits.

WELLSPRING OF EVIL

As they lay after in warm embrace, Jimmy started asking Sally what things like "surf tormented" and "pitiless wave" meant to her. He wondered aloud if "is all we see or seem but a dream within a dream?" Was that what he was feeling, what was clenching his insides and not letting go? Sally nodded and slept on.

About 3:00 AM Jimmy wandered into an interpretative review offered up by a site called GradeSaver which used descriptives like "evanescent," "inexorably," and "movement of time." Jimmy wondered if Poe's death related to his discovery of some new law of nature, keyed to those words, one that explained away his existence and put all mankind on a diminishing curve of relevance. Historians blamed Poe's demise on everything from alcoholism to rabies to suicide. Maybe the latter fit in the context of his "new law" and the immateriality of his life? Maybe it was because he had married his thirteen-year-old cousin. Maybe he was really, really, really drunk. All this heavy thinking was making Jimmy's hair hurt.

And then a phrase buried deep in the review caught his attention: "perception of reality occurs at two degrees detachment away from reality." *Bingo*, thought Jimmy. *That may describe my take on the dream within a dream construct.* Is that what happened in the garden that night as he faced the brutally severed rock art head and led him to fear for his family? Was that what happened when he dreamed he was sexing Sally and he really was without knowing what he was doing? He would have to contemplate this "two degrees detachment" some more, but for now he was spent. Intellectually and sexually.

Whatever, he concluded as he drifted into sleep, he would have to give up this "dream within a dream" terminology. Edgar Allan Poe already owned it.

Jimmy was quiet during the drive through western Kansas and eastern Colorado, turning the wheel over to Sally intermittently so he could nap. Sally didn't remember much about the previous night beyond her comfort in having Jimmy return as a gentle lover. They spent night two in Durango, Colorado, well within striking distance of their destination.

Bluff, Utah, is located in southeastern Utah alongside the San Juan River. It is a tiny little place without much to offer in terms of accommodation or food, but it is located in the heart of rock art country and home to a famous petroglyph tracker whom Jimmy had sought out on-line.

Naught, the Guide, would make himself available to Jimmy and Sally for the coming week. He would introduce them to such spiritual wonderlands as Comb Ridge, Cedar Mesa, and Mesa Verde and they would pay a very stiff price for the privilege. Call it the Rock Art Capital of the World Tour with Naught as curator.

Jimmy Jones didn't know what he was looking for, but was confident Naught could help him find it. Having Sally along for the ride lessened his sense of dread at what that might be.

Jimmy had booked them into a mid twentieth century vintage motel with the intent to also camp out at least several of the nights with Naught. Jimmy was relieved that he and Sally had gotten it on the previous night because his first floor room was located next to breakfast and check out. The bed placed directly beneath the window invited constant foot traffic and did not bode well for amorous undertakings. Then again, that wasn't the objective of this interlude in their lives.

Naught showed at 8:00 AM, as scheduled, for breakfast. Jimmy could hardly have picked him out of a lineup of tall, homeless drunks.

Naught stood about 6'7", was clad in an extended loin cloth that made his skinny legs look like redwood toothpicks, barefoot of course, wearing a nude-Katie Lee-emblazoned-poster t-shirt, and a floppy hat large enough to protect his shoulders from the sun. He sported a single rock art tattoo of stick figures and bloated quadrupeds descending from his loin cloth down the front of his thigh, knee, and shin, culminating with a giant serpent encircling his ankle. His long white ponytail and beard touched his chest and lower spine at about the same length respectively, and his eyes sparkled blue.

Naught stuck out his hand to Jimmy in welcome and gave Sally a warm hug, assuming that she was with Jimmy.

"Who is Katie Lee," Jimmy queried?

"A very great lady," was Naught's response.

Oh my, thought Jimmy Jones, *this is going to be an experience*, wondering if it was wise to spend a few nights in the wilds with a pterodactyl who sported photos of naked ladies atop his belly and rock art from his crotch to his feet.

Over coffee Naught embraced them with his reverence and respect for the "ancients," as he called them, putting all doubts associated with his appearance to rest. He was passionate, charismatic, and obviously one with his subject.

This day and the next they would scour Comb Ridge for petroglyphs that Naught in his many times on the ridge had not yet discovered. It was the thrill of the hunt which he treasured, and they were paying him not to guide but for the privilege of joining his exploration. Days three, four, and five would be spent doing the same around Cedar Mesa, camping two nights with the spirits. Then it would be off to the far reaches of Mesa Verde National Park, beyond tourist trails and Navajo guides. Naught said that if they were still standing and speaking by then, he would happily drive them down to Canyon de Chelly to sneak in up by Spider Rock and wander about in a tiny canyon offshoot only he knew about.

"Wow," was all Jimmy could muster.

Sally looked shell-shocked.

Jimmy then shared with Naught his purpose in digging deep into the ancient's rock art. He began with the dream within a dream in the garden that had so terrified him, triggered by the brutal rock art beheading recorded therein. He spoke of the fear he had felt, then and later, when a few instances of aberrant behavior had that same receding from reality sense that one feels when watching a wave roll back from the shore only to recharge and return, never freed from its clutches. He somehow felt that delving into the heart of the rock art world would connect him to the strange panel and the vibes associated with it in the garden, and free him of its haunting harassment.

Naught asked Jimmy if he was crazy, much to Sally's amusement. Jimmy responded that he didn't think so but until he could dig deeper into what was, in a sense, possessing him, he couldn't be sure. Naught promised only to find rare rock art panels, not solutions to Jimmy's obsessions. He simply couldn't relate to a thing Jimmy was saying.

"Good enough," was Jimmy's terse reply.

The road up Butler Wash along the eastern side of Comb Ridge is dirt and scarred with divots. The Ridge itself is almost like a toy mountain range that got knocked a little lopsided, broken slick rock rising at an angle from the east to over five hundred feet before dropping straight down and inwards facing west from the top. An impregnable sandstone fortress, some called it a monocline, unlike any rock formation in the country. There was more than one hundred miles of this stuff, according to Naught, lined with canyon slashes from Butler Wash, many with ruins, some with art, pocked with moki steps hand carved by the Anasazi, each with its own story.

The Anasazi story was indeed a long one and dated back several millennia, depending on who told it. Most agreed that they left their homeland suddenly and without obvious reason about 1300 AD, ceding it to the Navajo and other Native American tribes. Placement of their prehistoric villages in remote, often impregnable sandstone alcoves spoke to fear of something and assured the integrity of many of their ruins and the petroglyphs that embellished them. Many Navajo accorded them supernatural or magical powers and feared their ruins.

Naught, in fact, knew a lot about Comb Ridge and its Anasazi treasures. He, with several colleagues, was the first to hike the whole length of the ridge from south to north over a period of three weeks. Naught knew the ridge like his own back yard, yet remained confident that they would find something new today or tomorrow.

In fact, they did, at least three panels Naught had never seen before, some likely dating back to 700 AD. Nothing surprised Naught. And yet nothing resonated with Jimmy Jones' internal turmoil.

So it was on to Cedar Mesa for a couple of nights out. Each carried his own camping gear and Naught double back-packed the food and drink. No cold beer on this leg of the journey.

Jimmy had brought a little of his finest weed, which Naught was happy to share, to settle everyone down after supper. Naught then stood up, stripped naked, despite the falling temperatures, laid flat on an elevated patch of sandstone, almost molding into a single unit, and was out cold in a matter of seconds. This man was clearly one with this place and this time.

The next day involved hiking deeper into the half-million-acre mesa with thirteen thousand years of history. Naught was particularly excited to find an elevated cave with ruins and rock art that he had never seen before. Though it was early afternoon he decided to camp nearby to allow a thorough review of the premises and its treasures before and after supper, and even into next morning.

Jimmy broke out a little more weed, Naught stripped and molded into a sandstone rock again. Sally whispered it looked almost like he was copulating with it, which got Jimmy's juices to flowing and the two of them moving their sleeping bags around a nearby rock outcropping for some shared pleasure, just like in olden days. Sally was glad to have her Jimmy back.

Sally awakened alone and to the terrifying sound of Jimmy's shrill shrieks coming from the cave ruins. She ran into stark-naked Naught, headed toward the same bloodcurdling screams at full speed, dropping both of them into the red dust. With due apology Naught was up and going immediately, Sally trailing behind. When she caught up, she thought Naught was strangling Jimmy, given the latter's desperate gasping for breath. She grabbed a stick and began beating Naught on his bare backside to blunt the attack on her husband. But a closer look revealed that Naught was, in fact, trying to remove Jimmy Jones' hands off his very own throat before Jimmy strangled himself to death.

CHAPTER 21:
FATAL ATTRACTION

Sandy Smith and Bo Bevel had met for the first time in a bar in Spring Field. They were both looking for a girl to provide pleasure and entertainment.

Bo Bevel moved first, offering to buy Sandy Smith a drink. She knew immediately what he was up to and politely refused, noting that she only drank with ladies. Not used to being rebuffed, Bevel upped the ante and offered Smith money for sex. Would $1,000 pique her interest?

She again refused, causing Bevel to scratch his head and seethe inside.

"What do you want" he growled?

"The same thing you do—a girl," Sandy responded.

This really set Bo off. "Another freakin' lesbo," he spat at her. To which she replied, "Why not find someone to share?"

There was something about this lady that drew Bo to her. Maybe it was an undercurrent of menace beneath her reasonably attractive exterior. Maybe it was because he couldn't read her shallow poker face. In fact he couldn't figure out if she was really serious. Maybe because this was about power, not sex, about being up to no good.

"Let's have another beer, you buy to get that off the table," Bevel countered.

"Deal," confirmed Smith.

Five beers later they were on a first name basis, had shared most of their respective baggage, and fed their shared hatred-beast with mutual respect. They were well beyond their initial quest for short term pleasure and entertainment and into a darker conversation. How could they partner up to hurt someone? It had only taken two more beers to arrive at an answer.

They gathered again tonight as they had promised each other at the beginning, to continue their pilgrimage of pain and sadistic pleasure. Once a month they would vent their anger together, once a month someone would pay a higher price. They didn't see or communicate with each other month to month, yet somehow each knew the other would be there the next time around. A bond exclusive of love and sex had formed.

Bo Bevel had found his latest higher calling and Sandy Smith her new dark hero.

Their first victim had intentionally been two. The unknown blonde floozy whom they had left untouched, beyond her neck, and the feckless sheriff of Hardlyville whom Sandy called "Dad-ass."

They had picked her up at a bar in Spring Field, drinking alone but obviously in the market for company. Sandy had made the first move, and was soon in full control of the lonely lady traveling through from Amarillo on a cross country jaunt to New York City to become an actress. Two beers, an invitation to join Sandy and some friends at her apartment for some good ol' fashioned "fun" if the young lady would drive, and Bo took care of the rest.

He subjugated his own desires while chopping through her neck in an old barn outside Hardlyville, marveling at the feeling of power it provided. It actually felt better than shooting or just having his way with her. Perhaps he would make it his signature with other victims going forward, a mark to leave no doubt who was in control. He wondered aloud to Sandy, who was cheering him on throughout the process, if any others had ever done it this way, leaving a head barely hanging by a thread of skin.

"I'm guessing only someone really bad," Sandy laughed back in approval. Little did she know.

Bevel then disposed of her car in a nearby small lake, assuring that it sunk to the bottom before leaving the whole bloody mess behind.

It was all so easy, and just blind luck that the young lady was a unknown passerby and decent looker to present Sheriff Newt with his first murder to solve.

They would jerk his chain again, and again, and until Sandy Smith felt vindicated or Bo Bevel lost interest.

Number two was equally exhilarating, as was its delivery to dear daddy sheriff.

CHAPTER 22: A SUSPECT

Sheriff Newt reconvened his focus group as promised. And, as before, not much came of it. His parting instructions had been for each member to find something to criticize with one or another colleague's theory.

Anel Feckle and Feral Fister found fault with every conclusion except each other's, which both found plausible. This led Sheriff Newt to assume that, despite their respective ages and relative unfamiliarity, they had probably slept together the past week. He had seen the sparks between them last meeting and there weren't a whole lot of eligible sparklers of their vintage running loose in Hardlyville these days.

Pomp Peters discounted both of their respective hypotheses because he didn't know of anyone in Hardlyville who was gay. Sheriff Newt could only shake his head at the young man's naiveté.

Mona and Booray allowed that each and every theory—including the Tralfamadorian aliens—was possible, leading Sheriff Newt to conclude that focus groups were a waste of time. This was, of course, prior to dismissing them from this important civic duty with words of gratitude and another glass of Booray's Lebanese Red. On him.

In actual fact Sheriff Newton Diddle had been nursing a theory of his own. It would not be well received in the village as his suspected perpetrator was a much beloved, even adored, Hardlyvillain. But facts were facts, lineage was lineage, and the inner reaches of the psyche were deep and dark.

Sheriff Newt had spent most of his week researching the Evil Woman, the Devil Lady, the She with the piercing yellow eyes and graying ponytail who had wreaked havoc and hell on a previous generation of Hardlyvillains. Of course, very little was written down—it was mostly word of mouth. Beyond long-deceased Pierce Arrow's Pulitzer Prize-winning reports on the "coven of evil" and the bravery of Lucas Jones, the stories of horror, revenge, and violence were passed on as Ozarkian folk tales, a grain of truth in each, a heavy dose of exaggeration in most, and an underlay of dark humor throughout. And yet Sheriff Newt knew there was something there that fit uncomfortably within the context of his now-urgent investigation.

What if he couldn't bring the murderer(s) to justice? Would they kick him out of office, out of Hardlyville? Would he face a recall vote? What if the murderer(s) struck again? What if their next victim hit closer to home? What if it was a friend or loved one? It had been almost a month since the sheriff had first laid sight on the young, previously beautiful, unclad, nearly decapitated, and recently deceased victim. He knew nothing more about her or the circumstances of her demise than he had at that first nauseating glance. Sheriff Newt was flummoxed, which had led him to start over, and begin with the history of this place, a history that was bathed in blood, yet seasoned with hope and resiliency. Hardlyville, if nothing else, would never quit as a village, never give up or in.

In that a key remaining bridge to that previous generation was Ms. Billious Bloom, the sheriff reluctantly decided he needed to begin with her before going public with his suspicions. He was prepared to invest a painful amount of time with her.

When Sheriff Newt first asked Ms. Bloom to come to his office for serious interrogation, she wondered if she had finally gotten to him and he was setting out on the path of his famous predecessor Sheriff Sephus Adonis as a regionally acclaimed lover. She dressed in a provocative manner and even brought a bottle of wine for the interview. A little flirting might be fun.

When Ms. Bloom couldn't get sheriff to stop staring at his shoes or share even a half glass of vino she re-calibrated. She clearly had something he wanted and it wasn't the usual male fare. *Better find out what he has in mind*, she concluded, *and start teasing from there.*

When the sheriff spoke, she soon knew it was not a teasing matter. He wanted to know everything she knew about the Evil Woman, first, second, or third hand. Ms. Bloom pointed out that no one ever talked about the Devil Lady of lore and long ago but everyone in town knew the facts of her murderous and wanton ways, which Billious proceeded to recite. She had heard them straight from Lettie Jones who had heard them from Pierce Arrow and Sheriff Sephus Adonis, who had experienced some of them in the first person. It was nasty, horrible stuff indeed.

Sheriff Newt pushed Billious on what she knew about the many murders. Billious shared that she had heard that evil one's principal weapon of choice was a long knife with which she cut throats clear through the spine, often to the back of the neck, leaving heads dangling by a shred of skin. The Sheriff reasoned that this She must have been quite strong or have had a very sharp knife. Billious confirmed that she was purported to have unnatural strength and was rumored to have sharpened knife blades on her teeth.

This sent shivers up both their spines and even caused the sheriff to briefly look into Billious's eyes. Her quick wink brought an even a faster blush, gulp, and downward spiraling gaze.

Sheriff Newt's line of questioning soon shifted to the Evil One's daughter with Lucas Jones, Vixen Arrow, raised by Pierce and Lettie, and recently betrothed to Billious's son, Pres. This set off alarm bells all around. The sheriff knew Vixen had big yellow eyes but also wanted to know if Vixen possessed unusual strength, like her mother. Sheriff had heard rumors of a dramatic rescue on a fairly recent Skunk Creek float trip with Vixen as almost supernatural heroine. He wondered if Billious knew any of the details?

Billious shot back that she didn't and wondered what Sheriff Newt was intimating? If he was in any way relating beautiful innocent young Vixen to the murder of the naked young lady, he was wandering into dangerous waters. The sheriff acknowledged that obvious fact but stated that he was committed to pursuing justice wherever that led him. It led Ms. Billious Bloom to the front door, which she slammed in disgust as she exited.

Sheriff Newt's research had planted a seed of belief that fair Vixen had enough of her mother's evil blood flowing through her to commit a brutal murder, maybe even subconsciously, and the strength to replicate her mother's standard methodology of dealing death. Despite the lack of murder weapon, motive, or eyewitnesses, there was a clear genetic link to a very bad and supernaturally strong woman that could not be ignored. He wasn't sure how to piece it all together but knew he had to try.

It didn't take long for most of Hardlyville to hear that Vixen, the mayor's wife, daughter of hero Lucas Jones, gentle soul to all who knew her, was a prime suspect in the brutal murder case of the young naked victim.

Flam and Peli were not sure where to turn next either. Their encounter with Moon Child had left them astounded, inspired, touched, and wary. They wished to respect her privacy, given her lack of experience with mankind's ways, but felt compelled to help her reunite with her twin sister, which they knew must be Vixen Bloom if for no greater reason than the shared yellow eyes and unnatural strength. If Moon Child was even remotely as kind and gentle as Vixen, they were confident Hardlyville would take her in and shelter her through a transition to life in their world. Who could they trust with their secret and her future? All this they discussed aloud as she paddled them down through Skunk Creek rapid and dropped them beneath the bridge.

Moon Child hugged each of them, and her nod and pointed finger skyward implied that she would return next full moon to seek their continued counsel. She then paddled strongly back upstream. She had still not spoken a word. They thought back to the handwritten note she had shared, bearing the promise she must have made about not leaving her safe haven except under full lunar light, beyond gathering food in the immediate vicinity of the grotto. They knew she would keep that promise despite her growing suspicion that her twin sister was lighting up the immediate radar. She had waited this long and could surely last another month.

Peli had assured her that her step-father would forgive the indiscretion of her returning Flam and Peli to town in broad daylight. That she had not reclothed spoke to her innocence and naiveté whispered Flam. Peli even wondered if she had clothes, having seen none in her safe abode. That could present another challenge to reintegration into civilization. Thankfully no one was present at take out.

What neither Flam nor Peli realized was how long they had been gone and what a stir their absence had caused in Hardlyville.

Their car was encircled by yellow tape as in a TV murder scene. They decided to walk the half mile into town so as to not disturb things and were soon greeted with citizens running up to hug or touch assuring that they were okay. They shared a glance that said, *silence about Moon Child.*

Sheriff Newt was soon at their side demanding, to know where they had been and commenting that the village was worried sick.

"Hiking" was all Peli could think of to mutter.

Mayor Press and Vixen were not far behind, embracing the young couple with genuine relief.

"Give them room to breathe" ordered Dr. Abi, herding both quickly toward her office for inspection.

Neither Flam nor Peli said a word which added to the consternation of all around. The sheriff noted in parting that he needed to visit with them as soon as they were released by the doc.

When Flam asked Dr. Abi how long they had been gone she got a strange look and response. "Almost a week."

Flam and Peli were stunned and with a quick glance at each other decided to take Dr. Abi into their confidence.

They confessed to having no idea that they were gone that long although they admitted to a certain sense of timelessness, almost like a dream, filled with stick figures and ancient rhythms. They shared it all with Dr. Abi, from their first view of Moon Child to flagging her down a month later and disappearing into her hideaway for what apparently had been a week. They were never threatened nor harmed, only embraced by a wisp they took to be Vixen Arrow Bloom's twin sister. They shared her story as best they could recall, allowing that they must have slept a lot to have passed so much time in her hidden sanctuary. They added that Moon Child had promised to return the next full moon to perhaps meet her sister, if they thought it timely. And as a footnote of sorts, Flam smiled that she neither wore nor apparently owned any clothes. Dr. Abi looked as if she had fallen off a hay truck into a circus clown convention. Nothing she had just heard made any sense, and yet Flam and Peli appeared to be in excellent physical, if not mental, health.

Dr. Abi completed a cursory examination of both and pronounced them fit. She then urged the couple to sit on the couch in her office and take a deep breath. What she was about to share was not pleasant, nor particularly timely in the context of what she had just heard. It had evolved during the time they were missing.

Word on the streets of Hardlyville was that Sheriff Newton Diddle had fingered Vixen Bloom as a likely suspect in the recent brutal murder of the naked blonde lady. He refused to go public with the accusation for fear of repercussions but had intimated as much to Billious Bloom. Ms. Bloom had immediately called on the community in a searing editorial in yesterday's *Daily Hellbender* to stand up and protect their own from slanderous and unfounded innuendo from "outsiders."

"These are not Hardlyville values," Billious Bloom had railed. In fact, Ms. Bloom was so incensed that she raised the specter of a recall election unless Sheriff Newton Diddle would reveal his intentions as to further character assassination and whisper campaigns against the innocent.

No comment was all that emanated from the sheriff's Office. Most of Hardlyville was in an uproar.

Dr. Abi counseled that the time might not be right to unload the heavy news of a twin sister on Vixen just now. While Billious Bloom was incensed with Sheriff Newt's intimations, Vixen was crushed. She had never been anything but praised in her short life, with the exception of the time spent with her evil mother after the kidnapping. Even that experience had somewhat of a happy tragic ending.

When the sheriff had called her in for questioning, she appeared flanked by Pres and Billious Bloom. In that Pres had attended law school, he counseled her on every response. Vixen's inclination was to be open and honest as she had nothing to hide. Pres on the other hand was hostile and evasive in his proposed responses. Vixen told him that he was making her not only look but feel guilty of something. Pres advised her to not trust the sheriff or his motives, that he was on a witch hunt and would do his best to set her on a broom.

When asked where she had been when the murder had been committed Pres wanted to know when that was. When the sheriff guessed that it was sometime around the fourth of July, Pres advised her to respond that she couldn't remember with such a vague reference point. On and on in circles they went, sheriff and Pres bobbing and weaving, Vixen sniffling in the middle.

The sheriff threatened Vixen that he may have to bring her in for more intense questioning under oath.

"On what charges?" Pres shot back.

When the sheriff finally spat out the "M" word, Pres and Ms. Bloom grabbed Vixen's arms and marched her out of the Sheriff's Office, warning the sheriff of dire consequences if he moved forward without evidence, motive, or even time of death. The sheriff shrugged in mock defeat but was becoming even more convinced of Vixen's role in some form or fashion.

As Dr. Abi explained all of this to Flam and Peli, they showed their shock and disbelief. They agreed with Dr. Abi that now might not be the right time to introduce a twin sister into Vixen's life. If fact, it would just give Sheriff Newt another suspect.

Still, they had to come up with something by the time of the next full moon or they might lose Moon Child's trust, and even contact.

CHAPTER 23: NECK-ED

This time it was a shapely brunette. Young and naked again. And also "neck-ed," throat cut in a jagged line all the way through her spine. The crime scene was the front porch of the Sheriff's Office, with red spread all around. There were even Biblical Passover-type blood markings over the front door.

Sheriff Newt stumbled into the lifeless body early one morning as he was sneaking through the dark to avoid any needless encounters with citizens. He was shocked beyond his senses and could only sit down on the front steps and stare. He was there as the sun started to rise and the first pedestrians of the morning stirred. A crowd began to gather.

Sheriff Newt couldn't speak. He finally pointed in the direction of Dr. Abi's office and gurgled something.

She was quickly by his side, bending to confirm death before covering the body with a borrowed coat and asking the sheriff if it was okay to move the body from the crime scene to her office for further examination.

The sheriff nodded yes as Billious Bloom snapped graphic photos which would be edited for inclusion in the *Daily Hellbender*. The sheriff then asked all to leave so he could begin a formal investigation of the crime scene. He appeared dazed and confused, which presented Ms. Bloom another opportunity for an unflattering photograph for future use if recall became a necessity. He finally had the presence of mind to ask if anyone knew the young lady but most had left by then and only shrugs of negativity remained.

Dr. Abi was quick to advise the sheriff that once again there were no signs of sexual trauma.

Sheriff Newt demanded that Vixen report to his office immediately. With Pres and Ms. Bloom on either side, the dance began again. When Sheriff Newt asked what Vixen had been up to the previous twenty-four hours, Pres laughed out loud.

"You must be kidding," he sneered. "Let's see," he continued, "she urinated about seven and we made love at least twice." Would the sheriff like for him to be more specific?

The sheriff had had enough of her smart ass husband and told him so, finally gaining a grin from Vixen.

Sheriff Newt impulsively grabbed his gun, pointed it at Vixen, and advised her that he was placing her under arrest for obstructing justice or something like that, and that she would be spending the evening in the Hardlyville Jail.

Pres was quick to disarm the sheriff with a sharp kick to his groin and a simultaneous twist of his wrist. As Sheriff Newt writhed in pain on the floor, Pres dragged him into the smaller of the two jail cells in the Sheriff's Office and locked him in. Ms Bloom got photographs of it all and poor Vixen could only look on in disbelief and something close to horror. They left for lunch and for Billious to piece together a front page story about police brutality for the *Daily Hellbender*.

Pres returned a couple of hours later to release the sheriff on his own recognizance. They did agree to an uneasy truce which did not include the return of Sheriff Newton's firearm or any provision for further questioning of Vixen.

WELLSPRING OF EVIL

As life regained some sense of normalcy in Hardlyville, if two brutal murders in two months could be considered normal, Flam and Peli reached out to Vixen for an important conversation despite Dr. Abi's warnings. They sensed that there was a very small window about to close with the next full moon.

CHAPTER 24: CATATONIC CONTENTMENT

Jimmy Jones awoke in a hospital bed in Bland, Utah. He had been unconscious for almost three days.

Once Naught had removed Jimmy's hands from his own throat in the Cedar Mesa ruin, Jimmy sank into a lifeless trance, very much alive but not alert. Naught shared with Sally that he didn't think Jimmy was in danger but wanted to tie his hands behind his back to protect him from himself in the short term. They laid Jimmy on his bedroll and returned to the section of ruins where Jimmy's convulsions, for lack of a better term, had occurred.

A large rock art panel inside the cave-like opening revealed figures Naught referred to as "San Juan Anthropomorphic." He explained to Sally that these were among the oldest petroglyphs he had ever encountered and probably dated back to 500 B.C. He noted that a couple of the sections appeared very violent, but he couldn't tell much beyond that without investing some time. There were also several sherds of what looked like old pottery scattered about. He would definitely return here one day for additional exploration but was more concerned about getting Jimmy back to civilization for examination.

Naught left all of the camping gear at the remote site and carried Jimmy out, draped over his shoulder. The twenty-five mile trek back to his vehicle took Naught six hours to navigate.

While Jimmy did not regain consciousness the whole way, he was clearly alive and appeared almost serene in his suspended state. Sally didn't know whether to be frightened or envious.

Naught drove them directly to Bland, Utah where there was a regional health care provider. Sally promised to keep him apprised of Jimmy's condition and Naught in turn vowed to return to the ruin for additional interpretation at his earliest convenience. He admitted that he was a little spooked to go alone after what had happened to Jimmy and would probably take additional experts in rock art and ancient pottery for protection and consultation.

Doctors could find no signs of distress during their preliminary examination of Jimmy, beyond monitoring his vitals, could do nothing but provide around-the-clock observation.

Upon awakening, Jimmy remembered nothing.

CHAPTER 25: PINKY

Pinky Flawed was born in a hovel in northwest Arkansas twenty-three years earlier. He spent his entire life climbing out of that mess, hiding from his abusive father, missing his birth mother, who was dead on his arrival, and pitying a series of subservient, addicted step mothers, until he could run away and arrive dead broke and destitute at the feet of a similarly-aged, anarchistic death-star named Beauford Bevel, who fed him on hate for his circumstance, meth, and young women for his pleasure. This was pretty sweet for a young man whose vocabulary did not include that word. Yet for some reason he wanted something more.

Pinky clung to his unusual name for superstitious reasons. The Flawed part came from his nasty old man, Floyd Flawed. Rumor had it that "Flawed" had been scribbled in longhand across the top of his father's birth certificate by his unwed mother, who tried shortly after birth to trade him in for another model. When the hospital refused, she clung to the descriptive so at least her ill-conceived son would have a surname other than her own.

She raised Floyd Flawed as best she could on welfare checks and proceeds from prostitution, but he dropped out of school early on and began hanging with meth heads and their minions. Floyd sired several offspring with different wives, including young Pinky, losing or moving from one for another, and leaving destitution in his wake.

Pinky had a more logical reason for his given name. He was born with the little finger of his left hand splayed at a ninety degree angle from the rest of his fingers. His first stepmother, whose name he could never remember, explained that it had probably gotten caught in the uterus as he exited the womb, and was surely an omen of good things to come. And though he was often ridiculed for its unusual positioning, he sure as heck didn't want to screw up the only promising thing that anyone had ever said to him. So Pinky Flawed it was and would ever be.

It was inconvenient that he could never find a glove to fit it during cold weather, so he generally wore an oversize dirty sock on that hand to stay warm and keep others at arm's length.

Fast forward to Pinkie Flawed and Bo Bevel. When Pinkie's mentor sent him out to pleasure himself with six innocent Hispanic sex slaves before murdering them, something snapped. He had never killed before. And, nothing could get him high enough to do something so low. When he cut them free, he did the same for himself. A big balloon of hatred hissed wasted time and air into the cold night as he hustled them into the woods to hide.

One brown-eyed beauty clasped his hand and kissed it in parting. She looked through his eyes and saw what lay beneath. A needy heart.

Pinky felt her reaching out and threw it right back at her. A bonding occurred that would not be severed.

When Pinky realized this connection, he began to seek out the young, naked lady he had freed. His efforts culminated in a trip to Hardlyville where he easily identified the home base of the now-beloved illegal immigrants at the Donny Brook Inn. He rented a room and wandered the halls until he came upon the infant cap production line and saw that set of brown eyes ablaze with entrepreneurial fire which soon gave way to lust.

She slipped into his motel room that night to show her gratitude for her freedom. They spent each night for a week thereafter, sharing gratitude for each other. She also shared her name, as did he. He promised to return to her with a plan for the future. And, he did. Their shared past would remain their secret.

The wedding was simple and pure. Love.

Pastor Pat presided over yet another of his final ceremonies with that sullied white robe beside the banks of beautiful Skunk Creek.

Quatro, whose real name was Rosita, Hardlyvillized to Rosie, was resplendent in a full length yarn gown, hand-knitted by her sex-slave sister-entrepreneur-escapees. Her baby bump scarcely showed. The groom was dressed in hand me down 1960's hippie gear he had stolen from Bo Bevel's closet of anarchy just before escaping the compound.

Pomp Peters presented the beautiful bride as his and Uvi's own, and Rosie's sisters served as maids of honor. He rounded up several local boys to stand in as Pinky's best men, though he had to promise that no one would be asked to put on a tie. Peli Arrow was suspicious of a guy with such a freaky name, but let it drop when the love showed through.

Pinky was vaguely aware of traditional Ozarks shivaree antics and offered no resistance when the best men hoisted him on their shoulders, immediately following the kissing of the bride, and dumped him into Skunk Creek.

Rosie, on the other hand, had no idea what was going on, why all were laughing hysterically, and feared they were trying to drown her new husband. Despite being unable to swim, she jumped in to Pinky's rescue, or to drown with him, and before all was said and done several best men, including Peli, had to jump in to save her. This brought back buried memories of sexual assault which had been her lot before Hardlyville and she scratched at Peli's eyes, intending to drown him as well.

Pinky was finally able to get his arms around his distressed new bride and pull her ashore for an explanation, which did not translate well into Spanish and earned him a brisk slap in the face. He finally kissed her long and hard and led her off to The Donny Brook Inn for consummation of their marriage, which had, in fact, obviously been consummated many times before.

The wedding party was left with laughter, a bottle of aged Ol' Dill's finest donated by Greasy Spoons, and fond recollections of yet another memorable Skunk Creek shivaree. The obvious love shared by bride and groom sweetened the memory.

Pinky Flawed worried that Bevel might follow him and discover that the sex slave he had freed that night long ago had become his lawfully wedded wife. If that happened, Pinky knew that Bevel would have them both killed.

And yet he was drawn to make Hardlyville their new home despite the risk. Rosie had a steady, well-paying job knitting colorful yarn baby caps with her "sisters" and surely Pinky could figure out something constructive to do after a short life of bedlam and mayhem. To his knowledge, he had no skills or aptitude beyond making a baby, but it was clearly time to learn some.

Over coffee one morning with Pomp, his mentor and friend, a strange idea surfaced. Pomp suggested that maybe Pinky could start a rock band to entertain guests at the Donny Brook Inn. After all, he had a name that could be easily linked to historical star power, though Pinky had never heard of his near namesakes. Pomp guessed that Pinky's parents had been fans and probably just misspelled their tribute to the legendary English rock band.

Pinky allowed that they were probably so stoned that he was lucky they even came close to getting it right, but since he wasn't sure which of his old man's abused wives had named him, he couldn't say for sure.

Pomp guessed that if anyone knew about that music, it would be Jimmy Jones, who had spent much of his early years stoned. They would have Jimmy over for a beer and to pick his brain as soon as Jimmy was recovered from his strange seizures.

Pomp reasoned that Pinkie and his band could play in the bar on weekends when visitations from back east were at their highest, and provide an enjoyable diversion to guests who had to wait to get into Tiny Taylor's gourmet eatery, Spoons. Along with Uvi's Hardly Yoga Studio and the yarn baby cap production line, a Pinky Flawed Psychedelic Rock Show could round out his entertainment offering at the Donny Brook Inn. Now all they needed were some instruments and a few dudes to play them. Pomp Peter's entrepreneurial wheels were spinning and Pinky Floyd's future looked brighter than it ever had, which was not saying a whole lot.

Jimmy and Sally Jones' return to Hardlyville seemed strangely muted. They slipped into town silently, late one evening, and stayed to themselves for most of a week. Neither Girl Jones McHaffie nor Lucas Jones Junior II, could coax anything beyond perfunctory commentary from either of their parents. Sally just assured them that things were okay and that their trip had been both perplexing and revealing. Of what, she was not sure.

Jimmy and Sally didn't talk much either. There wasn't much to discuss, in that Jimmy did not remember a thing beyond the initial meeting with Naught the guide. When Sally walked through their explorations of Comb Ridge, the overnight trek into Cedar Mesa, and even their impassioned love making beneath a sandstone promontory which housed an old and eerie Anasazi ruin, she could not sense even a flicker of recognition. She was hesitant to bring up the grand finale of that strange evening for fear of sending Jimmy back into a coma. And she definitely didn't want to mention the colorful piece of pottery she had found in Jimmy's back pocket when undressing him at the hospital in Bland. It was as if sixty-two hours of their lives together had been wiped off Jimmy Jones' blackboard.

She finally sought help, but Dr. Abi could add little. Jimmy tested out healthy by any measure and the doctor could not explain why several days of his life had simply disappeared from view. Sally shared all with her in total confidentiality, to the point of Jimmy's self-strangulation attempt. Dr. Abi could only shake her head in confusion and disbelief, which led Jimmy to suggest that Sally had just made it all up for grins, which produced no grins from either.

Dr. Abi could only suggest that perhaps Jimmy had experienced a psychological phenomena known as a fugue, with a corresponding loss of time and place. She knew little about such things but would be happy to refer Jimmy to a psychiatrist friend in the big city for further evaluation.

Jimmy asked what would happen if they did nothing.

"Probably nothing," was Dr. Abi's response

That was good enough for him.

A few days later Jimmy received Pomp Peter's invitation to gather over a cold beer. This was an invite Jimmy would never turn down and he was soon gathered with Pomp and Pinky to explore their entrepreneurial idea.

Indeed Jimmy did remember the rock band "Pink Floyd." Sort of. He was generally semi-conscious when listening to their music, but thought he liked it . That was really a long time ago, he mused. Jimmy promised to go through his attic and see if any of their LPs had made it through Sally's frequent house cleanings and report back soon.

Ironically, the next morning Jimmy appeared at the Donny Brook Inn with an album entitled "Dark Side of the Moon," which he proudly lent to Pinky Flawed. Jimmy loved the name interplay between past artists and his new acquaintance and saw great potential in playing one off the other. Pinky Flawed and the Stoners covering "Pink Floyd." Beautiful. He liked it so much that he volunteered to fund the acquisition of instruments and the importation of a rock musician to tutor the aspirants. He quickly ran through his mental inventory of the "children of the creek," which would also be a catchy name for a second act if this went anywhere, and settled on asking Mayor Pres to screen "the children" for interest and aptitude. They would need five members in all to accurately ape the original band, which incidentally included no females beyond groupies. He would also secure the services of an attorney to assure that Pinky Flawed and the Stoners were not stepping into copyright issues. Perhaps a couple of non-groupie ladies in the band would help with that.

Jimmy Jones was as pumped about this entrepreneurial venture as he had been in years. His "fugue," or whatever it was, drifted into the subconscious of his suddenly alert mind. This was going to be fun, if not prosperous, which was also a remote possibility.

CHAPTER 26: FULL MOON

Their eyes met and both immediately leaked yellow tears. Vixen stretched forth her hands to her twin sister with a sob. Their embrace was frantic and supernatural. They almost seemed to meld into one another.

Vixen quickly took off her jacket and draped it over her naked sister, causing the latter confusion and a frightened step back. The full moon shone brightly on both as they subconsciously sought counsel on next moves, one from the other and back again.

Peli and Flam had approached Vixen with gentleness and caution. She had requested that Pres be included in their confidential conversation because she was so shaken about being a murder suspect she did not want to leave his side. Villagers jokingly began calling her deputy mayor without knowing fully what it was all about.

Peli began with a series of questions about Vixen's mother, which put them all on guard. Had the evil lady with the graying ponytail and yellow eyes who had terrorized all of Hardlyville ever mentioned a twin sister in the short time of Vixen's captivity? Vixen shook her head slightly in a confused "no." Had Vixen ever met another, evil or not, with her signature yellow eyes? Another "no." Pres Bloom pushed Peli to explain rather than play "Twenty Questions."

And Peli did. An hour later Vixen was begging Peli and Flam to take them to her twin sister, convinced that, in fact, that was who Moon Child must be.

Vixen obviously had no memory of her birth but had sensed on several occasions during her kidnapping and captivity that there was more to her mother's story than would ever be told. She had even caught moments of vulnerability, almost sensitivity, beneath the mean-spirited and nasty exterior. And, in the end, it had been that mother's love, buried so deep, that had saved Vixen's life and caused her mother to take her own.

That Vixen knew nothing of a potential twin sister with big yellow eyes only heightened her expectation and anticipation.

Peli had a couple of other things to explain. The potential twin didn't speak but explained things with elaborate sketches. The potential twin never wore clothing that Peli and Flam could tell. The potential twin only came out on full moonlit nights and could be seen from beneath Skunk Creek Bridge. The potential twin was expecting to meet them there under the next full moon.

Sheriff Newt was frustrated with the uncomfortable impasse reached with Pres Bloom over Vixen who, the sheriff was more certain of than ever, was a murderer. Whether she did it consciously or under the spell of her demon mother was not the point. Her alibis were weak and her ties to evil obvious. That her mother's signature method of murder, cutting through a victim's throat and through the spine, was how each of these murders was committed, was unusual, unprecedented, and beyond circumstantial evidence. Neither jury nor judge could fail to see the linkage.

Pres had returned the sheriff's gun with the proviso that he would personally use it on the sheriff if he did not lay off of his innocent wife, Vixen. And now the sheriff would take matters into his own hands. He had cut an agreement with his friend, the police chief of Spring Field. The chief would send two squad cars of officers to arrest Vixen and incarcerate her in the Spring Field city jail. She would be held without bail, pending a preliminary court date. Not even the pipsqueak, Mayor Pres, could do anything about it. And let that bitch editor mother-in-law, Billious Bloom, write all the whining editorials she wanted.

There would be no more brutal murders while the murderer was in jail, further solidifying both the case against her and Sheriff Newt's credibility. He and the chief would agree on a date to effect the transaction as soon as possible.

They had waited anxiously beneath Skunk Creek Bridge this night of the full moon, Peli and Flam, Pres and Vixen. As if on cue, Moon Child had drifted through Skunk Creek rapid and pulled up to the waiting party on the gravel bar below. What had followed was intensely emotional and inspiring.

As to Moon Child's nakedness, Vixen tried to explain she would be required to cover her body if she was to stay with her sister. Moon Child shrugged without conviction but remained covered by Vixen's coat. Vixen and Pres took Moon Child home with them immediately, expressing heartfelt thanks for bringing the sisters together for the first time since birth. No one knew what could have happened at that crazy moment, whether the demon lady had cast one baby aside or perhaps not even been aware of the other? But nothing mattered now beyond being together.

It didn't take long for the news to bubble around Hardlyville. Vixen was protective of Moon Child but slowly revealed her to trusted friends and neighbors, fully clothed, of course, since her clothes fit her sister perfectly.

Sheriff Newt Diddle took particular interest in the fact that there were now two known offspring of the Devil Lady in his community. He quickly added Moon Child to his list of murder suspects if for no other reason than she had no alibi for the occasion of each murder, and she surely had that evil blood coursing through her heart.

He quickly arranged for his friend, the Police Chief from Spring Field, to grab both suspects.

The snatch was scheduled for mid-morning the next day. The sheriff called a meeting with Mayor Pres and Billious Bloom to provide cover for his involvement. As they sat discussing the murders in Sheriff Newt's office, the Spring Field police swooped in quickly and without notice. In less than a minute, Vixen and Moon Child were covered in gunny sacks and thrust in the trunk of a police cruiser. No one saw. There was no one to serve as witness. The operation was flawless and clueless.

Pres assumed his ladies were out wandering down by Skunk Creek as they often did on sunny days, still trying to relate to one another beyond blood. When they did not show for lunch, he guessed picnic.

By supper time he had called the sheriff in a panic to file missing person reports. There was no sign of forced entry or a struggle. No sign of violence or coercion.

It was only as Pres lay alone in his bed, sleepless, panicked, that the alarms went off in his head. He was sure that Sheriff Newton Diddle had something to do with this.

CHAPTER 27: ROOTS

Jimmy Jones was stunned to learn that Feral Fister, town superhero, had played in a rock band in Colorado in his youth, and speechless when Feral noted in passing that banker Jamin had been his drummer. When Jimmy asked if they had done drugs to smooth the beat, Feral could only smile and confirm that even the silent one had sung back-ups back then.

Jimmy's approach to Pres Bloom for help in organizing a "Pink Floyd" cover band headlining Pinky Flawed had elicited only a tepid response. Pres was all in favor of starting a band, but who or what was this "Pink Floyd?" He had never heard of him and doubted that his fellow children of the creek had either. He would certainly ask but was skeptical of any serious degree of interest. Several hours later he confirmed the obvious. "Pink Floyd" was as foreign a concept to the children of the creek as a Pig CAFO.

Temporarily stymied, but still intrigued with the idea, Jimmy approached Billious Bloom to put an ad in The Daily Hellbender. Ms. Bloom was all in with the concept and volunteered that she had always wanted to be a groupie for a rock band, sleep with each of its members, and write a tell-all book about it. This was more information than Jimmy had requested but he was pleased with her enthusiasm. She would certainly be a valuable resource when it came to promoting the band in the overseas venues she was so comfortable cavorting around, if ever Pinky Flawed and the Stoners made it that far. She agreed to run an ad which read:

"Calling all rock-and-rollers . . . back to your roots . . . audition for Pinky Flawed and the Stoners by contacting Jimmy Jones immediately. Knowledge and exposure to Pink Floyd will provide a competitive advantage. No references or prior experience required."

Jimmy received only two additional inquiries, each of which blew him away. Feral Fister's acknowledgement that he and banker Jamin were former rockers was shock enough. But learning that Tiny Taylor had played bass guitar in a heavy metal outfit in Seattle was beyond comprehension. How could she even lift, let alone play, such an instrument with her diminutive frame? He knew that Tiny Taylor could fry the hell out of anything, but play the shit out of a stringed instrument? No way. And when Feral added that his live-in lover Anel Feckle had been a backup singer for the Beau Brummels way back when, Jimmy had his band. *They are all old*, he smiled, thinking of who had crawled out of the woodwork. *Old rockers never die, they just sink their roots in the closet and wait for the call*, he laughed.

Of course everyone had to audition but, since they were the only ones available to join Pinky Flawed, they would certainly make the cut.

Jimmy was pleasantly surprised at the audition, which was held in the Hardlyville High School gym. Everyone knocked the cobwebs off of their own instruments and, given their functionality, Jimmy surmised the owners probably had kept playing on the sly, though he just couldn't picture Banker Jamin slipping off into the bank vault to bang out a few rounds periodically. Nor did the good banker sing backups any more.

All were pretty good, generally familiar with Pink Floyd's "Dark Side of the Moon" album, and excellent mentors for Pinky, who had never played an instrument in his life. They reasoned that if he just huffed and puffed on a harmonica, while moving frenetically around the stage, he would stay out of trouble and add enough energy to warrant usage of his name, which was key to the whole charade.

Anel Feckle even taught him a few provocative dance moves she claimed to have learned from Tom Jones and pulled off the sock he often wore on his offending hand, rolled it in a elongated tube shape, unzipped his pants and inserted it next to the real thing. Another gift from her time with Tom Jones. Feral feigned jealousy but Anel promised him that he was every bit the equal of the short Welshman.

Pinky was still blushing from having his privates violated by an old lady, but calmed down when she assured him that his extended pinkie was cute and might even earn him a groupie or two. Pinky reminded Anel that he was happily married to Rosie.

Daily practices quickly became a drag for the veteran performers so Pinky Flawed and the Stoners were anxious to go live.

This was going to be wild.

CHAPTER 28: NECK-ED, AGAIN

This one was different. She had been violated. Brutally.

Otherwise it was the same gruesome scene. Young. Beautiful, in a dead sort of way. Neck cut clean through the spine. Body and blood spread all about the sheriff's front porch. This time at home, rather than work. He tripped over the body as he left for work and fell into pooled blood.

The sheriff's screams brought frightened neighbors and soon Dr Abi, who confirmed the obvious, including the sexual violation. Sheriff Newt couldn't stop moaning. A hypodermic needle through the now-bloodstained backside of his uniform knocked him down, and Dr. Abi had him carried to her office sleeping quarters for further observation.

He awoke later that day in a state of deep depression. He had been wrong. The twin spawn of the deceased evil one could not have done this. He had been so certain that it had been one or the other, or both. It fit their Devil Mother's M.O. to the nth degree. Except for the introduction of sex and the fact that the suspects were in the Spring Field city jail.

He asked to use Dr. Abi's phone. His call to Spring Field jail was short and sweet. The twins with the yellow eyes were to be released immediately. He would advise the one's husband to pick them up.

WELLSPRING OF EVIL

They were innocent of any wrongdoing.

He then walked home to change out his bloodstained uniform. As Sheriff Newton Diddle sat untying his shoes, it snapped. The steely resolve that had been his facade for decades cracked. He reached into the drawer of his dresser and pulled out a sealed bottle of Jack Daniels, twisting the lid as he lifted it toward his lips. It had been there untouched for scores of years. Held in reserve, for just this moment.

His first drink since the last violent rape of his pitiful ex-wife, that one in front of his sniffling fat daughter, only burned momentarily before spreading warmth and comfort throughout his tortured mind. His first drink since the subsequent rape of the kind lady who had helped him tackle his alcoholism. Both couldn't be "first," but they all blurred together back then. He knew this would lead to sex and violence, but perhaps he might keep it under wraps until he could relocate to a new community. His fate was sealed in Hardlyville.

Sandy Smith lay in hero Bo Bevel's arms, reveling in the success of their latest shared venture. She had never allowed Bevel to penetrate her, but she found great comfort in his embrace.

He was pretty spent anyway, having taken the young coed every way to Sunday including, eventually, her life.

Sandy Smith had nodded approvingly during the entire interaction in a trailer parked in the woods behind Diddle's house, guessing that the introduction of new evidence would likely drive her father mad. They had watched from the shadows as it did, before heading back to Bevel's cave hideout to celebrate. She would get hers from Bevel's current girlfriend who lay under his other arm, but pleasure could wait for now.

Revenge was sweeter. She had revenged the brutal abuse Newton Diddle had heaped on her mother. She had revenged his drunken ravages of her. She had revenged the relatively short but particularly painful part of her most formative years. The scales of justice had been balanced. Bo Bevel had helped her get there.

She greatly admired his cruel and creative mind, his conscienceless rationale for living, his passion for chaos, his abhorrence of authority.

She loved him in a way she could never love another man.

She was also intrigued by his vision of bringing sick Spring Field to its knees. He had not shared the underpinnings of his plan, just his hatred of the place. She was sure it would be brilliant and far reaching. She couldn't wait to find out more. *Get rid of Dad-ass, and watch out Spring Field. You are next.*

Billious Bloom slowly approached Sheriff Newt Diddle's front door. She was surprised to find it cracked. But that paled in comparison to what she found inside.

Upon finding that Vixen and Moon Child had been freed, Ms. Bloom felt a compulsive urge to thank the good sheriff for coming to his senses. While son Pres drove to Spring Field to get them, she decided to do so in person. She had heard all the details of the latest brutal murder, including the sex part, and knew that left the sheriff to start over. She admired a man who could admit he was wrong so quickly and not hang onto or defend his prior mistakes. She wrote a quick editorial to that effect for the *Daily Hellbender*, and wanted to run it by Sheriff Newt as her way of putting their differences aside. She was also anxious to offer her services, and those of her newspaper, to catching this hideous criminal.

Sheriff Newt was clearly intoxicated. Billious Bloom had never seen him so much as take a drink, let alone in a condition of drunkenness. He was sitting on his couch, wearing only boxer shorts and a cocky smile. As she was often wont to do, she quickly scanned his body, noting that it was not a bad one and reawakening memories of how she used to tease and taunt the young sheriff in days past. She had even wondered on occasion what kind of lover he might be, given her lack of choice in tiny Hardlyville. Despite her age she still got the hankering now and again, and he had clearly been available.

Sheriff Newton Diddle was not staring at his shoes now. The shyness was gone, replaced with a hint of sexual tension.

The sheriff invited her to take a seat across from him, threw on a discarded t-shirt and offered Billious Bloom a drink. Though she knew better, she nodded her concurrence and waited as he stumbled to the kitchen to fetch two glasses and load them with ice cubes before adding a healthy dollop of Prince Jack.

Sheriff Newt raised a glass to Ms. Bloom, apologizing for his almost compulsive insistence on the guilt of her daughter-in-law and/or her twin sister. Billious Bloom returned the toast with an assurance of forgiveness. She advised that Pres was on his way to Spring Field to hasten their return home, and she was grateful that the sheriff had returned to his senses.

They spent the next half hour discussing the details of the most recent brutal murder, including the sex part. Billious was surprised at what detail Sheriff Newt went into about the latter, given her status as a reporter. She asked if she and the *Daily*

Hellbender might be of service to the sheriff in solving these bloody crimes.

He nodded approvingly and poured them each another shot of Jack. Again, she knew better, but was enjoying the conversation, her first-ever constructive one with the sheriff. And despite his state of inebriation, or perhaps because of it, she found him vulnerable and a touch attractive. That he sensed it only heightened the energy in his living room.

Sheriff Newt finally popped the question. Did Ms. Bloom find him attractive? Her honest response brought a smile to his lips. He wondered aloud if she had ever thought of making love to him. Fortified with Jack, her response stirred a response from him. He stood and moved to sit on the arm of the chair, dropping his hand to Billious Bloom's uncovered knee.

Now, Billious Bloom feared no lover. When she wanted one, she took him. She always had and always would. Billious Bloom was a liberated woman in the fullest sense of the descriptive. And it was not fear that set the yellow light to blinking in her brain.

She removed Sheriff Newt's hand from her knee, expressing gratitude for his attentions, but noting that she must get back to welcome the twins home. Perhaps Sheriff Newt could join her for dinner at her house later in the week to become better acquainted?

Sheriff Newt shook his head no, drained what was in his glass, and proceeded to rape Billious Bloom, sticking a towel in her mouth to stifle her cries of dismay. Billious Bloom had never been raped before, and had only imagined the horror and inhumanity of what she was now experiencing. It was over quickly. As Sheriff Newt dismounted, he thanked her for the wonderful and exciting sex, and promised to kill Vixen if Ms. Bloom ever uttered a word about it. The sheriff said he would soon be moving on, and Ms. Bloom would never see him again, which was a pity for both of them, given the obvious animal attraction that existed.

Billious Bloom sat utterly defeated. She had brought this on herself. She should never have entered the front door of a man sitting before her drinking and clad only in his underwear. She should never have accepted a drink from such a man. She should never have leveled with him about her previous attraction to him. She should never have winked at him or invited him to her house for dinner. She did all the wrong things, but what he did was what was really wrong. He had forced himself onto and into her without her permission. That was rape in any language. He had bullied and hurt her. He had humiliated her. And he had the nerve to speak of their animal attraction.

Billious Bloom's options were limited, if even existent. She had alcohol on her breath and was in her attacker's house of her own accord. He would claim consensual sex and there was nothing in Ms. Bloom's liberated past to prove him wrong. She sobbed and threw her drink at him. She grabbed the panties which had been torn from beneath her dress just minutes earlier, wiped herself clean of most evidence, and threw them at his face before striding back out the door she should never have entered. She heard his sick laughter trailing behind.

Sheriff Newton Diddle was long gone before dawn, leaving behind a series of unsolved murders, a town without a sheriff, and a stunned and severely violated older woman.

CHAPTER 29: JUSTICE SERVED?

Despite her sense of shame and disbelief, Billious Bloom went directly to Dr. Abi for a vaginal swab. Dr. Abi cried when she saw the swollen evidence of Sheriff Newt's brutal attack.

Next Billious Bloom drove to Spring Field to file charges with the police chief against Sheriff Newton Diddle for rape. Chief Puddle was a friend of Sheriff Diddle and cast a disapproving eye at Ms. Bloom. His line of questioning began with "were you drinking" and spiraled down from there. Ms. Bloom knew this would go nowhere, but she gained a certain sense of freedom from her act alone.

Billious returned to Hardlyville. Then, after she welcomed Vixen and Moon Child home, she retired to the *Daily Hellbender* and began to write the lead editorial for the coming day. She shared it all in graphic and emotional language, including her reception at the Spring Field Police Department. She felt compelled to become a case study for other women, young or old, abused or not, knowing all were subject to this risk, beyond fairness, beyond justice.

Sheriff Newton Diddle changed out his license plates for ones he had confiscated from an old lady to keep her off the roads. He left everything but his weapons and several changes of clothes before driving due west as far as he could go, stopping only for an occasional nap along a side road, nursing a hangover migraine, and certain that he would drink and force sex again. It had been fun to cut loose for the first time in ages and be totally in control of everything within his grasp. That bitch, Bloom, would surely learn not to flirt and lead someone on without an expectation of culmination. It was she that had led him down the path to mutually satisfactory sex. Her second guessing was no more than rationalization and deserved to be overruled. Justice served.

Billious Bloom sat quietly contemplating life as a raped woman. A violated woman. An abused woman. A shamed woman. A used woman. She had never ever even entertained the possibility of having to do that in her lifetime.

Sure, she had been fast and free with sex after a late initiation to its pleasures by, of all people, Pastor Pat. She had been well into her thirties when he took her in the name of some strange iteration of religious philosophy, but she had enjoyed it too much to care. She would always be indebted to Pastor Pat for freeing her from the stigma of virginity.

She had used her wiles and allure to build the Rosebeam Foundation's collection of Latin antiquities and reputation around the world. She had enjoyed lovers of all cultures and from all corners of the globe, sampling as one might approach a box of chocolates or an appetizer tray, treasuring the variety and journey.

She had even slept with a sitting president of the United States to spare her dear friend, Lettie Jones, the indignity of cheating on her partner, Pierce Arrow, in the name of Skunk Creek. She still loved him as a dear friend and the father of her beloved Pres.

She had said no on many occasions, even up to the point of near consummation, and had never been turned down no matter how late in the courting ritual it came. All of which bred a certain naiveté, she supposed. She was naive no more.

She could contemplate all she wanted, but what had happened at the hands of Sheriff Newton Diddle would never go away. She even wondered if she could ever have sex again. This brought a brief smile to her face and even a hushed giggle. Of course she would. It would just be framed in a different context. No, rape had changed her life in ways she could probably not even imagine now. There was no justice in that.

When Sandy Smith picked up a copy of the Hardlyville *Daily Hellbender* in the Spring Field beauty shop to scan, while having her hair colored pink at Bo's request, she hardly expected the lead editorial.

Sheriff Newton Diddle accused of rape? Sheriff Newton Diddle vanished into thin air? Newton Diddle no longer Sheriff of tiny Hardlyville?

She leapt from her chair with joy and a blood curling scream of victory. She threw a $20 bill at the attendant and dashed off to the car with only half a head of pink.

Bo Bevel was busy observing the daily comings and goings at the Spring Field city hall, rolling around in his mind what nasty things he could do to disrupt business as usual when

Sandy thrust the *Daily Hellbender* through his open window. "Nice hair," he muttered to Sandy before scanning the lead editorial from Billious Bloom. A slight smile crossed his lips as he read of Sheriff Newt's demise and disappearance and Ms. Bloom's first rape. Sandy Smith even promised to have sex with him, her first man in years, if he wanted.

Why not he shrugged? Justice served all around.

Bo Bevel guessed aloud they would have to find another source of entertainment beyond cutting lovely coeds' heads nearly off, now that Diddle was history. He had his eye on Spring Field at some point. He wasn't sure how or when, but justice would be served to that butt end of a hick town sooner or later.

Sheriff Newton Diddle was never seen again.

Billious Bloom became the second editor of The Hardlyville *Daily Hellbender* to be nominated for a Pulitzer Prize for her personal exposé of being raped, following proudly in the steps of the now-deceased Pierce Arrow.

Sandy Smith didn't particularly enjoy her first experience with a man in decades, but it had seemed an appropriate way to say "thank you" to the only man in her life. Justice served?

CHAPTER 30: ROCK ON

As Hardlyville reeled in the chaos of three unsolved murders of beautiful young ladies, the rape of one of her finest citizens—an experience shared openly and honestly with all—the disappearance of rapist and former Sheriff Newton Diddle, the appearance of precious Vixen's long lost twin sister, and the apparent complicity of Spring Field police chief Omar Puddle in both the abduction of the twins and Diddle's escape, Mayor Pres Bloom declared a formal day of . . . something, but he wasn't quite sure what. Reconciliation? Fear? Retribution? Redemption? Repentance? Partying?

It was the latter that caught Pomp Peters' eye. He advised Mayor Pres that he would step in to serve as sheriff until a qualified replacement could be recruited. At least he knew how to handle a gun and occasionally look the other way, two traits that had served Hardlyvillain sheriffs well in the past.

And he knew exactly who to trot out for a party. Pinky Flawed and the Stoners. They were primed for a debut which could cleanse the village soul and move life forward, or backward, as wished for by each.

Pinky Flawed and the Stoners would debut for their Hardlyville neighbors only. A free outdoor concert for any Hardlyvillain who wished to attend. Jimmy Jones would provide kegs of beer and rolled joints, which was only natural since he now owned the Budweiser dealership and, of course, had long controlled weed distribution in the entire region. Interim sheriff Pomp Peters would look the other way.

A stage was set up just behind the Donny Brook Inn and pre-parties began early the morning of. All of Hardlyville was primed and ready when the band emerged from their dressing tent.

Unfortunately they too had partaken in several pre-parties and were not particularly steady on their feet as they mounted the stage to assorted hoots and hollers. That changed when Feral Fister, clad only in his signature super hero purple boxers emblazoned with the red BPM (Bi-Polar Man) initials, struck the first chords of "Money," specially requested by banker Jamin as their opening number. It was as if Fred, banker Jamin, Tiny Taylor, and Anel Feckle were transported back in time and space, dragging Pinky Flawed along for the ride. Hardlyvillains sensed transmigration and went there with them. Most shot flashlights like light sabers into the air, occasionally blinding the performers. A few sticks of dynamite were tossed on the sidelines and the whole affair took on the nature of a shivaree. After several songs the band took a short break to toke up and drink down.

Back on stage, they launched into "Time." Anel could stand it no more. The one-time, sexy, backup, lead singer placed the mic back onto its stand and ripped off her gauzy top to reveal what sagged beneath. She twirled her blouse around her head before unleashing it into the roaring crowd below, grabbed the mic, and began to strut back and forth among the band members. Banker Jamin was so astounded that he hit himself in the head with his drumsticks while trying to cover his eyes. Tiny Taylor, on a bass that was nearly as big as she was, got all caught up in the moment and followed Anel's lead. At least she didn't have much to sag. Banker Jamin again clunked himself in the head in a second feeble attempt at modesty while Pinkie Flawed laughed so hard he nearly choked on his harmonica. Only Feral Fister, who was well acquainted with Anel's saggy showpieces, didn't miss a beat.

Even Billious Bloom, positioned front and center like any good groupie, lost her bearings in time and place, unsnapped her bra from beneath her sweater and threw it at Banker Jamin, who hit his head on the drum stand trying to duck, opening up a bloody gash. Despite her spontaneous outburst, Ms. Bloom had already decided not to be groupie to anyone on that stage.

It was a scene straight out of Alice in Wonderland does Woodstock or some comparable anomaly.

A couple of old biddies sashaying topless atop a small rudimentary stage in the middle of nowhere, an old drummer bleeding from self-inflicted head wounds, a graying village superhero in monogrammed purple boxers pounding away at his guitar, and a twenty-three-year-old harmonica player, with his little finger splayed perpendicular to the rest of his hand, darting around and laughing maniacally in front of a village gone mad with rhythm and laughter. Dark side of the moon indeed!

There had been very few moments in Hardlyville history to rival this one, and all of Hardlyville was caught up in it. Let the healing begin.

Skunk Creek rippled to the beat and promoter Jimmy Jones was already counting $100 bills in his head.

WELLSPRING OF EVIL

The violent murders of beautiful, young, naked girls stopped as quickly and mysteriously as they began. From one per month for three months in a row to none over the subsequent three months was a joyous relief to the community.

Maybe sheriff Diddle had been the perpetrator. He was certainly no stranger to sexual violence, as witnessed by Ms. Bloom, and maybe he just laid off the first two cases to confuse the issue. He had certainly made up for lost time with the third and final murder victim and Ms. Bloom, if it had been him. There had been no violence since he left.

Interim Sheriff Pomp Peters had pushed Spring Field police chief Puddle to engage in active pursuit of Newton Diddle. Chief Puddle was evasive and abrasive. He had no idea about anything. Interim Sheriff Pomp was appalled, but powerless. These politics drove him crazy, but not as crazy as Newton Diddle was.

Billious Bloom struggled in her recovery from rape. She hadn't thought she would, but there was this shadow of guilt or shame or blame or something that lurked around the corner. Her normal high-flying sexual libido seemed sunk in the memory of her violation by a violent, drunk ex-sheriff. She found herself wondering if it would return. Unless she planned a trip soon, she would likely not find out for a while, as there was no one in Hardlyville to ignite the spark. She even had a passing thought about reaching out to Pastor Pat for one more soiree, since he was the one who had launched and blessed her journey from abstinence to fulfillment. But he was just so damn old. The more she stewed on it, the deeper she dove into the despair of unplanned celibacy. She needed a lover now. She just wasn't sure she wanted one.

Hardlyville history was rife with violence. Beginning with village founder Thomas Hardly's brutal execution. Some blamed it on money. Others named a woman. Still others added woman spurned. Whatever. His battered remains were found in his house without apparent reason or suspects.

There was Octavia Rosebeam's horrid rape. And, Lucas Jones was shot dead by an Evil Lady, who killed scores more during her reign of terror. The shoot-em-up bank robbery/kidnap that murdered an innocent Donny Brook tourist and almost cost banker Jamin and Jimmy Jones their lives. Aimless Bevel and his gang of anarchists had dished out their share, and the Freeload Twins focused on eliminating endangered species.

And now this. Innocent-looking young ladies carved up, and Billious Bloom raped into abstinence. On, and on, and on.

Yet despite this multi-century vicious cycle, Hardlyville displayed an other-worldly undercurrent of resilience. From village jester Dinky Doodle's antics, to octogenarian Ol' Dill Thomas's claims of paternity, to French porn star Florence Hormel's ministrations of passion, to Octavia Rosebeam's generosity—albeit it tainted with theft—to the Bull Rush Festival's annual inspiration, to Bedouin shivarees, to Pinky Flawed and the Stoners concerts, the village seemed always to find something to laugh at. Generally wounded but perpetually resilient, Hardlyvillains were constantly celebrating their way to survival of yet another day. Violence and humor seemed the eternal handmaidens of life in Hardlyville.

Unfortunately, there was more of the former to come.

CHAPTER 31:
SIGN OF THE TIMES

Pomp Peters was very proud of the new, large, electronic billboard that he had acquired for the Donny Brook Inn. With guests traveling long distances to dine at Tiny Taylor's Spoons and stay at the Donny Brook Inn, frequently for multiple nights, he was excited about the range of entertainment his facility could provide. From wife Uvi's Hardly Yoga Studio, which also offered in-room massages from newly recruited masseuse Bimbo B. Bailey, to hand-knit baby caps from Mexican Cap, LLC, to live weekend entertainment in the bar from Pinky Flawed and the Stoners when they weren't on the road soaking up their newly found regional acclaim, to day float trips on Skunk Creek in season led by Otis Hendricks, there was always "Something to do at The Donny Brook," as Pomp affectionately called it.

He was also proud of the prosperity his entrepreneurial ventures had brought to Hardlyvillain minorities. The cultural rainbow at his place alone showed the influence of Arab, African-American, Hispanic, with a sprinkling of traditional Caucasian—namely him, Paul Michael Peters, dubbed Pomp by his beloved Lebanese wife Uvi. This was a hillbilly stew not found elsewhere in the Ozarks. And he decided to put it all up in lights to wow his visitors from back east, a Hardlyville Time's Square of sorts.

Such diversity had not come easily to tiny Hardlyville. The first recorded resident of color had been a lady from the far east, Anny Qingdao, who it is told once attempted to seduce town founder Thomas Hardly, until reined in by her husband James. Some blamed Anny, directly or otherwise, for the brutal murder of Thomas.

It took over a hundred years for the next minority resident to appear. That was Otis Hendricks, illegitimate son of Sabrina Hendricks, who died in childbirth. Her mother, Flotilla, raised Otis as her own, and despite some early racial slurs, Otis earned his way into the heart of most Hardlyvillains, and his beloved wife, Mona Arrow. Otis became the first "child of the creek" to gain a college degree and currently ran the float trip concession at the Donny Brook Inn.

Booray Abdul was the next minority to stumble in. A first generation Lebanese-American, Booray fell head over heels in love with Rifleman and Steele's liberated daughter, Lil' Shooter, and followed her from Washington, DC, to Hardlyville to secure her hand in marriage. Pomp Peters, on the other hand, survived a calamitous trip to Lebanon and the Middle East to seek the hand of Booray's youngest sister Uvi in marriage and return her to Hardlyville to launch a yoga studio.

Booray and Lil' Shooter birthed a beautiful daughter Abi Abdul who went on to medical school and returned to the community to succeed Doc Karst as the local family physician. Shortly thereafter Sheriff Sephus married his long-lost first love, Airreal Flambeau, and doubled the African American community numbers. Their daughter Flam Adonis merely sweetened the colorful multi-cultural pot.

If you are keeping score at this point, that totals three Hardlyvillains of Lebanese descent, three African Americans and, if you include yellow-eyed Vixen and recently arrived Moon Child as minorities, given that there were certainly none like them in Hardlyville if even the world, you reach a net non-Caucasian count of eight.

With the influx of the six young Mexican sex slaves, the number had almost doubled overnight and was nearly five percent of the total population, not bad for a tiny burgh in the heart of the Ozarks. And given that young Rosie had recently revealed to husband Pinky Flawed that her baby bump was really two, their twins would move the needle ever further.

Pomp was proud of his community's progress and, given that much of Hardlyville's minority population labored at the Donny Brook, was pleased to show it off in lights.

Unfortunately for all of the above, Bo Bevel and Sandy Smith took notice as they were delivering dead naked ladies to Hardlyville and the now deposed sheriff Newton Diddle.

Bo Bevel hated minorities of any race, color, or mixture. He believed that they had no right to live in the Ozarks, and that allowing them to do so robbed him of his God-given right to live minority free. He came by this belief honestly, as it was the only thing he had in common with his worthless father, Aimless Bevel. It didn't seem to bother Bo that he had the blood of foreigners coursing through his veins. His father's was bad enough.

He also couldn't help but notice the mention of Pinky Flawed and the reference to an enterprise with the word Mexican in it.

Bo Bevel was many things, but stupid was not one. He quickly deduced that Pinky had freed the very sex slaves he claimed to have murdered months ago, which explained why he had disappeared from Bo's compound of evil-doing shortly thereafter. He was probably cohabitating with all those whores at the Donny Brook Inn and having a grand old time.

Sandy Smith had never seen her hero as angry as he was the night of the last dumped body on her abusive father's front doorstep. Pomp's sign had really set Bo off. He took it all out on the unfortunate young lady as Sandy watched in stunned silence. There had been no plans to rape the victim, as that was not part of standard operating procedure. But he did so, time and time again, before putting her out of her misery with a long knife to her neck.

On their return to the compound, Bo promised Sandy he would find every last minority in Hardlyville and eliminate them from his Ozarks.

This frightened Sandy because her own mother had been the illegitimate child of an illegal Mexican immigrant, but all physical signs of her lineage had been diluted over time. She did know that if Bo ever found out, she would move to the top of his hit list.

With the successful purge of Sandy's abusive father, Newton Diddle, from the landscape, and Bo's continuing ruminations about how to harm Spring Field in flux, he had time and energy to devote his full attention to cleansing Hardlyville.

He decided to begin, as most wise men do, with a market assessment. He quickly disbursed his most trusted lieutenant, Johnny Protem, to Hardlyville and the Donny Brook Inn to do a thorough inventory of Hardlyville's minority population, including color, age, and vulnerability. He was not to return until he was certain of his findings or with the traitor, Pinky Flawed. Success would bring Johnny newfound fortune, women, and fame. Failure would cost him his life.

CHAPTER 32:
RESEARCH AND DESTROY

Johnny began his interrogatories at the *Daily Hellbender*. He met first with publisher Billious Bloom, explaining that he was working on a project about minorities in the Ozarks for his graduate school thesis. This caught Ms. Bloom's ear as much as young Johnny caught her eye. She even had a passing thought as to flirt with this handsome young hunk of a man. She quickly sloughed that off to maybe thirty years ago, or even twenty. At least she was pleased to feel that sleepy libido showing signs of stirring again. It had been a while.

Johnny was a natural con and Billious a willing conned. Within an hour Johnny had the names of every minority citizen Billious could think of and even learned that Billious had initiated a course at Hardlyville High School on Sex Ed and Diversity, which still stood as part of the curriculum. Johnny let it be known that he so wished he could have had such a course of study with such an attractive professor, which only greased Ms. Bloom's tongue more. She was figuratively licking the crumbs from his hand by the time she turned him over to son and editor, Pres, to assure that she hadn't left anyone out and that she didn't make any further advances to a young man barely half her age, if that. Johnny promised in leaving to return with an update for Ms. Bloom before he left town.

Pres Bloom confirmed that Billious's count of fourteen, plus twins in the hopper was accurate, and a source of great pride for the village. He was particularly excited about the recent marriage of Pinky Flawed to Rosey and the news of twins that preceded it. Pres shared the story of Pomp Peters' rescue of the six Mexican sex slaves, of which Rosey was one, and his hope that the other young ladies could find similar happiness in Hardlyville. Their arrival had nearly doubled the village's minority population and any further betrothals that yielded offspring would impact diversity in Hardlyville geometrically. Johnny could only smile that white-washed-toothpaste gleamer and nod enthusiastically.

Pres placed most of Hardlyville's minority citizens at the Donny Brook Inn, either as residents or employees. He further suggested that the affable Mr. Protem might benefit from spending a couple of days at the Donny Brook interviewing some of Hardlyville's minorities to gain deeper insight into their experiences. He was sure they would cooperate, as they were as proud as the village of their acceptance and seamless assimilation.

Pres was thinking night-stays equaled revenues. Johnny was thinking personal "ID-ing" of these inferior bitches and bastards. The fox was headed into the henhouse which waited with open doors.

Johnny Protem struck up a comfortable and personal conversation with inn manager Pomp Peters. He silently wondered if he might be one of those God-forsaken minorities with a name like that, but quickly learned it was no more than a nickname bestowed with affection by his beloved Lebanese wife, Uvi. That he was tall and blonde with blue eyes sealed his innocence but condemned his wife to additional scrutiny.

Pomp ended up inviting Johnny for a traditional Lebanese dinner prepared by Uvi's older brother Booray. They were joined by Booray's wife, Lil' Shooter, their daughter, Dr. Abi, and her "partner," Priscella, who was an attorney in Spring Field.

Johnny was particularly cordial to the latter and curious as to how their relationship had been greeted in a small Ozarkian town. Pomp took the lead in responding, and having had a couple of Bud Lites, was straight to the point. He didn't think much of this same sex stuff, but Dr. Abi was blood relative of his wife. This was gosh darn America where individual rights mattered most and if his cousin-in-law wanted to sleep with a smart, attractive, female lawyer more than someone like himself, that was her right under the constitution. Besides, "blood is thicker than sex," he finished with a large punctuation point. This diatribe set all of them to giggling and earned Pomp a peck on the cheek from Dr. Abi, which Pomp promptly presented as evidence that she was not totally gay.

Johnny thanked all for a wonderful and informative evening which, in fact, it had been. The food and Lebanese red had been superb, and Johnny had learned all he needed to put the three fucking Arabs, including a lesbo, at the top of Bo Bevel's Hardlyville extermination list.

Over the next several days, Johnny Protem wandered the halls of the Donny Brook, visiting with whomever he could find. A delightful lunch with Otis Hendricks earned him a subsequent interview with Flambeau Adonis and thorough background data on both.

Johnny's attempts at inroads with Hardlyville's Hispanic population required more patience. Though his Spanish was passable, they were shy and retiring. He wandered through their cap production line daily but they would avert his eyes and pretend to not comprehend his questions.

Then one night in the bar, Pomp introduced him to Pinky Flawed between sets of music. Pinky had been long gone by the time Johnny had joined up with Bo Bevel and had no idea of the immediate and grave danger he was in. He too look a liking to Johnny and agreed to introduce him to his beloved Rosie next morning, believing that she could get the others to open up to him for his research.

Rosie was cautious at first. She had been around a lot of mean and dangerous men in her life and could almost sense their presence, There was something about this Johnny that jiggled her internal alarms, but his charm and naiveté eventually won her trust and soon thereafter that of her "sisters." All began to open up to him and one, formerly number "Dos" as Hardlyvillized to Doseta, actually took a shine to him. This was a new word in her vocabulary and pretty much a new concept to one who had been used and degraded all her life. Johnny Protem was a predator of the basest kind, and it didn't take long for him to shine right back at pretty Doseta.

Over the next several days Johnny hung out with the sisters a good bit, and as might be expected, seduced poor Doseta before she even had time to think "no."

Johnny had a tougher time squeezing out information about Editor Pres's wife, Vixen, and her mysterious sister with the fairy tale name. While he was never able to formally meet either he pieced, together that their deformity was "yellow eyes," and that they had been conceived in an unholy alliance between an evil lady and a local hayseed whom she had immediately murdered. That made them was sure-enough minorities in his book.

Research completed, Johnny had only to nab Pinky Flawed and return him to Bo Bevel for proper punitive action. This would not be pretty.

The problem was that Pinky and his band the Stoners had just set off on a two-week tour of three adjoining states. Johnny had to give it to them. They were pretty good, especially the older but somewhat sexy lead singer who he was certain once really knew how to strut her stuff. Pinky Flawed was an idiot with a catchy name but enough marketing sense to know they had a flashy and unusual product to cash in on. Problem was, Johnny couldn't wait that long. He had given some thought to moving in on the old broad and getting invited on the bus tour for an easy snatch of Pinky on the road. But he had a bad dream about what that well-used body might look and feel like and decided against it. He would find a different way to bring Pinky to justice, even if he had to come back to this God-forsaken town to do so.

Johnny Protem's final tally was fifteen confirmed infidels, including six Mexicans with two more on the way, probably all Catholics, three Arab Muslims, two young, black half breeds, and two yellow-eyed bitches. All were relatively young and in decent health. All seemed to possess a certain naiveté and vulnerability to manipulation, probably owing to their primitive surroundings and association with fellow Hardlyvillains. All would be easy marks for Bo Bevel, however he chose to cleanse their sick souls.

Only one task remained. A parting kiss for the lovely whore, Doseta.

Vixen and Moon Child were spared Johnny Protem's intrusion into their simple lives because of Vixen's insistence on shielding her twin sister from, Hardlyville, the world, and beyond until she could wipe the innocence and naiveté from her eyes.

Though Vixen didn't tell Pres, she believed that she loved this sister of hers more than anything in the world. This beautiful and totally natural sharer of roots and blood was special beyond belief. She had told Pres before they wed that she was reticent to have children because of the genetic taint of her evil mother. She would not be guilty of unleashing another of her kind on the world. Pres argued that the dilution of that strain had already assured there could never be another, but Vixen was hesitant to accept that risk. She loved Pres for who he was, not who he might sire, and he must feel the same about her or theirs was not to be. Pres reluctantly agreed, assuming he could change her mind along the way. And while their love deepened and grew as husband and wife, Vixen clung to her birth control like a coon dog to a bone. No, Moon Child would be the only one with whom she would share DNA. Theirs would be a bond like no other.

Vixen became both friend and mother to her sister.

As friend, she provided a warmth and grounding Moon Child had never known. In actual fact, Moon Child had never known anyone, beyond the kind old hermit who had raised her. This was a huge emotional void to fill and Vixen knew she needed to do so fully and quickly.

As mother, her tasks were even more daunting. Here Vixen needed to be more authoritative. Those first couple of weeks were otherworldly.

First was the name. Moon Child was ethereal but impractical. The poor child needed a real name. Vixen settled on Robin, Robin Jones, Jones in honor of deceased father Lucas, Robin as harbinger of spring. What could be more appropriate? She taught Robin to both say and spell her first name with ease, the first words she had ever spoken or written. "Vixen" was the next. Robin would learn to speak and write quickly.

Second was clothing. Robin had never worn any except what she pictured in a drawing as a large bear skin wrapped for warmth in the dead of winter. Since Robin indicated no immediate interest in returning to her hidden retreat, confirmation of that article of clothing would have to wait.

Explaining to Robin why she had to wear clothing was more complicated than Vixen had anticipated. When Vixen draped a nightgown over Robin's shoulders that first night together, Robin simply shook her head no and removed it, walking nude by a stunned Pres on her way to the sink for water. It was not as if Pres hadn't seen that beautiful, lithe body with an animal-like sheen before. It was Vixen's, down to the last curve he observed before Vixen playfully clamped her hand over his eyes. Robin seemed to be oblivious to both temperature and gaze. With regard to the latter, Vixen placed her under house arrest.

Vixen was anxious to introduce Robin to others and to the world outside. But clothing optional, even in Hardlyville, would not do.

Vixen began modeling the process of dressing, naming items of clothing, trying to make a game of it.

That first lesson on underwear degenerated quickly. Vixen started by standing naked, face to face, nose to nose, bosom to bosom with her twin sister. She took a pair of panties and pulled them up her long legs. Robin took the pair that Vixen handed to her and pulled them over her head, placing them like a face mask over her nose, setting first Vixen then Robin into shrieks of laughter. Pres rushed in thinking something was amiss and quickly ascertained that he was in the wrong place at the wrong time.

"Vixen" he whispered, looking at the one on the right who shook her head no and pointed to the one on the left. His beet-red blush set them both to laughing again as he ran for cover.

Vixen gave up on underwear and moved to pullovers and jeans. Commando would just have to suffice in the short term. Once Robin was reasonably covered, Vixen slipped sandals on her feet and led her out into the sunlight.

Vixen gradually began to make the rounds with her twin sister, introducing her to all of Hardlyville, person by person, over several weeks, but refusing to let her out of sight or control.

Several young men began to follow them about, almost lurking in the shadows of neighboring trees, waiting for the front door to open. Vixen began to vary her departure times, but there always seemed to be at least one waiting around. Since they didn't know which was Vixen, they were hesitant to speak for fear of appearing to flirt with a married woman. But they were always there, one or another.

Vixen knew this was not a problem that would go away. Robin was young and beautiful, like Vixen herself. She was ripe for pickin' and every unattached male in Hardlyville knew it. Men and sex would be the next lessons Vixen would tackle.

It didn't take long for the latter to move up the syllabus.

One late night as Pres and Vixen were doing what they often did late at night, Vixen's sounds of pleasure awakened Robin, who walked from her bedroom into theirs unannounced and sat on their bed without prior notice. This presented a problem as consummation was imminent.

A quick glance between Pres and Vixen confirmed the obvious. They would finish. As both sighed in contentment for a moment, Robin blurted out "What, why, how?" This was going to be difficult to reduce to "birds and bees."

Vixen huddled beneath the covers in Pres's arms. Ironically Robin was the only one with clothes on. Maybe they were making progress?

Vixen asked Robin to return to her bedroom while they dressed and she promised to join her for an explanation of "what, why, and how."

Vixen started by asking Robin what she thought. Had she been frightened by what she walked in on? Had it embarrassed her? Had she ever seen anything like it before? Robin shook her head "no" to all of the above.

It struck Vixen at that very moment how fortunate Robin was. The kind hermit who had raised her could have taken advantage and worse of her. But, he didn't. He had shielded her from the very things that caused him to drop out of sight—greed, avarice, abuse, deceit, hatred—and nurtured her love of all things natural. What a gift he had given her.

Vixen began with the "what." Making love. That's what she and Pres had been doing when Robin walked in on them. It was a very private moment of intimacy. Robin shook her head not understanding that word. Nor did she get why you had to hide to do intimacy. Vixen explained intimacy as best she could and moved on to "why?"

This was an easier pitch. She told Robin it felt good and it generally made the participants feel closer together. People made love to bring pleasure and intimacy into their lives. There was that word again, but Robin nodded as if she got it. Some people made love with a lot of partners because they wanted to share good feelings. Others made love to just a few because they considered it a special gift. Most who were married made love a lot before the ceremony and in the heady early days before children were born. Lovemaking generally decreased with age and offspring. Maybe that is why she and Pres were still so active. They enjoyed each other and the pleasure each brought to the other, without children. This brought a gentle smile to Robin's face. She liked that idea, the concept that pleasing another can bring pleasure to yourself. That was something she could understand.

The "how" was the hardest part, but she had promised. Vixen thought back to who explained it all to her and their approach to doing so. It had been stepmother Lettie and she had done it over a period of several years, timing her observations to Vixen's stages of development. Vixen didn't have the luxury of time with Robin. She would have to walk a thin line between celibacy and promiscuity. She didn't want to frighten Robin, but she wanted to assure that Robin understood the risks related to sexual activity. And she had to get Robin on birth control if for no other reason than to extinguish her evil mother's genetic markers.

Vixen decided to draw stick figures. This was brilliant in that Robin had grown up looking at rock art in her benefactor's grotto, some of which explicitly displayed sex acts. Robin just hadn't known what they meant. An hour later she did.

Vixen closed her middle of the night class on Sex Ed by promising to speak openly and honestly about sex going forward and to answer each and every question Robin might have. In return she asked Robin to promise her that she would never make love to someone without clearing it first with Vixen. In that Vixen knew from experience that this would be an empty promise, she handed Robin a bottle of pills and made her promise she would take one first thing in the morning for the rest of her life. She assured Robin that this would likely be the most important promise Robin would ever make. And since Robin understood the gravity of the word promise, she nodded her commitment vigorously.

Vixen tucked Robin back into bed and crawled in close to Pres for warmth and reassurance. This got Pres excited again and led to a replay of their previous romp. Robin slept through this lesson.

Despite Pres's repeated encouragement that Vixen and Robin would enjoy being interviewed by the pleasant grad student hanging out at the Donny Brook Inn and Billious Bloom's fixation with his "cuteness," Vixen refused even the briefest of conversations. A slick-talking, good-looking bad boy like Johnny Protem would not cross into their sanctuary. At least for now.

So, while Johnny Protem's exercise in racial profiling progressed, Vixen was fixated on catching Robin up on twenty-five years of the facts of life. In thirty days.

CHAPTER 33:
ALL FOR NAUGHT

Jimmy Jones choked on his beer as he sat watching the evening news. He spewed foam across the room as he screamed at Sally to come immediately . Sally didn't know what was wrong but recognized the sense of panic in his voice. She halfway expected to find his hands around his own throat again, gasping for life. What she found instead was death.

There on the flat screen in front of them was a picture of Naught the Guide, the quirky grin and intense blue eyes, frozen in the midst of a horror story. He was flanked by two colleagues described as petroglyphists of world renown. All had been murdered at a remote Anasazi ruin in the Cedar Mesa area of southern Utah. Strangled to death. No clues. No motive. No suspects. No survivors. Jimmy stared at the screen, then at Sally, then back at the screen again. He could only mutter something about knowing what must have happened. Sally was frankly scared of the moment, scared of Jimmy, scared of the memory of Naught prying Jimmy's hands from around his very own neck to save his life.

Sally asked Jimmy how he could know what happened if he couldn't remember anything about the forty-eight-hour period surrounding his Cedar Mesa fugue. Jimmy acknowledged he wasn't sure but needed to go back out there to find out. It was Sally who screamed then. She called Jimmy crazy, possessed, and obsessed, and warned him she was leaving if he ever got near one of those crazy ruins again. She just couldn't take any more of his hocus-pocus subconscious bullshit.

Jimmy smiled gently through his tears. He sobbed with sadness at Naught's death, while remembering with affection his odd appearance, sleeping habits, and mannerisms. No, Jimmy wouldn't go back to Cedar Mesa, but he did need to talk with Naught's widow, whom he had met and taken a genuine liking to. He needed to tell her how sorry he was and how much he had come to admire Naught in a very short time.

He wondered too if maybe there was something she could share that would bring order to the neurons bursting in his brain, something that would settle the disconnect between reality and dream, something that would explain what happened to Naught and his colleagues in cold, logical terms, no matter how brutal or violent.

Pastor Pat was in a reflective state of mind, as he often was these days.

He was contemplating prayer. On this particular day his focus was on whether prayer was a linear or horizontal construct? Does one pray directly to God, bypassing competing petitioners to reach the front of the line? This had almost a capitalistic ring to it but raised questions as well. Why would God choose Pastor Pat over another? What if God chose him second or third or fiftieth? How long does that queue take to process? We all know God is omniscient and other-worldly powerful, but answering millions and billions of requests at once was the pinnacle of multitasking. Maybe that was why there were so many different Gods, to spread the load and shorten response time.

Pastor Pat's mind was a bear-greased mobius strip when he started asking deep, confusing questions about his faith. But, he continued, as he often did. At this stage in his life he lived beyond fear, believing that the many missteps he had taken in life had led him to this time and place for a reason. Fear was not part of this construct. Only hope.

So, what if prayer was a horizontal concept? One spreads their prayers as a giant condor flexes its wings, seeking forgiveness across a broad spectrum of entreaty, almost as if God is in each of us rather than lording over from above. This would allow a prayer to roll forth like an ocean and touch points of holy response across the entire universe. This theory intrigued him and seemed more socialist in nature.

What got him started down this path today was his heartfelt concern over the rape of Ms. Billious Bloom. He had always felt a deep affection for Ms. Bloom, and their brief affair represented one of the highlights of his life. At the same time he carried immense guilt for taking advantage of her sexual naiveté and vulnerability. Theirs had been a consensual relationship but he had always carried the upper hand because of his religious trappings, a man of God relieving a suffering practitioner of her burden of near-middle-aged virginity so she would never have to worry about it again. And he, finding great pleasure in each and every outing.

He knew he had freed her inner longings and spirit for a lifetime of guiltless frolic and he felt good about that. He had also enjoyed their exploits immensely, probably more than with any other partner in his life. She was a passionate, bold, fearless, creative lover, and he missed that with the others.

That said, there weren't supposed to be others. There wasn't even supposed to be her. He had broken his vows of celibacy too many times for too many good causes, and it was time for him to pray to his God for forgiveness. Again. Which set him to thinking about whether he should just go straight for the Gold, directly to the Almighty—"God forgive me for I have sinned," and hope he eventually made it to the front of the line—or should he spread his prayer across a level playing field, sort of sneaking around to the back door and begging forgiveness with humility, praying to God within?

And, there was also another urge at work. His friend and former lover, Ms. Billious Bloom, had been brutally and forcefully raped. He just wanted to hold her, to comfort her, to provide warmth and understanding. And he had a pretty good sense of where that might lead. Again.

So this flawed servant of God must first decide how to approach his God for forgiveness of a lifetime of weakness for the fairer sex.

And then he must decide about whether to face temptation straight on and reach out to comfort Ms. Bloom in her time of distress.

The life of a country preacher was filled with challenge and contradiction. That said, he loved the wiggle room it provided.

Pastor Pat decided he would pray for forgiveness both ways, direct and indirect. That he would trust in a God beyond his understanding. That he would love and be loved, with a heart full of gratitude. And that he would stay away from Ms. Bloom. For now.

Jimmy called the number on Naught's business card and teared up when he heard the soft frail voice answer. It was Naught's wife alright, and though he couldn't remember her first name and forgot to tell her his, he proceeded with a heartfelt, sob-laced statement of condolence. She surprised him by calmly thanking him by name and asking him how Sally was doing. All he could do was gulp, and thank her for asking. What was it about these folks that related so closely to the ancients? Did they live in a different space and time? That is surely how Naught struck him. And now his wife. It was as if they were sitting across from one another, sharing thoughts and signs.

She asked if Jimmy was calling to learn more about Naught's death. Jimmy gave a subdued "yes," and she confirmed that was what she thought.

"It was all so strange," she began. As her story unfolded, pieces of Jimmy's memory began to connect again, as if being knitted back together by the sad voice on the other end of the phone.

She shared that Naught had been perplexed by Jimmy's incident at the remote ruin several weeks before, the very site where Naught and his colleagues were found strangled. He became fixated on returning as soon as he could gather the two petroglyph experts he trusted most to join him. With their schedules it had taken a while, but other projects were shunted aside because of Naught's insistence on this one being profoundly intriguing.

Naught had spent hours reading and studying the really old rock art, which he was convinced this was. Maybe "Basketmaker" (500 BC - AD 700)? Maybe older? "Archaic" (4000 - 500 BC)? He also immersed himself in legends of the ancients.

He rarely left the chair beneath his favorite Katie Lee poster, his heroine, the singer, actress, song writer, and environmental activist who had compromised her career to become a Colorado River runner, only the third woman, and one-hundred-and seventy-fifth human being, to follow John Wesley Powell down the dangerous rapids of the Grand Canyon.

Katie Lee, at age 96, was still trying to get the Glen Canyon Dam decommissioned and destroyed to free the upper Colorado River to run through beautiful Glen Canyon as it had until mankind had "fucked it up," her words, Naught's wife laughed aloud. Jimmy mentioned that he remembered the poster-emblazoned t-shirt of Katie, in all of her naked splendor of half a century earlier, posed between two equally bare and beautiful sheer canyon walls that Naught had worn that first day they met. She had authorized commercial use of the image to raise money for her Glen Canyon quest. Besides, she wasn't hard to look at back then, Naught's wife added. She noted with a chuckle Naught's observation that it was a good thing he and Miss Katie hadn't gotten together in her prime. She agreed.

Naught was wearing that shirt the last time Naught's wife saw him, she recalled. He had five or six of them and wore them for good luck. It had run out on him this time, she whispered softly. Jimmy was struck by her calmness.

They had planned to stay three or four days, photographing and cataloguing specimens, before returning for deeper research. He considered this site literally untouched by modern hands or influences and wanted to assure that it remained that way.

Naught's wife found it particularly odd that a small sherd of apparently ancient pottery was found stuffed in the pocket of his shorts. She knew he could not have put it there. He would rather die than violate the 1906 Antiquities Act, which rendered it illegal to remove artifacts from any federal or protected lands. And here he had died doing so? It just didn't compute. Naught was one of those purists who knocked down every cairn he encountered. These guideposts, left in good will by and for fellow hikers, were a deviation from what was natural and true. If a hiker couldn't get where they wanted to go without mankind's signposts, no matter how primitive, they had no business even trying. None of any of it made sense.

Naught's wife shared that the sherd of pottery seemed transcendent when handed to her by authorities. She kept it with her at all times and was torn between hanging on to it as a final link to Naught or returning it to its rightful home as he would have done. For some reason she could not bring herself to do the latter, complying with a subtle sense of subservience that drew her to it.

This connected another dot in Jimmy's brain-locked scattergram. He remembered kneeling in the dark amidst an ancient Anasazi ruin and reverently grasping a tiny piece of pottery reflecting the full moon light. It was an isolated memory but he knew it could merge with others with more stimuli. For now it lay surrounded by darkness in the deepest recesses of his mind, flanked by a subtle sense of foreboding.

It was how they died that troubled Naught's wife the most. Jimmy's skin began to crawl. "Strangled," he asked hesitantly?

"Yes," Naught's wife confirmed. "Apparently each by their own individual hands, just like he saved you from," she concluded.

Jimmy Jones' brain exploded with this chain recollection. He remembered it all for one brief crisp moment: the ruin they had wondered onto, tucked high and deep in a hidden corner of a large overhang, the faint moki steps up steep, slick rock. He and Sally had followed Naught up, Naught in another world of wonder and awe at this newly discovered and very old remains of shelter. The hours of exploration before a quick supper, lingering over weed, then diving into bedrolls before he and Sally slipped off for an unusually passionate session of love and returned to sleep. The dream of pre-historic violence within a dream of petroglyphic death, a sherd of pottery, gasping for air as his own hands sought to shut it off, Sally screaming, Naught clawing, then nothing.

He dropped the phone and sank to his knees for stability. He couldn't respond to Naught's wife's entreaties before the phone finally went dead. He still hadn't asked her first name.

Jimmy called Naught's wife back after he regained his composure. He apologized to her for falling apart but thanked her for unlocking a closed door in his memory with her account of Naught's demise. He knew it wasn't easy for her to go there, but frightening or not, it had grounded him in the reality of his experience. He shared with her that beyond the shared ritual of self-strangulation, attempted in his case, he had another thing in common with her husband. Sally too had found a sherd of ancient pottery tucked in his pants at the hospital in southern Utah and ultimately returned it to him. Her term transcendent seemed an apt descriptive. It rested in the nightstand next to his bed. It seemed to have a hold on him that would not release, almost laying in wait for something or someone else. He simply couldn't be far from it.

Naught's wife marveled at the coincidence and added that there was one more strange wrinkle she might as well share, though she doubted it would mean anything to Jimmy. Another item authorities turned over to her was a document written in Naught's hand entitled "Notes from an Interview." It bore the very date of his demise and was discovered stuffed in the corner of his back pack. It was scribbled in pencil and included a bold notation at the top - FORWARD! It didn't say to whom or when. She added that it seemed to be some sort of Navajo folk tale from her initial scan. And there had been a printed page, likely torn from an old book or journal, affixed to it. Jimmy asked if she could read it all to him and she suggested she mail it instead. Who knows, maybe it was Jimmy Jones who Naught wished to forward it to. It would be in the mail the next day.

Naught's wife noted in closing that Naught's ashes had been sprinkled from a small plane over the vast expanse of Cedar Mesa, as he would have wished. She was confident that his gentle spirit was aligning with others to confront the evil that had taken his life.

This eternal battle between right and wrong, good and evil, natural and unnatural had been waged forever, with advantage shifting back and forth between combatants in timeless surges of momentum. This was a vision of eternity that chilled Jimmy Jones' soul and set him to wondering where he would fit in, particularly if he was now part of some apocryphal equation.

After thanking Naught's wife, and sharing tears over her loss, Jimmy Jones slowly hung up and sat still in the dark, contemplating all that had been his life the past several months. Naught. Good. Evil. Native American rock art. Sherds of pottery. Self-strangulation. Fugue.

His mind drifted back to the magical "Rock On" concert just days back.

There had been words from a song that had singed his subconscious amidst the glory of celebration and escape. Something about brain or brains.

Jimmy retreated to his room and activated the antique record player with Pink Floyd's "Dark Side of the Moon" resting on it. He singled out a song entitled "Brain Damage." Yes, this was the one. He listened to it three times before crawling into his bed and hiding his head beneath the covers.

Sally crawled in next to him as he quietly mouthed the words, again, and again.

"The lunatic is in my head.

The lunatic is in my head . . .

There's someone in my head but it's not me."

When they awoke entangled in each other, for reassurance more than pleasure, Sally suggested that Jimmy visit Uvi at Hardly Yoga for some temporary relief. It was the only thing in their current lives that seemed harmless and beyond fear. The "Omming" did help. Jimmy walked out of Uvi's class with at least a flicker of inner peace in his soul. Until he heard a muffled sound coming from what apparently was a storage closet.

The low-pitched hum was more vibration than noise, but there was an undertone of hurt attached. He walked past then turned back. Something wasn't right in there. The door was locked, so he went in search of Pomp for a key.

Both gasped when they opened the heavy door. There in front of them was a pitiful mess. Little Doseta was tied to a wooden chair, a sock stuffed into her mouth, moaning softly, actually more of a hum than moan. She had been stripped naked. Cigarette burns covered much of her body.

Slick Johnny Protem had checked out that very morning.

As soon as Rosie cried out the story to Pinky Flawed, he knew immediately who was behind the humiliation of poor Doseta. He didn't recall a Johnny Protem per se, but knew his kind, slick, conscienceless, just mean. These were the ones Bo Bevel attracted to his outpost of evil. These were the ilk that served without question. These were the ones that Pinky Flawed could never be like.

Pinky couldn't begin to guess what Bevel was up to, but it worried him personally, and more broadly, that he had sent an emissary to Hardlyville who had harmed one of the sex slaves who Pinky had helped escape from his clutches. It could just as easily have been Rosie and the twins. It probably would be next time. Bo Bevel needed to be confronted and put out of business.

Pinky Flawed returned home immediately, then went straight to interim sheriff Pomp Peters.

The mailing from Naught's wife arrived as Jimmy stewed over the maelstrom his life had swirled into, and before he could visit Lucas and The Garden. He opened it with trepidation juiced with hope. Maybe it would contain some answers rather than raise questions, the latter of which seemed to be the order of most days. She had summarized the contents accurately: Handwritten notes of an interview, a yellowed printed page of text, and an italicized heading atop the interview - *Keet Seel*.

Jimmy immediately looked it up on-line. He found a National Monument of that name tucked into northern Arizona, a well preserved Anasazi ruin dating back to the 14th century.

But what caught his eye as he dug deeper was the phrase itself,

Navajo for "broken pottery scattered around." He wondered whether Naught's notes related to the ruin or the words, shivering at the implications of the latter, given the presence of pottery sherds in each of their possessions. Navajo interpretations of the ancients' words would be confined by neither time nor intent.

Jimmy Jones dove head first into Naught's notes, not knowing where the path would lead, but assured it was one he must follow. He started with the printed document which laid out in almost melodious tones a legend involving an ancient Shaman, his beautiful daughter, a people who had just prevailed in a battle with evil forces, and their subsequent descent into death and their village into ruins.

Jimmy Jones scanned this from the yellowed printed page, then read it more carefully again and again. Though there was no reference from which to identify the document, he thought it must have come from a compilation of Native American lore, maybe one that Naught had carried with him to the site. The similarities to the images embedded in his mind of the ruins they had discovered with Naught were unmistakable.

He then turned to the handwritten interview notes. Beneath the *Keet Seel* title was a handwritten reference to an old Navajo sheep herder who had agreed to allow Naught to question him. He had refused to provide his name out of fear that the evil spirits most Navajo associate with Anasazi ruins might bring their ire to bear on him. Naught began with a question related to the specific site they were investigating.

Three pages of his flowing cursive followed.

The old shepherd was apparently aware of the legend Naught used as a reference point. He had heard of the powerful Shaman and his beautiful daughter, of the battle between the ancient ones and invaders from a dimension beyond which ended in victory, of the sealing of the portal by the ancient ones that had been opened from darkness by evil forces with sinister intentions, the ceremonial entombment of the ashes of their soulless leader, the quake of destruction which immediately followed which freed the evil essence from its place of captivity, and the strange deaths of the daughter and her lover shortly thereafter. This was all part of Navajo lore that kept them from ever visiting or even revealing the location of this cursed ruin. That he was even near it was causing the old shepherd great anxiety.

Then he began sharing the extension of the story. Navajo legend had it that the evil essence entombed in the ashes had seeped into the clay jar and was released when it broke apart in the tremor, that every potsherd was cursed to human touch, beginning with the Shaman's daughter and her lover, that others who removed the sherds from the site met similar fates, and over time these sherds had made their way to other sites and locales beyond the mesa, spreading violence and evil in their wake.

Navajo legend proclaimed that the evil essence occasionally propagated his demonic inclinations through spiritual intercourse with human souls weakened by accelerated sexual impulses, who in turn distributed his madness biologically and ruthlessly among certain people of the earth.

Navajo legend specified the evil essence's signature marker as consistent with the demon's own yellow eyes.

This pushed Jimmy Jones over the edge. Pierce Arrow always attributed the Demon Lady's eyes, the evil one who had murdered cousin Lucas in cold blood, to a natural phenomenon called "wolf eyes," an extremely rare concentration of lipochrome. He had looked it up online and concluded that he preferred natural to supernatural when it came to evil.

That she was more likely the genetic spawn of an evil presence released from broken pottery at an ancient Anasazi site millennia earlier, a site and sherds of pottery that had most recently intruded on Jimmy's sanity and probably cost three men their lives, and that her yellow-eyed daughters were probably two of the gentlest humans Jimmy had ever met, were variables in an equation with no rational solution.

Jimmy raced to his bed stand, grabbed the ancient pottery sherd with the mysterious hold on him. It almost resonated in his hand. And then he saw the colors. The blue and brown on gray were straight out of the Navajo legend. Jimmy hopped into his truck and drove to Skunk Creek as fast as he could. He leapt from the truck and drew back to fling the polychromed sherd as far down stream as he could, hoping it would be carried to big water below and ultimately to the Gulf of Mexico as quickly as current could move. And then it dawned on him that this act of escape would do nothing more than perpetuate the lineage of evil, that he would simply pass it on to another unsuspecting soul who would see its colors glittering in the water and fall under its spell. A reality beyond legend that would never end.

He stuffed the colorful sherd carefully and slowly back into his pocket, unsure of what to do next.

He would ask cousin Lucas.

CHAPTER 34:
BACK TO THE GARDEN

Jimmy Jones was in desperate need to get back to The Garden. That's where all of the craziness in his brain had begun. The dream within a dream stuff. He needed to be in the garden and feel the spirit of cousin Lucas Jones' steady hand on his shoulder, to steal some stability from him for his own life.

It wasn't just the conversation with Naught's wife. It wasn't just the memories of his own near demise that she had helped him conjure up.

It wasn't just Pink Floyd lyrics. It wasn't just Naught's notes, the shared sherds of ancient pottery, the tales of yellow-eyed markers of the evil essence's spawn. It wasn't just what he stumbled into at the Donny Brook Inn on his way back from Hardly Yoga. It was all of it, just circling around him like a pack of hungry wolves.

Interim sheriff Pomp Peters and former bad guy Pinky Flawed were strategizing about how to stop Bo Bevel.

They were certain that he now knew about the Mexican sex slaves Pinky had rescued and Pomp and Uvi had adopted as their own. Pinky was quite certain their lives, as well as his, Rosetta's, and the twins', were in grave danger. And, while they couldn't confirm the details, they guessed that any human being that evil probably was connected in some way to all of the bad things that had hit Hardlyville the past several months, from three brutal murders to Dolsetta's torture.

Pinky thought he might still remember how to get to Bevel's den of thieves and worse, and wondered how they could infiltrate his inner circle to secure proof and intercept future evil doings before they could be executed. Speaking of which, maybe they should do just that. Assassinate the mean spirited son of a bitch. Pomp, as interim sheriff, could do no such thing without proof, and Pinky wouldn't have a chance in hell of breaching Bo's security, so that approach was tabled.

How to get to Bevel? Pinky knew nothing about his current hangers-on, only that he had a weakness for women, if abusing them qualified under that definition, and a hatred for anything not Caucasian. Within those parameters, what could they do to smoke the bastard out before he struck again? Who was a strategic enough thinker to sort this challenge out? Jimmy Jones popped to mind simultaneously. They needed to bring Jimmy into their circle as soon as possible, like right now.

Jimmy was packing a backpack to take down into the Garden. He felt he had to stay there until he got some answers or at least his thinking cleared. He would tell Sally he was going out camping for a day or two to get his bearings.

Pomp and Pinky caught Jimmy just as he was leaving. The offer of a beer was too good to turn down, even in Jimmy's state of confusion. In fact, it might help him focus. And as hoped, Jimmy had an idea as to how to get to Beauford Bevel. He remembered the tracker who had managed to corner Bevel's criminal father in his prime, many years back, and was close friends with his son. Ozarks trackers were a breed apart, and Clavical Autrey was the pick of the litter.

Clavical Autrey was the son of Angle and Angel Autrey, and learned to track at the knee of his famous tracker father, Angle. Angle was part of a unique band of brothers, and one sister, with roots so deep in the Ozarks that tracking anyone or anything through the bramble-laced rugged Ozark hills, where peaks were short but valleys deep, was second nature. There was nothing that Angle Autry, Normal Ned, Whipple Night, a man with no name, and sister Sarcoxie Combs could not find in the Ozarks. Nothing. They travelled by foot or swung through trees when undergrowth got too confining.

It was this quintet that had tracked down the lair of Bo's father, Aimless Bevel, after a massive manhunt for Jimmy and Sally's only daughter, Girl.

Angle, hence Clavical, were thought to have descended from Hardlyville's early rootstock. Their Native American bearing and instincts were distinct among Hardlyvillains.

They were all gone now except Angle's son, Clavical, so named after the human body part that binds together shoulders the way Clavical connected leads in a hunt. They needed more than just a location this time around. They need information and they needed it quickly.

Could Clavical Autrey not only locate Bo Bevel's hideout, but could he also follow Bevel's every movement, to and from the compound, without being detected? Could he prove past sins and isolate plans for future ones?

Clavical was often hard to locate, generally being out in the wilds tracking something. Like most trackers before him, he had never married, had no kids, and few friends. In fact, his parents were the only married tracker couple anyone could document, and that only because Angle Bevel had seen a young lady who touched his heart, had tracked her down in the big city, and saved her from an abusive rich-kid suitor. Angle felt he really had no choice but to marry someone he had tracked down and rescued. Clavical had been their only offspring as tracking left little time for frivolous pursuits like propagation. Trackers were loners through and through.

Because of their friendship, Jimmy had been given a special high frequency siren that when sounded could be heard by no human, but some dogs, at a distance of up to thirty miles. He hoped that Clavical was in the area.

Jimmy sounded the siren setting off frenetic dog barking all over Hardlyville and sending residents to storm shelters as many had been raised with the old saw that dogs could foresee tornados. As panic engulfed the community, Jimmy finally backed off, confident that if Clavical was near he would soon make an appearance. In fact it took him less than thirty minutes to come running up in full tracker mode, camo'd out, face blackened with soot, knife drawn. Clavical was a very scary-looking creature in full tracking array. Several citizens emerged from their storm cellars but quickly returned when they saw Clavical, presuming a terrorist attack.

Clavical knew something important was up or Jimmy would never have signaled him.

It took interim sheriff Pomp and Pinky Flawed more than an hour to weave together their circumstantial case against Bo Bevel and his gruesome band of followers. Clavical sat stone still throughout the presentation. He then nodded in a yes sort of way, indicating he could do it, find and follow the bad guy to whatever nasty ends he was pursuing. Clavical would not kill him, only report back what he learned on a frequent and timely basis. He would charge a flat fee of one thousand dollars, no matter how long it took.

All shook hands over the deal and Pinky Flawed offered to get him started toward the compound, but Clavical shrugged him off and headed out into the woods in the general direction signaled by Pinky. He would get back to them when he knew something.

Lurking in the back of Jimmy's mind was another thought trying to find form. Something about loosing evil on evil, but it was still a vague notion, without substance or definition.

Little yellow-eyed Robin's first real date was a doozy.

Vixen and Pres had been intensely protective of her, not once allowing her to be in the company of a young man alone. And this was not an easy task, given the number of males of all ages circling the house with increasing frequency. Robin couldn't help but take notice and wonder what all the fuss was about. She also liked the looks and smile of one suitor in particular and occasionally smiled back at him.

One beautiful day, when she and Vixen were out walking, she noticed him drop a piece of paper alongside the sidewalk and quickly move on. She checked to see if Vixen had noticed and concluded that she hadn't. She stopped to tie her shoes, having advanced from flip flops, next to the note and effortlessly scooped it up and into her pocket in one motion.

Later at home she read it through with a smile.

Dere butiful lady, I am sur yu have many offers but I would like to invite you to a picnic on the banks of the creek. I bring it all to yu and we will sit on a blanket and eat lunch. How bout next munday?

WELLSPRING OF EVIL

I will walk by yur house tonight at nine. Look out yur front windo and signal me yes with 1 finger or no with 2. Please make it yes. yur friend damon

Robin was both touched and a little excited. She showed the note to Vixen, who cringed then laughed out loud. This must be eighteen-year-old Damon Crank, whose parents were among Hardlyville's nicest citizens. Surely he would be okay.

Vixen knew that, sooner or later, she must open this door and she would rather it be with a known quantity than a stranger. Vixen okayed the picnic, but only if Robin would allow her to watch from cover, in case she was wrong about Damon.

Robin shrugged her concurrence and, at nine o'clock, threw up one finger from her front window. She told Vixen she thought she saw Damon jump up and click the heels of his boots. This was going to be fun.

A little before noon on Monday, Damon appeared at the front door with a picnic basket. Robin had dressed in a comfortable yellow sun dress which almost matched the color of her eyes. She looked stunning and Damon could not crack the smile on his face. Vixen guessed it might be his first date as well.

She followed them down to Skunk Creek, being careful not to attract attention. Damon spread a blanket right next to a deep beautifully blue stretch of slow water and begin to distribute fried chicken on paper plates. Vixen settled in to enjoy the scenery.

Robin rose slowly, looked longingly at the clear cool water on a hot day, raised her sundress over her head, and jumped in with a shriek of joy, leaving poor Damon gawking at her nakedness and spirit. He didn't have a clue as to what to do next.

Fortunately Vixen had recognized the glow of freedom in Robin's yellow eyes, and in anticipation of her return to roots quickly stripped off her own clothes and came flying in from the bushes to join her. This caused Damon to faint as the sisters splashed joyously in the clear, cool water, laughing aloud and playfully hugging one another.

When Damon came to, he took one more X-rated glance, turned tail, and ran all the way home to the safety of his room. No one would ever believe what he had just witnessed.

Jimmy resumed his efforts to return to the Garden. He would go alone and stay until he could regain his footing, sort his way through the mess in his mind, with or without help from the spirit of Cousin Lucas.

And then the final shoe fell.

CHAPTER 35:
A MORE PERFECT UNION

Amidst all the chaos that was Hardlyville at the moment, an undercurrent of almost revolutionary chatter was circulating. The world outside was continuing to go to hell with gun violence, mass shootings, and random acts of terrorism dominating most news daily. Global warming continued to ratchet up the misery index for many around the world. As the succumbing of California and other points west to encroaching desert conditions continued and Florida began to wallow in sea water, the fresh-water-rich Midwest was looking a lot like paradise.

Several in Hardlyville worried that, despite the strict controls they had placed on property transfer and ownership, the almighty dollar would find a way to corrupt even the simplest and most straightforward of population and inflation control strategies.

Hardlyville was grounded in the most basic of American founding principles: Life, Liberty, and the pursuit of Happiness. Though some Hardlyvillains argued there was at times a little too much focus on the latter, most felt it was perhaps the most important of leg of the old milking stool. Without Happiness, what were life and liberty worth. At best, a diluted version of the American Dream?

Most children of the creek hung around after growing up, content with the life they were raised within, making babies without the babies before they got hitched, and having those babies after they took the vows, living off the land, the creek, and Jimmy Jones' distribution networks, settling for less as more, and finding peace in Skunk Creek valley between bouts of natural and unnatural misfortune.

What was happening in the world beyond Hardlyville didn't seem very American to her patriotic citizens, and some even wondered, *Why bother with the outside world? We've got ours: our history, our love, our water, our pride, our sense of humor, our resilience, our guns, our warts. Why would we want to dilute or water down what was good about our village with what was going on outside it?*

Mayor Pres Bloom had always been the ambitious sort. Named, sort of, for his father, a former president of the United States, who had just found out about his illegitimate son at the recent wedding to gentle yellow-eyed Vixen, Pres came by this ambition naturally.

The former president came running from Washington, DC, immediately upon learning of Billious Bloom's rape. She welcomed him with open arms and appreciated the emotional comfort he provided, but was just not ready yet to resume the intimacy of their prior relationship. This afforded the president more time to spend with his newly discovered boy, and it didn't take long for their wheels to start turning.

Pres was delighted to serve as mayor of Hardlyville, but felt his capacity to govern exceeded the challenge at hand. The former president agreed.

Maybe Pres should take a shot at running for a seat in the Congress as a next step. Legendary Pierce Arrow had beaten all the odds and a corrupt politician funded by Big Pork to serve in that capacity for one term a long, long time ago. The one term had been a campaign promise and Congressman Arrow kept it. He had been more liberal than most of his constituents but had earned their trust by simply telling the truth and fighting for their precious Skunk Creek. Every time. In every way. With all things. Why couldn't Pres do the same the former president wondered?

But then what could a freshman congressman hope to accomplish? He or she got to kiss ass, play the game, vote for things he or she abhorred to pacify party brass regardless of side of the aisle, and in general push dirt around rather than clean house.

Pres and the former president wondered to each other aloud what might happen to this sometimes idyllic and generally satisfied little community if they just decided to go it on their own. There was little the outside world had that they wanted, and there was plenty they had that the outside world had begun to covet.

Why not declare independence from the toxic union of American states, secede and seek a more perfect union along the banks of Skunk Creek amongst our own? Both Pres and the former president acknowledged that this was a radical course for a generally conservative constituency, but marveled about how, throughout Hardlyville's colorful history, Skunk Creek had been the precious variable that crossed party lines, that aligned disparate interests for a common goal, that brought Hardlyvillains together in grief, in love, in tragedy, and in celebration.

"Think about it," Pres said to his father. "From settling on her banks, to isolation because of her remote location, to national refuge status because of her near destruction by self-serving corporate interests, to her recovery under federal protection to near-pristine water quality, to the bull's-eye on her back because of clean water shrinkage elsewhere, to the almost sacred aura her waters dispensed among those closest to her, Skunk Creek has always centered her people." Pres was really getting wound up now. Father and past president were nodding vigorously at every treasonous thought and utterance he shared.

"What if we prepared our own Declaration of Independence," Pres mused. "We could declare our own set of self-evident truths in the context of life, liberty, and happiness," he continued.

Among the truths he extolled for a Hardlyville different from most places were:

A reverence for Skunk Creek and those who reside next to her.

An independent, resilient, and hardy group of descendants from founding days.

Financial security provided by the stash of ancient silver dollars which serves as the Hardlyville Federal Reserve Branch and hedges against inflation and deflation.

A willingness to forego short term profits and the folly of speculative gain in the interest of stable housing stock and prices.

A belief in small government, no taxes, limited public services, and a generous safety net provided by citizens themselves, one on one, one to another.

Abundant water, food, and complimentary natural resources.

No gun control. Everyone packs who wants to.(There had never been a deadly shooting by a Hardlyvillain in the village's entire history.)

Pres finally had to stop for breath as his proud father beamed.

"What if we seceded from the sick and corrupt US of A and formed our own Republic of Skunk Creek, established within the boundaries of the Skunk Creek watershed already defined as the Skunk Creek Watershed National Refuge. This would give us control of our own destiny and our most precious natural resource," Pres concluded. "And you could run for president of The Republic of Skunk Creek," Pres challenged the former president of the United States.

He just smiled back and shook his head no, observing that he had already had all the women in his life that one man should, and that he was growing increasingly fond of Pres's own mother, Billious Bloom. "I might even ask her to marry me one day," the former president confided.

And then he turned the tables on son Pres, challenging him to pick up the mantle of leadership in the new Republic. It would be a daunting task, leading a small band of revolutionaries through secession from the United States of America and forming their own unique form of governance aligned with their self-evident truths, but he felt Pres was up to it. He would, of course, be always available for counsel and advice.

Pres wondered aloud what the powerful, if corrupt, government of the US of A might do? He knew they would object, if for no other reason than avoiding precedent. Would they invade? Would they drop a bomb? Would they wipe out the entire village? After all, we fought a bloody Civil War over the same issue in centuries past.

The former president laughed out loud and countered, "None of the above. How would you like to be the commander-in-chief who wiped out a tiny village of God-fearing Americans for simply wanting to be free? How would you like to go down in history as the Skunk Creek Butcher? How would you like to run for re-election on a platform of eliminating the weak and the powerless? Not me, I can assure you."

The former president went on to describe how the secession scenario might play out. First of all, it would take years for anyone in Washington, DC, to notice. Government was so removed from the people they were elected to serve that a tiny movement toward local autonomy, even in a federal wildlife preserve, wouldn't even create a ripple. Hardlyville could approve its Declaration of Independence, hold leadership elections, implement its own system of governance, and stop paying state and federal taxes, as long as they just kept it quiet. The last thing anyone in Washington would want in the current state of turmoil in the country would be to create a band of idealistic dead martyrs. No, Washington, DC, would surely turn its head the other way, even after learning of the clandestine secession. Life would go on as usual in Hardlyville and the Republic of Skunk Creek while chaos would continue to reign outside its borders.

Pres thought the former president's analysis was brilliant and was certainly credible, given his eight years behind the big desk with all that power and authority.

Both the former president and Mayor Pres agreed to keep their thoughts of rebellion between themselves and stew on them further. Hardlyville faced its own immediate challenges from the three recent unsolved murders, the torture of a young Hispanic girl, to Jimmy Jones' aberrant rock art based behavior and rantings about evil. There was no need to foment revolution in the midst of such distress, no matter how crazy things were getting in the outside world.

Yet both agreed that their pipe dream had merit and warranted further discussion at a later time, be it months, years, or beyond. It had certainly been stimulating, even fun, to dream large.

CHAPTER 36:
THE LOSS OF A CHILD

The entire Hardlyville community was in mourning. One of their own, a precious child of the creek, had been killed in a tragic automobile accident.

Lucas Jones Junior II had swerved to avoid a dog as he drove home from a hunt, lost control of his old Ford pickup, veered off the dirt road that ran alongside Skunk Creek just south of town, and flipped upside down into the water. Interim sheriff Pomp Peters found him submerged and lifeless in the creek they all loved.

It was only natural.

This Lucas loved dogs. All dogs. He never turned down a stray for a meal. He generally had no fewer than three living full time with him. This thing for dogs may have been the reason he had never married. He was a good looking, well-built, hunk of a man with a ready smile and easy going way. He had plenty of girlfriends, most of whom would have said yes if he had asked. But he never had. Maybe he didn't have enough love to share all the way around, and knew it would be unfair in the long run. To the girl, not the dogs. His current girl friend, Lili, had lived with him for a year, just waiting to say yes. And now, she would never have the chance. No, this Lucas would never run into a dog.

And this Lucas last gasped in Skunk Creek.

As a child of the creek, one of the namesakes of village hero Lucas Jones, Jimmy and Sally Jones' only son, and just a damn good guy in the mold of his father and his uncle, the loss of this Lucas hit particularly close to Hardlyville's roots.

Pastor Pat's eulogy was particularly poignant.

In a community like Hardlyville, such loss was a burden shared by all. Whether you knew him or not, you mourned. Whether you liked him or not, you mourned. Whether you didn't like to mourn or not, you mourned. This was the way of a small town, the way to survive tragedy, the way to wake up next morning and move forward.

He recalled the community's loss of the original Lucas Jones. And was he ever an original. After his murder at the hands of the Demon Lady, all had gathered arms around broken-hearted widow Lettie and her children by Lucas. All had propped up cousin Jimmy, who had idolized Lucas and was distraught beyond capacity to function. Each supported each other in time of loss. And, in the end, it had been a mourner, Pierce Arrow, who had stepped in to fill the void in Lettie that Lucas had left, and give them both a fuller life.

Filling voids. That's what life and death in Hardlyville was all about. It had been that way with Ms. Bloom for Ms. Rosebeam. It had been that way with Tiny Taylor for Ol' Dill Thomas. It had been that way with Pres Bloom for Pierce Arrow. It had been that way with one lovely lady after another between bouts of celibacy in his life, thought Pastor Pat, before assuring all that, "It will be that way forever in Hardlyville. The beauty of life is that it just keeps going on," he quoted Lettie Jones in closing, before rumbling out a heartfelt "Amen."

Beyond Jimmy and Sally, and older sister Girl, who were inconsolable, the other children of the creek were particularly hard hit. Lucas Junior II was one of them, the first one to go. They were the last to leave his grave, which was placed just south of the original Lucas's headstone. As they gathered around it, the circle was uneven. They were twelve instead of thirteen. The ring was broken and they leaned on each other for balance and grounding.

Jimmy and Sally went home and jumped into bed. They held each other so tightly as to bruise.

The ringing of the doorbell was persistent and beyond ignoring. Jimmy finally rose, threw on his jeans and opened the door to find Lucas's girlfriend Lili there, wracked with sobs, then reaching to embrace Jimmy. Sally invited her in and offered a seat. She finally took a deep breath and gasped out the word "son." This was almost irritating to Jimmy as he muttered that he knew he once had one. His only one.

"No," Lily continued. "Son," she repeated, patting her belly. "Your grandson. I found out the gender just two days ago and I hadn't even worked up the nerve to tell Lucas about the pregnancy yet. I hoped he would see fit to marry me, but I just didn't know, with those dogs of his and all."

"He would have," responded Jimmy, tears leaking from his eyes.

Sally was sobbing now as Jimmy reached over and patted his grandson in Lili's belly. "He would have," repeated Jimmy.

Lili assured them both that it was an accident, that she had not set up their son. She had loved their son as no one before in her life, but she would never have imposed herself on him. Somehow, it just happened, and the timing seemed particularly prophetic. She went on that she couldn't say that she would never marry another. She was young with her full life ahead. But she could and would promise that the baby would bear Lucas's name, both first and last, no matter who she might marry in the future. She felt a strange but genuine responsibility for preserving the lineage into a new generation of children of the creek. She would do just that.

Jimmy could only hug his appreciation and thank Lili for her commitment. He offered to help financially or in any way she needed.

Lucas Jones Junior II would live on through the son he never even knew he had, and another child of the creek would soon fill a void.

CHAPTER 37:
REPORTING BACK

Clavical Autrey had no problem locating Beauford's hideaway deep in the heart of the Ozarks. He could almost smell it. And it was an evil stench.

As Clavical scouted the perimeter he began to formulate a plan. It was keyed to Bevel's exits and entrances, his mode of transportation, and the tiny "bug" in his own vest pocket.

He watched from his perch atop a facing bluff as an old pickup truck pulling an antique Airstream Trailer pulled up to the compound and slid up next to the camouflaged netting. He heard a scream of fear as a young, dark-skinned lady was pushed out of the trailer. She appeared to have been beaten, and probably more. Behind her, a heavy set young lady pushed her forward, followed by a tall skinny shell of a man he immediately recognized as Bevel. He simply exuded hatred.

The driver of the pickup proceeded to pull the whole rig into the woods.

He ripped the clothes that remained on the young lady off, and shouted to his commune mates to help themselves before he penned the kaffir. He added in a loud voice that she would be an excellent test case for his new Minority Prison Camp of the Ozarks which he would soon populate with all the scumbag half breeds from Hardlyville.

It was then that Clavical noted the barbed-wire-topped, fenced-in block of cages just beyond the commune and the single plank-boarded outhouse in their midst. This accommodation was not fit for dogs, let alone human beings. This is where the Hardlyville harlots would spend the rest of their God forsaken lives, Bo spouted in closing.

It was hard for Clavical to simply sit by and do nothing while several grungy looking characters shed their overalls and had their way with the shell-shocked young lady, but there was too much at stake here in the long run to blow his cover just yet. Her cries had been reduced to helpless whimpers, and soon ceased all together. When they finished with her, Bevel's lady companion, who he called Sandy, shoved her into the makeshift prison and threw a blanket and roll of toilet paper at her, making a hissing sound all the while. She locked the single gate entrance with a large padlock.

Clavical decided he would risk slipping down and trying to free her once her captors were asleep. At the same time he would install the "bug" in the Airstream, in that it appeared that was where Bevel hung out when being chauffeured around. He would deliver the poor victim and a receptor to interim sheriff Peters so he could eavesdrop on Bevel whenever he was in transit, and then return to personal surveillance of this very troubling situation.

About 2AM, after a long and riotous night of beer, drugs, and sex, the compound as a whole descended into quiet.

Clavical stealthily slipped into the unlocked Airstream trailer and secured the transmitter beneath a couch. He tested reception and, satisfied with his work, snuck up to the young prisoner who sat huddled in the corner of the pen, sobbing quietly, wrapped only in a blanket. He frightened her initially but was able to convince her that he would soon set her free.

His short but powerful shears clipped through the lock and he motioned her to join him. She cautiously stepped toward him, trying to trust this stranger in the fog of the past twenty-four hours, but unable to take the last step.

Clavical immediately scooped her up in his strong arms, kicked the gate closed, and carried her into the woods. After escaping the night lights of the compound he asked if she would clasp her arms around his neck and ride on his back to safety. It would be a long trip and he might have to stop and sleep briefly, but she would soon be free again. The blank stare that accompanied her nod of concurrence spoke of the horror she had been through. He wrapped her body tightly in the blanket, leaving only her arms and head uncovered, turned his back to her, and helped her climb aboard.

He walked steadily through woods and fields, up and down hills, and across several small streams for the next eight hours. Clavical finally collapsed on the ground beneath a large sycamore tree and fell into the deep, short sleep that only trackers know. When he awoke an hour later, fully recharged, he found that the young victim had covered them both with her blanket and she lay snuggled next to him for warmth. This was the beginning of an unusual and eventually unprecedented relationship for both victim and rescuer.

As Clavical rewrapped and reloaded his passenger, he had to laugh out loud at the steady stream of vulgarity presenting on his receiver. The "bug" worked, and an angry Bevel was pissed. He was spouting bile to his partner about how he would find the whore who had busted out of The Minority Prison Camp of the Ozarks. He would hang her naked from a tree after wrapping her in left-over barbed wire. He would let her twist in the wind until she breathed no more. He would also install a lock on the gate that no set of shears could clip. His partner,

Sandy, comforted him that this had been a good lesson for all, one better learned now than when he had all the Hardlyville half-breeds in his captivity. It sounded like he slapped her and told her to shut up.

Clavical's passenger cringed at the sound of their voices. She opened the blanket, draped it over her shoulders, and pressed her naked body into his back with renewed urgency.

Dr. Abi was first. After she looked after the swollen vestiges of rape and provided pain medicine, Uvi and Vixen lent comfort, cleaned, fed, and clothed her. Then interim sheriff Peters, Pinky Flawed, Jimmy Jones, and Clavical sat listening to the sad tale of this young African American girl who had fallen into the clutches of Bevel. Clavical had wanted to return to surveillance of the compound but the young lady would not leave his side and clung tightly to his hand, even during the medical examination and treatment. Her story brought tears to his eyes. Clavical didn't ever remember crying before.

Her name was April and she was a second year student at the community college in Spring Field. She wanted to become a nurse. She was the first of her lineage to set foot in an institution of higher learning. She was working full time, so it was going to take her a little longer, but she would get into nursing school. She just knew it. At least she used to. She didn't know anything now. Except that a man in a camouflage vest had saved her life.

It was her job that had gotten her in trouble. She was a pole dancer at Spunky's in Spring Field. She loved to dance, but she hated who she danced for. Men. Old men. Fat men. Gross men.

Men that didn't get any good loving at home. At least she didn't have to give any of that up, and they all still tipped well.

Until this weaselly looking guy with a chunky girlfriend showed up and tipped her beyond well. She kind of wondered why he had his woman with him at a strip place but guessed it must just get them going.

She noticed that they came every Wednesday for about a month before he reached out to her and stuck three $100 bills in her tight little g-string. This obviously had gotten her attention. It was a month's rent. She expressed her gratitude with a kiss on the dude's forehead.

They introduced themselves as Bo and Sandy. He asked to buy her a drink. She politely refused, confessing that she had a big test in the morning. "How about a coke," he countered. "Sure," was the response that cost her the most damaging loss of time and innocence in her life.

She remembered sitting at a table with Bo and Sandy and exchanging pleasantries. Then nothing. The next recollection was awakening with her wrists bound to a bed, a strong male hand around her throat with a threat to be quiet or die, and the vision of a naked Sandy slobbering all over her. Bo was next. And he wasn't slobbering. And so it was for some period of time that lost all bearing.

Her next memory had been awakening in an old smelly trailer or something, and everything happening all over again.

They shushed April as a Bevel transmission caught everyone's ear.

". . . burn fucking Spring Field to the ground."

He would blow up fucking Spring Field, Bevel crowed to Sandy Smith, and he explained to her in detail what he was up to. Many would die, and fucking Homer Simpson would shit a brick. He had dreamed it and it had finally happened. He hated all Spring Fields, but the one closest to him, the one that served as the model for the useless TV series that he was forced to watch most of his young life, would pay the price.

The whole thing had kind of dropped in his lap. And now they were headed to Spring Field to meet the woman with the sexy foreign accent who would deliver the B-54 SADM nuclear device, the one that Bo had just acquired over his secret NRA internet site. The one that Navy SEALs carried around during the Cold War unbeknownst to any beyond the tight cocoon of top secret military intelligence. A nuclear device that would fit into a backpack and obliterate and irradiate a defined area.

The B-54 Special Atomic Demolition Munition had been formally eliminated from battlefield strategy at the end of the Cold War, but for more than twenty-five years Special Forces had packed real heat. No live usage was ever authorized. As these battlefield nukes were retired from the field, it was only inevitable that a few would be lost in the shuffle. Several terrorist organizations and rogue states claimed to have them, but none had ever surfaced publicly. Large scale mass casualty events in India and western Africa were always blamed on chemical leaks or toxic waste. The more Bo Bevel researched them, the more he questioned those conclusions. He had also heard about "red mercury" but when he got into the alternatives his focus tightened.

Bevel cast about for months on the internet after watching a revealing documentary about Navy SEALs on a history channel and digging deep into the history of B-54 SADMs. He finally got a hit from an unidentified source who claimed to have one available for purchase.

Bevel had wired the $1,000,000 asking price to his newly established joint bank account in Switzerland from what remained of the spoils of the career of his worthless father, Aimless Bevel, as a bank robber. Aimless and his slut partner in crime had always been so stoned they hadn't a clue as to what Bo was doing. Bo reasoned that Aimless would be proud in an odd sort of way if he knew, though he would probably have preferred that Bo stick to eliminating minorities from the Ozarks, a peculiar passion of his that had passed straight to Bo Bevel.

The Hardlyville Harlots would have to wait for now. This was entirely too big. Who could have dreamed it? Only a true visionary like himself.

Bevel would remove his name and partial ownership position from the joint account once the device was in his possession and activation instructions were clearly understood.

Interim sheriff Peters, Pinky Flawed, Jimmy Jones, and Clavical looked at each other in stone silence, not believing what they were hearing. April was squeezing Clavical's hand so tightly he had to loosen her fingers.

A conscienceless mind so toxic it could jump from imprisoning and torturing innocent minorities to wiping out a whole city because of a TV show was beyond evil. Or was it?

Pomp thought they needed to bring in federal authorities as soon as possible. He wondered if they moved quickly enough they might be able to intervene at the closing of the deal. Clavical's "bug" would allow them to follow the whole transaction to conclusion. Clavical worried briefly about planting a bug without a warrant, but agreed that legal procedure was not important in a situation like this.

One problem was that not a single one in the room knew a federal contact. "What do you do," wondered Jimmy aloud, "look it up in the phone book? How does one report a national emergency, to whom, and how?" No one knew the answer. Nor did anyone trust the Spring Field chief of police after his handling of Billious Bloom's rape case.

Clavical felt that the four of them should intervene personally. They could stop the deal at point of sale and handle legal and federal formalities later. Pinky worried that intervention might push someone to trigger the device prematurely. Clavical acknowledged that he hadn't thought about that. He wondered what would happen if they intercepted Bevel and his girlfriend on the way and posed as them at the closing. Checking the digital map device attached to the receptor showed the Bevel vehicle only fifteen minutes away from Spring Field.

Clearly not enough time. They were stuck and the clock was ticking.

Jimmy Jones was struck simultaneously by two different ideas. They both ran through Pres Bloom. Jimmy ran to the *Daily Hellbender*, urging the others to sit tight, and hoping to catch Pres in his office. He did and returned with him immediately. He filled Pres in on the details of the two sinister plots that were unfolding simultaneously: the acquisition of a small nuclear device to unleash on the city of Spring Field, and the kidnapping, incarceration, torturing, and who knew what else of every minority citizen of Hardlyville.

He also advised Pres that the worthless son of Aimless Bevel, Bo, was behind both. Pres had never heard of the latter but recalled hearing tall tales of Aimless Bevel. Aimless, the Agenda 21'er. Aimless, the racist who tried to lynch Booray Abdul. Aimless, the leader of a pack that staged a gun battle in which Sheriff Sephus Adonis was shot. Aimless, the bank robber. He knew that Aimless Bevel had been one bad dude. It sounded like his sick spawn was worse.

Jimmy Jones' first request was for immediate and direct access to the former president of the United States, and he knew that Pres's mother, Billious Bloom, could provide that. They needed to know where to go in the faceless bureaucracy that was their federal government to get quick, decisive action.

Jimmy's second request was a bit more obtuse. He needed to sit down with Vixen and Robin as soon as possible to discuss Native American legends and lore. Pres looked puzzled but suggested that they get together in an hour to allow time for his mother to get on the presidential track. They would meet at Pres and Vixen's cabin to assure confidentiality.

CHAPTER 38:
EVIL V. EVIL, FOR REAL

Bo Bevel and Sandy Smith checked into the old Spring Field Inn downtown as they had been instructed to do. They proceeded to the bar for a beer and to await the 5:00 PM meeting with their emissary in the lobby. They were anxious, but excited.

About five they began to wander back and forth through the old lobby. They had been told to look for someone strange. Then they saw her. It wasn't often that a statuesque woman covered from head to toe in a black burka, showing only flashing black eyes, walked into the Spring Field Inn. Actually, probably never, until that very moment.

She motioned for them to join her at a corner table. As soon as she was seated, she uncovered one of the most beautiful and alluring faces either had ever seen. Thankfully she was Caucasian and not Arabic as Bevel feared, for he would have had to kill her after closing the deal. Instead thoughts of sex leapt into both Bo and Sandy's minds before the lady refocused them on the matter at hand. Her name was Aliya, which she explained translated as "sublime" in Arabic, and she had come to do business. There was no dispute from either about the translation, and the disguise as a conservative Arab woman in dress and name was brilliant.

WELLSPRING OF EVIL

Jimmy sat nervously on the couch in Pres and Vixen's home. They sat across from him, with Robin soon moving in to sit cross-legged on the floor.

Pres let Jimmy know that his mother had indeed made contact with the former president, who was nearly always personally accessible to her. She had explained as best she could the backpack nuke threat to unsuspecting Spring Field and he had turned directly to Captain Jack at Code Spode, which had been his personal security attachment for eight years. He reported through Ms. Bloom that Captain Jack would reluctantly call Jimmy on a secure line at precisely 0200. The "reluctant" stemmed from Captain Jack's last and only experience in Hardlyville. He had been called in by the president, who was "sitting" at that time, to track down some mysterious evil lady with yellow eyes as a special favor to the president's supposed lover, Lettie Jones. Not only had Code Spode failed in their mission, but Captain Jack had lost one of his ace Special Forces warriors to a severed neck, purportedly executed by the target herself. He did not have pleasant memories of this crazy place, Hardlyville. Nonetheless, he would call as ordered and assemble his team for immediate action if needed.

Jimmy expressed his gratitude for the quick and direct response. He begged their patience for what would be a more difficult conversation regarding his sanity.

Jimmy began at the beginning with his dream within a dream experience with Native American rock art in the Garden. Since none of them even knew of the existence of such a place, in fact banker Jamin was the only living soul beyond Jimmy who did, it took a while to even set the stage for the weirdness which followed.

He carried through with his trip to Bluff, Utah, his and Sally's explorations of rock art panels with now-deceased Naught, who had in fact saved Jimmy from strangling himself only to end up murdered the same way. He shared "The Dark Side of the Moon" lyrics of Pink Floyd which were also stirring inside his head. And he closed with Naught's wife's discovery of legend and lore about ancient Anasazi evil embedded in pottery sherds.

Jimmy could have turned off all the lights in the cabin at midnight and been able to read the serial numbers on a $1 bill. He had never seen four yellow eyes open so wide. They were like headlights. Pres could only shake his head in disbelief and offer Jimmy a word of sympathy for his personal struggles.

Jimmy reached into his pocket and pulled out the sherd of ancient pottery. He asked if either of the twins had ever seen anything like it?

Vixen shook her head no. Robin rose slowly from the floor and headed back to her room. Jimmy wasn't sure whether he had offended or bored her.

When she returned she went straight to Jimmy and opened her clenched hand. Laying on the palm was a sherd of monochrome pottery of the same look and apparent vintage that Jimmy held in his hand, which began to shake. She explained that the old man who had raised her gave it to her long ago with the admonition that she should be careful because it made him feel funny. He had found it on the floor of the cave where he had found the young twin just after her birth. Robin confessed that, while she had sensed evil from time to time, she had felt secure enough in her own skin to deflect it.

Jimmy was about to come unglued, but needed to bring closure so he launched into the legend of an evil presence with yellow eyes propagating its species through spiritual intercourse with like-minded humans. Jimmy wondered whether either Vixen or Robin had ever heard such a legend or tale? Neither had, but each looked into the other's bright yellow eyes with confusion and guilt. If the legend of the evil presence was true, how had they been spared such a horrid outcome? Had Lucas Jones' goodness voided their mother's evil? Was it still lurking somewhere deep inside them. Why did the ancient pottery sherd not grab them as it had Jimmy Jones, as it had Naught and his colleagues? Were they spared its evil aura because of natural immunities? So many questions emanating from an ancient legend and its physical presence among them.

"I just wish I could get this sherd of nasty stuff in Bo Bevel's bed with his ugly girlfriend," mused Jimmy. "Maybe they would awaken with their own hands around each of their throats. Or better yet, maybe they wouldn't awaken at all." Jimmy rushed to conclude he hadn't a clue as to how to plant the haunted piece and certainly didn't know anyone he would wish in Bevel's bed anyway. Except the whore that was already there. Did anyone have any ideas? No one did.

The disguised one with the flashing black eyes explained in her sexy voice that Bo and Sandy would have to wait for their backpack nuke for at least forty-eight hours. Shipping had been delayed because of a failed bribe to a customs official. He had been dispensed with and his replacement had graciously accepted what he had turned down. She expected the device to arrive by truck day after tomorrow. One had to be very careful shipping such volatile cargo. The funds in Switzerland would remain in the joint account until the deal was consummated.

In closing she promised to make the wait worth their time, motioning them to follow to her hotel room. Once inside, she slowly pulled the Burka over her head revealing nothing beneath beyond her exquisite naked body. Neither Bo nor Sandy had ever seen anything so desirable and began to free themselves from clothing as well.

The 2:00 AM call from Captain Jack did not go well.

He reminded Jimmy Jones that his daughter, Girl, had played a major part in the loss of his trusted warrior many years ago. He expressed doubt that anyone could have obtained a backpack nuke, because they were all accounted for in a clandestine storage unit in northern Utah. He acknowledged that several terrorist organizations laid claim to inventory slippage but none had ever employed a battlefield nuke in their line of work. He sincerely hoped Special Forces like his own would be authorized to carry them again but doubted that current military leadership had the chutzpah to reissue. And he sincerely hoped that this allayed Jimmy Jones' concerns because he never wanted to visit the hillbilly backwater of Hardlyville, with its multiple village idiots, again.

Jimmy thanked Captain Jack for his input and asked if there was a number he could call back after his brain trust processed the information that the good captain had shared.

"No," he was informed. Captain Jack would contact him if he needed to.

Aliya indeed proved to be sublime.

WELLSPRING OF EVIL

Jimmy gathered his tired but frightened brain trust to share Captain Jack's intelligence report. He wasn't sure if the prickly Captain was just blowing him off or correct in his report that Bo Bevel was being defrauded. Whatever, it was clear that it would take more presidential lobbying to move Code Spode to action.

While there had been no further transmissions from Bevel's Airstream, it didn't mean that they had much time to squander.

Clavicle offered to track down Bevel and his girlfriend in Spring Field, which all except April thought was a good idea. If they could just keep them on the radar it would buy time to look at alternative strategies.

April refused to leave his side, so Clavicle just took her with him.

He was able to report back later that morning that Bevel and his girlfriend had booked a room at the Spring Field Inn, were seen talking to a tall lady in a burka, but had not been seen since. Clavicle would also check into the Inn with April where she would obviously have to stay hidden. Clavicle would rotate between the lobby and the bar, while trying not to arouse suspicion, until he could confirm a sighting.

She knew what she had to do. It would be dangerous, but many lives, including her own, depended on it.

Vixen shared breakfast with Robin while Pres grabbed a nap. She also shared her plan.

Robin would just have to trust her, she began. She would need to keep what she was about to hear to herself, to tell no one. She had to promise that. Robin nodded her agreement, pleased to be so trusted by her twin sister.

Vixen laid it all out in great detail. Robin would have to be Vixen for the next twenty-four hours. She would have to fool Pres into believing she was his wife. Robin giggled at this. Vixen said that it was not a laughing matter, which erased Robin's ornery grin.

Vixen assured Robin that standing in for her did not include having sex with Pres. She cautioned Robin that Pres was a handsy son of a gun and a very sexual husband. Vixen admired and enjoyed this in Pres. Except with a stand-in wife who was her twin sister.

Vixen ordered Robin to keep her clothes on at all times. She knew this was not her natural proclivity, but did not want to present Pres with any distractions. She was to sleep in a bulky granny-gown nightie, to not go to the bathroom at the same time, and to not utter a provocative word in his presence. Pres would move in under the slightest pretense. Again, Vixen loved this about him, but not with another. And if he just wouldn't take a NO, Vixen advised Robin to tell him she was in her period. This set both of them to laughing.

Pres had been Vixen's only lover, despite having a pretty good run himself before they became engaged. He had been true to her ever since. Of that she was certain. But it got a little tricky when an identical twin entered the bed.

That Robin was smiling again made Vixen think twice, but her course was set. She added that Robin as Vixen should tell

Pres that Robin was spending the night with Aunt Billious and would be home the following morning. That was the only place Vixen allowed her to go alone. She would have to take Billious Bloom into her confidence as well, without going into too much detail.

When Robin asked what was going on, Vixen could only shrug and promise that she would tell her later. She then asked Robin for her sherd of ancient pottery. Another "why" earned a similar answer. Now Robin was confused and maybe even a bit concerned, but would honor her sister's confidence in her.

Pres was awakened with a phone call from Jimmy confirming a Bo Bevel sighting in the hotel lobby. Clavicle and April now had him clearly on their radar. They also had caught a clipped conversation between Bevel and his girlfriend during a brief retreat to the Airstream for additional clothes. They laughed about their new Arab friend "Sublime" and their plans to introduce her to Spunk's this very evening. There was no mention of a nuke. Pres shared the update with the twins before heading back to The *Daily Hellbender*. He would be home later in the afternoon and winked an "I'm coming to get you then" message of amour to Robin who he thought was Vixen.

Vixen retreated to her bedroom and was barely recognizable to Robin when she emerged. She had covered her beautiful yellow eyes with blue contact lenses, had frizzed her hair in a provocative manner, and wore tight jeans with high heels. Her shirt was unbuttoned to her breast and she wore no bra. Robin had never seen a woman who looked like this, let alone her twin sister.

Bevel and Sandy met their partner and new best friend in the bar. She was dressed in western clothes that left nothing to the imagination of the observer. They each ordered a beer. "DADDY'S" was a local micro-brewery and produced a unique and favorable line of beverages, as colorful as the name itself. And its logo, a canoe with a keg in it, was killer.

Aliya assured them that her freight tracking device confirmed a late morning arrival tomorrow. She would meet the truck at its dock, claim her package, and have it their hands before noon. She would train them in its activation and triggering before requiring that they remove their ownership claim in the Swiss banking account. She would even help them set the timing device and place the backpack nuke in the garbage can across from city hall. She strongly recommended that they all exit very quickly thereafter as there would soon be very little left of Spring Field.

Bevel questioned her as to what if it didn't work? What if their million dollar purchase didn't blow Spring Field to smithereens? She assured them that it would and that she was clearly a woman of her word as evidenced the previous night. All night long. Bevel and Sandy smiled at her and then each other. It had been quite a night.

She added that there was a twenty-four-hour waiting period before one party could access an account of that magnitude after a joint party relinquished ownership. International banking rules ruled, even in Switzerland. If they were not completely satisfied they simply would revoke their change of ownership and resume joint possession. Bevel couldn't recall the exact wording of ownership reclamation and made a note to himself to check the account paperwork which was hidden in the Airstream. They had more pleasurable activities to attend to this evening.

On their last visit to Spunks, Bevel and Sandy had scored with an African-American scoundrel who was naive enough to get drugged. She had been an easy target, and her eventual incarceration in Bevel's new Minority Prison Camp of the Ozarks had been a most fitting end to an evening of racial cleansing. At least until someone had let her out. They had learned a valuable lesson from that one.

Maybe they could hook up another minority with Aliya tonight. She seemed to share their intense dislike of people of color and might enjoy a Negro man if they could find one. He could then be stored in the Airstream while they concluded their business, and returned to the prison camp as its second enrollee.

After a second, third, and fourth DADDY'S, the trio headed over to Spunks for some fun.

She was sitting alone at a corner table in the back. She recognized them immediately though she had never met any of them. It was as if a sinister cloud hung above them. Bevel's eyes came to rest on her, lingered on her eyes, which made her wonder for a moment if she had lost a contact, then moved down to her breasts which were all but wearing an "open for business" sign. He smiled at her without taking his eyes off them.

Vixen was walking into the valley of evil with her disguised yellow eyes wide open.

As promised, Pres burst through the front door with energy and enthusiasm. His eyes lit up when he saw only one of the twins and asked where the other was. He was advised that Robin was spending the night at his mother's. "Oh my," was all he could smile.

Robin had dinner waiting on the table, which bought her a little time. She had roasted some squirrel and situated it on a bed of nuts and berries. Pres should have known right then that something was amiss. Vixen had never cooked wild game in her life, but it was the only thing that Robin knew how to prepare. Pres complimented the chef and pinched her derrière causing Robin to yelp. No one had ever done that to her before and it hurt. So she pinched Pres back. This was a cue for love making that Robin hadn't intended. When Pres grabbed Robin's breast she gasped and excused herself to the bathroom.

Pres was hot on the trail of his wife. She was the most exciting and exquisite lover in the world and she was all his. The locked bathroom door only heightened his excitement. He pounded with all his might, demanding to see the most sexy woman in the world.

Robin finally opened the door wearing a purple granny nightgown and rushed toward the bedroom. Pres chased her with a growl. He loved it when Vixen played shy doe to his man cheetah.

Robin knew she was in trouble now. Cornered and about to be captured.

Bo Bevel bought the sexy stranger in the corner a drink. Sandy was set on finding Aliya a horse of a different color to ride, one that could be captured and incarcerated at the end of the day. All was rocking at Spunks.

As Pres encircled the billowing granny gown and attempted to lift it over Robin's head, she played the "in my period" card. This confused Pres greatly. "That was two weeks ago," he recalled, wondering what Vixen was up to. He looked deep into her yellow eyes and saw confusion there as well. Robin had never been touched, let alone fondled, by a man before and it felt kind of good.

"Robin here, not Vixen," she blurted out. This stopped Pres in his tracks. He dropped the granny gown back down to cover her body and paused to assess the screwy situation. Either Vixen was playing a new game that bordered on weird, or she didn't love him anymore, or this was really Robin, not Vixen. He settled on the latter conclusion.

"You're supposed to be at Mom's for the night," he said with a hint of exasperation, followed by "where is my wife?"

Robin thanked Pres for believing her then answered "I don't know." She proceeded to share Vixen's strange appearance and request to borrow her sherd of antique pottery.

"Oh no," bellowed Pres, quickly throwing on his clothes and ordering Robin to do the same. "She's gone after the bad guys in Spring Field. We've got to find her before it is too late."

Bo Bevel was mesmerized by the cute little hooker at the table in the corner who continued to flirt with him in almost a little girl sort of way. He finally walked up to her table and sat down, offering to buy her another drink. "I'll have what you're having," she responded. He motioned to a waitress to bring them three "DADDY'S" as Sandy joined them. This might be fun, she muttered.

Aliya had disappeared with a tall good looking Caucasian dude which had caused Bevel and Sandy to lose interest in her for the moment. She could do what she wanted tonight, but tomorrow she was all theirs until the backpack nuke was safely in their possession.

Sandy Smith engaged the hooker in animated conversation. Out of the corner of her eye, Vixen saw Bevel slide a small tablet from his pocket toward her beer and deftly drop it in. This was how they had nailed April, the bastards. Vixen excused herself to go to the ladies room, staggered and tripped on the way there, falling into the lap of a totally surprised elderly man. She let out a small scream which brought Bevel and Sandy running. "The little hooker is mine, old man," shouted Bevel as Sandy restrained him. Vixen hurried back to the corner table and switched beers with Bevel. Since the old man wanted nothing of what any of them had to offer, Sandy let him go and returned with Bevel, who downed half of his DADDY'S in one gulp.

"Asshole," he muttered to Vixen, who nodded in agreement and excused herself for another try for the ladies room. She lingered as long as she thought she could get away with then returned to find Bevel's beer gone and him leaning on an elbow, telling Sandy that he didn't feel all that well. Sandy asked Vixen to help get him to their room, thinking a little action might perk him up. They were literally dragging him by the time they reached the room.

Sandy was worried now and went to the bathroom to fetch a wash cloth. Vixen quickly slipped the mono-chromed sherd under his pillow with a silent wish for that evil to prevail over their evil.

Bevel was now passed out cold, as Vixen could imagine little April had been when they turned loose on her. Vixen was fuming inside, fighting to maintain her poise. Sandy asked Vixen if she was ready for a little one-on-one action to warm up for the big boy when he awoke. Vixen said she didn't do women. Sandy wanted to know why not and began to fondle Vixen's breasts. Vixen said she had tried it once and found the experience lacking as she brushed Sandy's hands away.

Vixen said she would return the following night and make up for tonight's loss in ways Bevel couldn't imagine. Sandy sighed in disappointment because she was really turned on and she knew Bevel would be wild with lust when he awoke. She might even have to do him for what would be only the second time in their relationship. For now, she would lay down and comfort him as best she could.

Vixen ran down the stairs to the lobby, buttoning her blouse as far up as it would go. She went back to the corner table in the bar, ordered a glass of white wine, breathed deeply, and tried to re-enter real life, life as she knew it.

There was a commotion in the lobby and she heard voices she knew.

Pres ran through the bar, casting a glance at her table before moving on. And then he was back, rushing headlong toward her, toppling her from the chair with his embrace. He was crying real tears, wanting to know if she was okay, why she was dressed as a whore, and whether she had done it with anyone, all in the same sentence.

Robin was close behind, promising that she had not done it with Pres.

Clavical and April were looking on, trying to figure out who had done what with whom, and not really wanting to know.

Vixen finally stood and silenced all. She said that she had done what she had to do, and all would be well. Pres wanted to know about Bevel, and Vixen said "let him be." Clavical wanted to go to Bevel's room, and Vixen said "let him be." April said that she hoped justice would be served, and Vixen said "let him be."

The headline in the *Spring Field Daily* next morning read:
COUPLE FOUND DEAD AT INN
Apparent Self-Strangulation Suicide
No witnesses, No motive

CHAPTER 39: SERENDIPITY

A couple of good things came out of the whole sordid mess. Serendipity is the optimist's word for "show me something good" whatever the surrounding circumstances. It speaks to pleasant and unexpected surprises that emerge from difficult situations. It derives from an old folk tale but carries real world implications, like most folk tales do.

Okay. What possible good could come of a young college student being brutally raped, intimidated, and incarcerated because of the color of her skin? How about true love? How about marriage? How about a partner for life? April found Clavicle, the handsome young Ozarks tracker who rescued her from the sinister world of Bo Bevel and rarely left his side thereafter. Clavicle found a love which he had never experienced or seen. They were married before the year of her rescue was out.

Speaking of which, the world was rid of Bo Bevel. And his mean spirited sidekick, Sandy Smith. Their evil was of this world. It fell prey to another evil that was timeless and other worldly. Their sick dreams of destruction of a city and a prison camp for minorities in the heart of the Ozarks died with them. Their infested compound was rid of its transient population of goons and mercenaries, including Johnny Protem who was killed in the shootout that shut the place down forever. Founding bonehead Aimless Bevel and his simpleton blonde sidekick were left standing naked outside the cave fortress in a state of stoned stupor while interim sheriff Peters and his posse blew it up.

No one much cared what happened to them and they were certainly not worth utilizing precious Hardlyville jail space on. They were ultimately found dead in the woods of exposure. Billious Bloom insisted that the sign Minority Prison Camp of the Ozarks be permanently displayed at the Rosebeam Center for Latin Studies to remind all that civilization's eternal fixation with enslavement and racial discrimination was alive and well in modern times.

As for Ms. Bloom, the crisis had brought her and her former presidential lover back together again. Since her rape at the hands of former sheriff Newton Diddle, Billious Bloom had reluctantly steered clear of sex and the pleasures it had brought her over the decades. She just didn't know if she could ever accept penetration again after the shameful and painful experience that had befallen her. This is not how Ms. Bloom expected to react to being raped. She knew it had hurt physically and had left her feeling embarrassed and stupid. But she was a big girl. What she did not anticipate was the emotional scarring, a general sense of fear, that just would not go away.

She remained in touch with, and she guessed sort of in love with, the retired president of the United States of America, but steered clear of what had brought them together in the first place. A shared sense of pleasure and history. Hearing his powerful voice over the phone when she had sought his help in bringing federal power to bear on what was unfolding in Hardlyville, had stirred, even awakened, her longings to hold him tight. When he had visited two weeks later at her invitation, "hold tight" escalated quickly to shared intimacy. She later told him it was as if he had cleansed her open wound, stemmed the bleeding, and salved her heart. They began discussing marriage shortly thereafter, a first for either.

Aliya, Miss Sublime, had been the fraud Captain Jack had predicted. She did not have access to B-54 SADM backpack nuclear weapons, only to the joint bank account through an inside connection, which she quickly accessed upon reading the headlines in the morning Spring Field Daily. The unexpected surprise in this instance was that when she visited the deceased couple's suite the morning after, utilizing the card key they had given her, she had been attracted to a tiny sherd of pretty pottery laying next to the entangled bodies and had tucked it into her pocket before leaving the little piss ants to their own self inflicted demise. Soon after, it earned her the same.

More complicated was Robin's discovery of her own sexual yearnings brought on by Pres's unsuspecting attempts at foreplay. She had never felt the flash of passion or the flush of excitement at the point of touch before. When Pres had fondled her breasts, thinking they were Vixen's, it had stirred longings deep within. She sat on this discovery for days before coming clean with sister, Vixen, who could only smile and grab her hand. Vixen shared her journey into sexuality, confessing that she had been fortunate to have a lover as patient and passionate as Pres. They simply needed to find one of those for Robin. And she needed to keep taking that little pill daily for the rest of her life. Vixen had known that this day would come, and having arrived, she would be more proactive than defensive going forward.

And it was indeed serendipitous that Vixen Jones emerged as an unlikely village hero, the third of her name after father Lucas Jones and the grand lady who raised her Lettie Jones. She had risked everything, just as they had, in the higher interest of Hardlyville. Hero was the last word in her vocabulary describing herself, and the only outcome she had sought was the elimination of Bevel and his sidekick from the Hardlyville way of life. What her selfless act had accomplished instead was to elevate her to a pedestal in the Hardlyville hall of unpretentious champions.

All in all, enough pleasant surprises and serendipitous outcomes dotted the landscape of this journey into near darkness to render it exceptional in the history of Hardlyville.

CHAPTER 40:
INTO THE GARDEN, FINALLY

One unintended consequence of the Bevel Crisis, as it became known to most, was the addition of Pres Bloom, Vixen Bloom, and Robin Jones to the most exclusive club in all of Hardlyville. Prior to Jimmy Jones sharing his experiences with rock art and ancient pottery with the three of them, the only other living citizen with even a hint of the secret was Banker Jamin Bennell.

The garden had been discovered by Jimmy, and later shared with the now-deceased Pierce Arrow and Sheriff Sephus Adonis. There had been the unfortunate intrusion by the Deadbeat Twins to assassinate innocent hellbenders after they had trailed Jimmy Jones there one night, but they had been dispensed back to Texas by Sheriff Sephus Adonis decades ago with the admonition to never return. They were probably and hopefully dead by now, so Jimmy didn't count them.

After consulting with banker Jamin, Jimmy determined that they should introduce the young ones to the Ozarks' very own Garden of Eden. They represented the next generation of vested interest in this unique paradise and the best hope for preserving it into the future. Banker Jamin also insisted on bringing his banker daughter, Uvella, in that she would one day assume the mantle of Hardlyville Federal Reserve Branch Bank president. Jimmy was also hopeful that the twins might be able to help him interpret the rock art panel and sherds of pottery beneath it. He would have to keep the rest of the party from that site for fear of risking their exposure to embedded evil. He had no idea what to do about the spirit of cousin Lucas, which had been absent his last visit. He guessed Lucas would keep to himself as Jimmy was the only one with whom he had ever communed.

The six loaded into Jimmy Jones' old pickup and struck out for the rock fortress where so much of Hardlyville's history had evolved over the past several decades. From Skunk Creek Ranch pig farm, to evil lady cult pavilion where she had spewed her venom and murdered cousin Lucas, to stash of old silver dollars that provided security to Hardlyville, to subterranean cave complex where the evil mother had birthed and later held her child, Vixen, captive and left baby Robin behind, no single locale in the Skunk Creek watershed had served as a more important venue. And most amazing of all was the garden, far below the rock surface, where life went on as it had for most of Ozarks history. Jimmy shared all of this with his travelers, omitting only cousin Lucas and the rock art panel. Those were for Vixen and Robin alone.

He led them to the boulder that they rolled away to leave a dark entrance to the underworld. He tied a knotted rope to the large adjacent tree and led his party on its descent into the depths. He helped banker Jamin navigate the rope part and soon all were gathered on a mud bank, trying to take it all in, surrounded by the soft natural light that Jimmy had never been able to source. He shone his flashlight briefly on the water, identifying hellbenders and other extinct species swimming in the crystal clear water. This was the largest gathering of modern humanity ever recorded in the garden.

WELLSPRING OF EVIL

As she was prone to do, Robin stripped off all of her clothes and waded into the waters, soon to lay on her belly and wiggle like a hellbender. This set all to laughing except an embarrassed banker Jamin who tried to pirouette around a rock and instead fell face first into the mud. He raised his hands to cover his eyes, depositing more globs of mud on and in them and temporarily rendering himself blind, which suited him just fine. He slowly rose to a sitting position, unable to see or hear, and resembling a character from the "Swamp Thing" or "Creature of the Black Lagoon" horror movies of his youth. He wondered out loud why people couldn't just wear clothes like they did in the good old days.

Jimmy Jones modestly averted his eyes but recalled warmly he and Sally frolicking naked in these very same waters on their first visit to the Garden several decades past. Their escapades that day eventually resulted in their first child, Girl Jones. *This is a most magical place*, he smiled.

Jimmy asked Uvella to clean up her dad so he could introduce her and Pres to the nineteenth-century silver coins that made up Hardlyville's financial reserves. He promised that Robin would put her clothes back on. He would take the twins and explore another passage while they were counting coins. He cautioned her about the copperhead nest that stood guard over the treasure trove and how to avoid it.

Jimmy got Robin reclothed and took her and Vixen down the narrow passage where Jimmy had found the spirit of Lucas before, not expecting to encounter him before veering off into the side cave that contained the rock art panel.

But, lo and behold, there sitting on the big rock, flipping a silver dollar, back turned to them all, was the shadow of Lucas Jones himself.

Sparks of spontaneous emotion filled the airways. Nothing was said but everyone knew. Lucas and his two daughters connected on the spot. No one knew what to do, so Jimmy Jones just sat and watched as first Vixen, then Robin, advanced to Lucas and placed a single hand on each broad shoulder. Then all three sobbed. Lucas turned and swept his daughters into his arms in one motion. They each clung to his neck and wrapped their long legs around him. They were home with their daddy.

No words were spoken as Lucas slowly set them on the ground and turned back around. His daughters both knew that the moment had passed and that they had been given a preternatural gift. They stared at each other with joy and amazement, yellow tears streaming down from their eyes. Lucas rose and walked slowly away down the narrow corridor to who knew where. Vixen and Robin enveloped each other in a cocoon of love borne of a brief encounter with their deceased father. They would never be the same again.

Jimmy was totally wrung out. There was no energy or emotion left to deal with rock art panels and sherds of evil. He would bring the twins back another day to tackle what now seemed less pressing. He would always remember these few moments and had no regrets about sharing cousin Lucas with his very own daughters.

All were quiet on the return trip to Hardlyville, each in their own world of wonder. A literal Garden of Eden stuck right in the heart of the Ozarks. A magical space that had survived intrusion but from a few and the destruction wrought by human kind. If their thoughts crossed on the way home, it was at the junction of protection and preservation.

They must never share this special place beyond their immediate circle and must always be vigilant in its interest.

CHAPTER 41: LOOSE ENDS

Jimmy promised the twins that he would return to the garden with them soon. He needed their wisdom and guidance in trying to decode the petroglyph and dispose of the sherd that had sent his equilibrium tumbling. He couldn't promise that their deceased father would make another appearance but wouldn't rule it out.

Until then, he sought their help in sorting out some inconsistencies in handling sherds of ancient pottery.

First of all, how could they do it without negative or fatal consequence?

He reasoned that they must have some innate immunity to the evil essence therein. Both agreed, but admitted that they felt uncomfortable when handling the pieces. There was clearly something lurking within the inanimate and irregular objects that caused anxiety to them and drove others to kill themselves.

How had they ducked the genetic evil that accompanied their yellow eyes? The only possible explanation was that Octavia Rosebeam, who was raped at an early age by an evil one and gave away the baby at birth who would grow into the

Demon Lady, and Lucas Jones the twins' father, taken together, had co-opted the evil lineage with extraordinary goodness. That yellow eyes were the only genetic marker that survived this particular mingling of good and evil implied that the ancient curse had been diluted in the process. In simple recipe terms: take one part evil, merge it with two parts good, add a little yellow food coloring for history's sake, and the twins had escaped unscathed. Did this mean their offspring would be culled of the origins of their lineage? No guarantees about that, all concluded.

Jimmy also wondered how the kind old hermit who had raised Robin as Moonchild had been able to transport a sherd to pass to her without losing his mind to it. No one had an answer for this one beyond, "He was just an odd, lovable, old coot."

Jimmy wondered if there had been other "touches" in Hardlyville? There had been no apparent suicides that he had heard of, so he doubted it. That Feral Fister had experienced a single episode after saving Jimmy's daughter's dog from drowning would surface in later conversations, again with no reason. Maybe heroes wearing embroidered purple boxers were granted a special exemption.

One thing was for certain. The legend, the lore, the lineage of evil, the dastardly outcomes from handling ancient pieces of pottery, were powerful and real. To understand it all would place one above time and history. Pastor Pat would call that God. Jimmy Jones would leave it at that for now.

Jimmy did resolve to return to the Garden with the twins to seek additional clues and understanding. And more time with Lucas.

WELLSPRING OF EVIL

And then there was the matter of finding a man for Robin. Vixen and Robin hadn't spoken of it since their single discussion of Robin's surfacing sexual feelings and Vixen's promise to be there for her along the journey. But the stirrings had not subsided. Vixen had racked her brain for a Hardlyville male who might be trusted with one so innocent as Robin and had come up empty. Vixen had been lucky to find Pres, and there simply weren't any like him among the many who lurked around their doorstep daily. Poor what's-his-name who had taken her on that inaugural date, the now-famous Skunk Creek picnic, had leaked the story of the daring skinny dipper and her sister which had gained Robin additional wannabes. Vixen didn't even know what she was looking for as a friend, mentor, and potentially first lover for her sister, who was well past that stage chronologically if not emotionally. Fact was, Robin Jones was a beautiful, full grown, full bodied, fully "hormoned" woman in her mid twenties, and she wanted to be treated like one.

Vixen remembered Banker Jamin mentioning in clipped phrases on their recent outing to the Garden that his youngest son Wendell would be returning from college for a break about now. No one Vixen knew seemed to know much about him, so she went straight to his mother, Mabel, who could say more in five minutes than Banker Jamin would in a full workweek.

Mabel couldn't stop talking about Wendell. He was her baby boy and she was so very proud of him. He was different from the rest of the Bennells. He was handsome like HER father, smart like HIS dad, and passionate like HERSELF. He had no interest in business, which perplexed his father to no end, and was studying art at a small, highly regarded, regional liberal arts college. When Vixen asked if he was married or had a serious girlfriend, Mabel laughed out loud. He simply didn't have time for such trivial pursuits at this stage in his academic career. Vixen could sense that she was on to something. She mentioned casually that her twin sister, Robin, was somewhat bored with the Hardlyvillain smörgåsbord of potential suitors and wondered if maybe Wendell and Vixen might enjoy getting to know one another.

Mabel nodded enthusiastically, adding that Wendell was due home the very next day for several weeks and that he too was generally very bored during his visits, sitting for hours in the woods, sketching whatever caught his fancy, from people to animals to landscapes. Vixen asked if Wendell might come over for dinner after he was settled in. Mabel said to forget about settling in, he would be there tomorrow night—if that suited Vixen. Vixen nodded a delighted approval and added that she wouldn't give Robin the slightest heads up. Both women were aware of what the other was looking for and pleased that their agendas aligned so well.

When the doorbell chimed, Pres started to answer but backed down after an admonishing look from Vixen. He didn't know what was up but knew that look. Robin finally tired of hearing the bell ring and popped up from the book she was reading.

Robin opened the door. Their eyes met. Something passed between them. Vixen became concerned that no one was talking and rushed up behind Robin, only to back away and give them space. Wendell introduced himself and thanked

Robin for the invitation to dinner, adding that she had saved him from a very boring evening. Robin introduced herself as the twin sister who knew nothing about what he was talking about. This set them both to laughing. Wendell asked Robin why her eyes were yellow. He had never seen such a thing. She asked Wendell why he wore glasses so thick she couldn't even make out the color of his. Another round of laughter. "Come on in, you two," intervened Vixen, introducing Pres and herself to Wendell. She confessed to having invited Wendell to dinner because Robin was bored too.

Small conversation became large quickly as Wendell's passion for his studies and his love of art spewed forth like a bubbling spring. Robin was enchanted and made no attempt to hide it. She told Wendell she loved art too but was limited to what she could draw from innate instinctual memory on cave walls. Wendell was floored and lit up like a candle.

"Petroglyphs," Wendell smiled, adding that he was intrigued with all manner of human figures, from stick to voluptuous, and particularly enjoyed portraiture. He wondered if Robin might sit for him tomorrow in the woods at a special spot next to a spring that he loved. This brash invitation after only ten minutes.

Robin looked to Vixen for permission, sort of. It was obvious she wanted to. And would likely do so, granted or not. Vixen could do nothing but nod slightly.

The rest of the evening, the rest of Wendell's stay, went as quickly, all looped together with an energy and spirituality that befit both young people.

There was no overt touching or affection, but it was easy to see that a link had occurred, a bond had formed, a shared light had been lit.

Mabel and Vixen tittered like two old maids, comparing notes daily, sharing observations. "He looked at her with genuine amusement." "She blushed just slightly." "His smile melted into her and was absorbed like hot butter on bread." "Her yellow eyes leaked a yellow tear." They took turns hosting dinner. Pres talked politics, Jamin didn't talk at all, Robin and Wendell talked, and listened, art.

One splendid day Vixen noticed that Robin's antique handcrafted canoe was missing from the garage, where it had rested since Moon Child joined their family months ago. Pres guessed that Robin was giving Wendell a canoeing lesson on Skunk Creek. Vixen presumed it was more, and wondered if Robin had paddled Wendell up to the secret cavern where she had been raised. They did show up late for dinner, looking very tired and happy, but she didn't ask.

When Vixen asked Robin nearly every day if there was anything she could help with she always earned a smile, but no more.

When it was time to depart, there were no tears, just happy smiles, and a brief embrace. There was no discussion of when they would meet again, of future plans to communicate, of anything beyond that embrace. Mabel looked at Vixen and sighed. Vixen shrugged back as Wendell drove away and Robin went back to mundane chores.

A couple of days later Vixen was looking for a special bra that Pres had given her and that she may have misplaced. Robin didn't often wear one, but maybe it had slipped into the wrong laundry basket. Vixen wanted to wear it, and have him remove it tonight, in honor of Pres's 26th birthday so, having searched the rest of the house, she rooted around in Robin's room

As she looked under Robin's dresser on her hands and knees, the corner of what appeared to be a canvas of sorts caught her eye.

She pulled the dresser from the wall and came upon a cheap plastic portfolio which appeared to have material in it.

She hesitated before opening it, wondering if Robin had been experimenting with some new petroglyphic designs. And then she saw a corner of blue sky, not the gray of a cave wall, and reached inside.

One by one she pulled the most beautiful nude portraits she had ever seen from the portfolio. They were of Robin. Robin perched on a boulder mid-stream, Robin spread-eagling a fallen log that was diverting current, Robin flashing her lean backside from behind a tree in deep woods. Her sister, Robin, with her lithe, supple little body in every pose imaginable, at least twelve of them. One a day? Robin posing for the artist, holding the pose long enough for him to capture the essence of her beauty and the nature that enveloped her. Robin being Robin again, Robin as she was raised, one with the stream, the spring, the woods, in all of her natural beauty. Vixen was breathless.

It was then she heard the intentional rustle behind her and turned to find Robin smiling. "You are so beautiful," was all Vixen could say. "You too," Robin responded. And then she reached into her jeans pocket and pulled out the bottle of little pills, grinned, and shook it proudly. Robin and her first lover, Wendell Bennell, had enjoyed a really good time over break.

CHAPTER 42: FREE AT LAST

Loss was not finished with Hardlyville. It never was. Not since founding father Thomas Hardly's brutal beating and death.

Pastor Pat passed away of a heart attack, and with a smile on his face. At least that is what she said, she being a distressed alto in the Skunk Creek Church of Christ choir. They had been making love in the narthex and the good Reverend gave one last push, took on a heavenly glow, shut his eyes in ecstasy and glory, and inhaled his last breath.

"Think of what Michelangelo could have done with this one," quipped Billious Bloom, recalling her own glorious induction into Pastor Pat's hall of liberated women. He had done so much for her, all in the selfless name of salvation, of course, and it had been so much fun. She laughed out loud at the prospect of a colorful mural on the back wall of the church detailing Pastor Pat's previous dalliances with members of his flock and his ascension on angel's wings to a smiling and forgiving God, awaiting him with open arms. A man of the cloth, a prodigal son, a much beloved, if imperfect, preacher and practitioner of the word embraced by glory.

The alto was in tears as she ran to Dr. Abi's office for help, pulling on her clothes along the way. As they walked toward the church, she explained her gratitude for Pastor Pat's intervention in her life at a desperate moment of need. Her worthless husband, who had been cheating on her regularly, at least that was what Pastor Pat gleaned from his frequent confessions, had left her for a younger lady in Spring Field. She was heartbroken, lonely, and occasionally horny. Pastor Pat had stepped up to fill the void with tenderness and affection. He had taken a broken woman and made her whole again, and she would be forever grateful. To have been part of his glorious exit from the bounds of earth would forever rank as one of her proudest moments.

Dr. Abi could only smile. The old goat had apparently saved many lonely women over the course of his career, at least that was the village line, and somehow left most feeling better about themselves along the way.

But this was hardly tragedy, at least in a Hardlyvillain sense. This was actually a victory of good over evil. At least if one considered engaging in illicit love trysts with married congregants evil. Or if one counted as evil being seduced by a third tier French porn star name of Flo. Or if it was freeing several local citizens from the burden of virginity that was creating anxiety and costing them precious pleasure started with the "e" word. Most Hardlyvillains didn't, or if they did, were so wracked with guilt over the duplicities in their own lives that they refrained from passing judgment.

Pastor Pat was now free of his all-too-human obsessions and impulses, which was the good in this equation. Freedom. Free from temptation, free from backsliding, free from impassioned repentance that bore repeating on far too many occasions for a holy man.

At least this was all about good over evil, and not the latter over its evil counterpart. This seemed more natural than dreams within dreams, tales within tales, and evil triumphing over evil.

Pastor Pat was indeed dead of a heart attack, Dr. Abi could confirm. And a huge smile was frozen on his face.

CHAPTER 43: RULES

The village of Hardlyville had a rule. It was kind of the flip side of the Golden Rule. If something bad happens to one of their own, celebrate something good. It did not foreclose grieving, but required an answering celebration somewhere down the road. The freeing of Pastor Pat was not necessarily something bad, but it did warrant a party.

Billious Bloom stepped up. She and her long time lover, the former president of the United States, suddenly announced that they were getting married. He had seen her suffer the ignominy of rape and wallow in its fearsome debris. She had seen him bring patience and gentleness to her recovery and help reignite the passion that had always marked her sexual proclivities. They had always been grounded in pleasure, but growth into an emotional and psychological realm of interdependence drew attention to what they had been leaving on the relationship table for so long and spawned action.

They would have liked to get married the following day, but as a former president, albeit decades past, neither his private life nor the secret service agents assigned to his protection were his own. Nor was the timeline to his life events, most of which required national media coverage. So they postponed for a week to allow dignitaries and press to book travel, arrange for accommodation and, in some instances, time to figure out where tiny Hardlyville was even located on a map.

Besides, a week would give them time to relive some of their more precious memories in anticipation of the real thing.

They laughed out loud at the elaborate ruse that led to their first coupling. The president's fixation on little Lettie Jones, her obsession with earning the designation of "National Refuge" for the Skunk Creek watershed, her natural marketing instincts which knew that an official presidential visit would seal the deal forever, her offering of sex in return for such an honor, their walk to the community root cellar for that very purpose, the stand-in of Ms. Billious Bloom for Lettie to protect her friend's marital fidelity and in the interest of Hardlyville history, the encounter that carried such pleasure it earned a repeat visit with Lettie of course, the president's obvious surprise when press photos of Miss Lettie waving at the president in full dress clothing mode at the very time he had been making love to her, or Billious as it were, the second trip to the White House to seek presidential favors in tracking down Lettie's own kidnapped step-daughter, and the true confessions which followed.

It took the former president and Billious two hours to get through the whole sordid tale, laughing at every twisting turn and clever deception. It took them less time to sneak off to the root cellar for a commemorative romp. The week flew by in a haze of sweet memories and lost ones along the way. First Lettie and Pierce, now Pastor Pat, whom they had wanted to marry them. As usual, entrepreneur, interim sheriff, and jack-of-all-trades Pomp Peters would do the honors. He could get his marrying certificate on-line in a matter of hours and would be honored to preside.

Billious prepped the president for what might await him by sharing the tale of Booray Abdul's marriage to Lil' Shooter, the first and only Bedouin shivaree in the history of the Ozarks. He loved the cultural interplay, the camel, and the merging of Muslim and Christian religious custom in a day and time when many were set on exacerbating the differences. He wasn't sure about the dump in Skunk Creek but, if that is what tradition required, he wouldn't object. No doubt Jimmy Jones would be up to no good, and the press would be all over it.

Logistics were a nightmare. Hardlyville had approximately one-hundred-and-thirty rooms to rent at the Donnybrook Inn. Security for visiting dignitaries would use up half of them. There were only two restaurants in town, Greasy Spoons, which was always on a stand-in-line basis anyway, and Country Lebanese. Tiny Taylor and Booray Abdul, respectively, were willing to try anything but the numbers were daunting. Former Cabinet members and foreign dignitaries for the president, Latin aficionados and former lovers from around the world for Ms. Bloom.

One-time close friend and fellow bad guy, the former prime minister from England had called immediately to announce his congratulations and attendance, wondering how in the hell one could get from London to Hardlyville?

"With difficulty," was how the former president responded.

The ex-prime minister also wanted to know on the QT if the ex-president was really settling down. After all there were still birds to bed and single malt Scotch to gargle.

The former president affirmed his intentions to stay true to a woman he had come to love and admire, acknowledging that the two former leaders of the free world had enjoyed one hell of a time doing both back in the day.

Pomp and Uvi jumped in to organize logistics. The only way this could possibly work was to consolidate transportation, accommodation, and food preparation. Jimmy Jones volunteered to coordinate entertainment, or in other words, shivaree.

The beautiful weather that welcomed celebrants presented the Ozarks at its best. Fall colors were vibrant, temperatures moderate, blue sky almost azure with the slanting sun tingeing it with a touch of cyan.

The view from 1000 feet would have been mind-boggling. A virtual tent city had been erected on Jimmy Jones' old weed patch just outside town. Most Hardlyvillains enjoyed the occasional campout and had tents to fit their circumstance, from military issue pup tents to grandiose contraptions with front porches and sleeping room for ten. Uvi commandeered every tent in Hardlyville, arranged for the Mexican Cap girls to clean each one, and the Hardlyville High School basketball team to set them up. It would be first come, first serve for visiting dignitaries. Porta-potties lined the perimeter of the field. Cots and bedrolls were provided in similar fashion. Security and press would be accommodated in the Donny Brook Inn. Visitors could seek to share their shower facilities or simply bathe in chilly Skunk Creek, sans polluting soap of course.

"World leaders, persons of rank, and veteran globe trotters will have never been to a wedding like this," mused Mr. Ex-president to his bride to be. They both chuckled at the thought, glad to finally be getting married, and pleased that they chosen to do it in Hardlyville rather than Washington, DC, as Mr. Ex-president's former handlers had advised.

Tiny Taylor and Booray Abdul set up a full kitchen under a cover of tarps strung together with cord. They shut their respective restaurants down for two days and began preparing massive quantities of fried chicken and catfish, baked beans, and coleslaw, all seasoned with distinctive flavors from Booray's Lebanese spice collection, for the wedding feast. Jimmy Jones provided cases and cases of beer and wine from his distributorship as a wedding gift. Tiny's coup de grace was a fried chocolate wedding cake five feet high and three feet wide, with red, white, and blue icing unfurled flag-like about it There would be plenty to eat and drink for all the village and its guests at the celebratory meal following the ceremony. Until then it was pretty much ham sandwiches and chips.

Most guests were aware of the spare arrangements and did not begin arriving until the day before. Pomp recruited drivers to meet all guests at the Spring Field airport with a continuous twenty-four-hour shuttle of Hardlyville High school buses. All told he expected to transport up to two hundred dignitaries which, when joined with Hardlyville's own two-hundred-plus residents, would swell the wedding party to nearly five hundred celebrants.

Prince El Fatheade, single son of the deceased Saudi leader who had been one of Mr. Ex-president's staunchest allies, had his palatial tent flown in by private jet and delivered by his handlers in an eighteen wheeler. It required a separate weed field for full erection. Which was generally the Prince's normal condition as he cruised the other tents, seeking companionship.

The Prince's tent soon became the place to be for out-of-towners, and not for the reason he wished. The rumor of a fully stocked bar, soft oriental rugs on which to sleep, and ivory bathroom amenities proved quite the draw. Spiritual doctrine had never constrained the Prince.

"I have to sleep in this?" one diplomat's wife moaned upon seeing the pup tent they were assigned to.

"No, my dear," intoned the former ambassador. "Just wander over to Saudi Prince El Fatheade's Bedouin palace, pretend like you want to sleep with him, and you can spend the night in comfort . . . probably with many more just like you."

The Prince himself was a short, bulbous man, and women visitors in particular did flock to his tent for its creature comforts rather than for him. In fact, the night before the wedding he slept with more than fifty women without getting lucky with a single one. Finally, just before daybreak on the big day, the wife of Mr. Ex-president's dear friend, the Prime Minister of a small republic in eastern Europe, feeling sorry for the much put upon Prince El Fatheade, snuck into his robes and gave him what he wanted. She carried somewhat of a load herself but was substantially younger than her antique husband. Sort of "any port in a storm," she confessed to him later with a laugh. She did insist on covering her face with one of the Prince's scarves throughout the brief exchange, leaving the Prince pining for more yet not knowing who to seek out to get it.

The formal ceremony was slated for high noon. Pomp would officiate on a grassy knoll in the middle of tent city, with guests encircling them without respect to rank or gender. It was the Hardlyville way, if not exactly diplomatic protocol. The crowd parted like the Red Sea as the wedding party moved toward the site.

Billious Bloom was radiant in the bright red, silver-sequined, tight-fitting sheath that showed off her aging, but well maintained, hind quarters.

Tears were shed by friends and former lovers from around the world, most in joy for her obvious happiness, several in sadness that they would never again sample her unbridled passion in bed.

She smiled at her lover-soon-to-be-husband-former-president, sensing from his gaze that he was finally ready for this.

The "I do's" were crisp and to the point, including Mr. Ex-president's whispered wish that his wife wear her gown to bed with him this wedding night. Their celebratory kiss was that of a young couple wanting to get down to business.

The spread prepared by Tiny Taylor and Booray Abdul was memorable for its melding of Ozarkian and Lebanese flavors and scents. It lasted barely an hour before the deep fried chocolate wedding cake, encased in patriotic icing, was carted in on a horse-drawn wagon. Most thought it romantic until the horses did their thing in unison, casting a pungent odor on the immediate premises that was not of Lebanese origin. All in all, a memorable wedding feast.

Many in the crowd left immediately thereafter in search of a hot shower in Spring Field. Those who remained got incredibly drunk before stumbling or crawling off to their respective home tents, or that of a new acquaintance. Again many females opted for Prince Fatheade's luxurious tent home to curl up on an oriental rug and sip one last Courvoisier from his well-stocked bar. Unfortunately for the good prince, no one stepped up or slipped in to reward him for his magnanimous hospitality as they had the previous night.

About midnight all hell broke loose. A band of hooded horsemen swooped in on Billious Bloom's cabin, grabbed the naked Mr. President from the arms of his lover-wife, strapped him on the back of a feisty horse, and paraded him through tent city, firearms blazing, dynamite sticks bursting around the perimeter, on the way to Skunk Creek for a good old fashioned wake up shivaree dip.

Jimmy Jones and his band of renegades had planned their mission well. Though some fell off their horses due to excessive alcohol consumption, enough remained upright to steer the presidential steed toward Skunk Creek. Security and Press had been forewarned about the ancient Ozarkian custom and were positioned creekside to enjoy the spectacle. Several even shot roman candles over the creek to shed light on the groom's ordeal as he was dismounted and tossed like a rag doll into a deep pool.

The photo of the former president, emerging from the chilly waters of Skunk Creek, buck naked, screaming in frozen agony, privates covered by his trembling hands, made the front page of the *Washington Post*, the *Daily Hellbender*, and all form and fashion of written and digital communication in between.

CHAPTER 44: BIG APPLE

The baby cap business was booming. Uvi had taken over full management of that enterprise in addition to Hardly Yoga and the Donny Brook Inn because Pomp, as interim sheriff, simply didn't have any free time. Plus, there was a natural synergy between the caps and her wealthy weekend yoga clientele.

Uvi wanted to assure that the former Mexican sex slaves got a fair share of the profits, which were soaring. She wanted part of the proceeds set aside for recruiting additional skilled labor from the young ladies' village of origin and to expand production capacity, maybe even a new building. Finally, she wanted to share some of the cash flow with the village of Hardlyville for a rainy day fund. Yes, there was that much money rolling in.

She began with the six young ladies. She would school them in the foreign language of financial statements so that everyone knew how they were doing and was empowered to implement improvements to increase efficiency and widen profit margins. She called her system SHARE (Systematic Holistic Accountability and Responsibility for Everyone). She could not believe how quickly several of the girls caught on and dragged the rest to financial literacy along with them.

With the help of Dr. Abi's lawyer-partner and girlfriend in Spring Field, they established an ESOP (Employee Stock Ownership Program), which gave equal shares of ownership in Mexican Cap, Inc to the girls and she and Pomp. She paid bonuses to each for their level of production. Some girls were faster than others and earned more.

Finally she established savings accounts for each young lady at the Bank of Hardlyville and direct deposited their hourly wage and monthly bonus. In that they were paying no room rental at the Donny Brook Inn and had very few living expenses, their accounts grew exponentially.

Five percent of all profits were set aside for recruiting additional ladies from their village in Mexico who would also receive proportionate ownership shares. They could stay put and ship product if it met standard, which it did almost all of the time. Ten percent went directly to the Hardlyville operating reserve. These payouts were substantial.

Pomp was amazed at his wife's creativity and fairness. Mexican Cap, Inc. was humming along like a mosquito on a plump backside. They had come so far from their cruel and dismal introduction to America. This was what free enterprise, and Hardlyville, was all about.

Out of the blue Uvi received an official-looking personal letter to her with a Macy's Inc. return address. It was from the president of the company, and she wanted to proudly invite the entire staff of Mexican Cap to New York City for a week, culminating with being the guests of honor in the annual Macy's Holiday Parade. A check for $20,000 was included to cover expenses.

Uvi Peters sat in stunned silence as she reread the invitation. The Macy's Holiday Parade? The nation's largest? Seen by millions in person and on TV? The guests of honor? Uvi thought this had to be a hoax, a mean-spirited joke, something Bo Bevel thought up before his death. She ran down to get Pomp's reaction.

"Who's Macy?"

Sometimes her husband's naiveté made her laugh. Sometimes it made her wonder how in the world he ever flew to Lebanon and talked her into coming back to Hardlyville with him. She couldn't help but love the hayseed with all of her heart.

"Oh, the ones that buy all our baby caps," he said. "Where's New York? Don't have to get on a dang airplane again do I?"

This flashback got them both to laughing. From Pomp's physical encounter with TSA when they asked for his wallet, to throwing up all over himself, to near incarceration for attempting to bathe in a sink at Heathrow, to the plane sliding off the runway in Beirut, to Uvi's warm embrace despite his foul appearance and odor, to secret interludes of Namaste as Pomp thought it was called in Arabic, Pomp's courtship of Uvi had been an adventure wherein truth was stranger than fiction. They decided to celebrate the warm memory with a little spontaneous Namaste of their own.

"No, dear Pomp, you don't have to fly to the Big Apple! We'll drive," Uvi promised in the afterglow. This sent Pomp into confusion again. He didn't even like apples.

Uvi gathered her adopted children to share the news. They all spoke rudimentary English peppered with hill folk colloquialisms by now. In fact, each had moved on from their numerical names to proper ones.

Uno through Seis were now Rosie through Doseta with Ethel, Opal, Walli, and Urma in between. Walli was intended to be Walleye, named for a tasty local fish, but somehow got misspelled in the process. It stuck. Only Rosie had wed but all except Walli were in various stages of romance with local boys. Uvi assured Walli that it was only a matter of time before she found the right one for herself. She was a stunning beauty, after all.

The children were at first confused, but soon elated. They would be traveling to famous New York City, because of the fame their knitted baby caps had brought them, and ride on a float in a big parade. A couple were perplexed that they would be taking a float trip in weather this cold so Uvi had to reassure them this float was a different animal than the float trips Otis Hendricks provided to guests at the Donny Brook during the summer.

Rosie expressed concern about taking a long trip so close to her twins' delivery date but Uvi promised that she and they would be okay.

Rosie wondered if husband Pinky could tag along. Uvi nodded her concurrence.

Uvi brought in Billious Bloom and her new husband for help with logistics, as both had traveled to NYC extensively. The former president had been close friends with the mayor and would turn to him for help with security. Macy's contact point would be a young intern named Buford and he would handle lodging, in-town transportation, and food over the two-week stay. Billious had always loved to party in NYC and would coordinate entertainment, albeit in toned-down fashion. Never would such an unlikely party of first time visitors to the Big Apple receive logistical support of such depth. It was nearly on a par with a visit from the Pope, observed the former president.

But they still had to get there, and since flying was not an option, Pomp turned to Hardlyville High School and their fleet of yellow school buses. Surely they could spare one for the cross country trek. Two days out, two back, and two weeks parked in a safe haven. The principal enthusiastically agreed, smiling at the thought of all the publicity that would be accorded the Hardlyville-High-School-lettered yellow school bus along the way.

Time was of the essence and Uvi decreed they would depart in forty-eight hours to allow plenty of time to explore the city before the grand parade. They would drive straight through and Pomp and Pinky would alternate driving shifts. Everyone should bring at least four changes of warm clothes, including comfortable ones to sleep in along the way.

All of Hardlyville was atwitter with pride in their Mexican sex slave survivors who had turned tragedy and abuse into national exposure and fame.

About half way through Illinois, the big yellow school bus broke down.

It was about 2:00 AM. It didn't help that, as Pomp fiddled with things under the hood, a pickup truck full of local yahoos joy riding the night away screeched to a stop behind the bus. They could see pretty young faces peering at them through frosted windows and took that as a come-on of sorts. As they piled out of the pickup, lust showed in their eyes and menace in their step. Rosie whispered to husband Pinky that there was trouble a'brewing outside.

Pinky Flawed grabbed the handgun that interim sheriff Pomp Peters had stashed beneath the driver's seat, opened the bus door, and stepped out to confront the drunken locals. He had dealt with this kind before and realized he might need to shoot a couple to get their attention. Whatever. He would not let them get to the girls. They had seen this kind before as well, and each was balled into a fetal position at the memory.

Pomp quickly sensed what was going down and slipped silently down the back side of the bus to get behind the gang of ne'er-do-wells.

Pomp signaled to Pinky to fire a round over their heads. While this got their attention, it did not blunt their momentum. In fact, one in the middle of the pack pulled out a pistol of his own and returned the favor, firing skyward with a loud laugh.

Pomp plowed into the scrum of drunken lads, scattering them like bowling pins, and disarming the shooter with a crack to his wrist. As that one wailed in pain Pomp quickly moved through the rest with vicious blows to heads and knees to groins. Pinky resumed firing over their heads as the girls curled into tighter balls on the bus, not knowing who would walk through the open bus door next. Only Uvi could see the carnage her husband was leaving in his wake. She smiled broadly. She had seen him handle hostility before and had always marveled at his calm in dispensing troublemakers.

The sound of a truck engine coming to life mingled with moans and pleas for mercy brought the girls of Mexican Cap out of the fetal position. When Pomp walked through the bus door he was embraced by each and every one on board. Pinky got a similar reception. Crisis averted, bus still disabled.

Pinky finally was able to flag down a passing car for a ride to the nearest town. The girls insisted that Pomp stay with them for security purposes.

Twelve hours later they resumed their journey east. The bus broke down once more, but Pomp was able to crank it back up this time.

They rolled into the Big Apple during the middle of rush hour. A large, obsolete, yellow school bus belching foul black smoke during the morning rush was not well received by many cabbies. Horns blazed, middle fingers flashed, and there were even a few fist pounds on the sides of the bus when traffic jammed. The girls thought it humorous and simply smiled and winked at those so offended.

Arrival and check in at the elegant hotel was relatively uneventful until they entered their rooms. Neither the girls nor their escorts, excepting Uvi, had ever witnessed such luxury. Heated toilet seats? Jacuzzi bathtubs? Silk sheets? Boskinosie Chocolates on their pillows? Uvi was constantly on the move between rooms to try to explain it all. She finally gave up and just watched, enjoying the spectacle of secular overload.

Buford could not take his eyes off of Walli. This was new for her and she liked it, staring shyly at her hands as they sat on the tour bus carrying them to the boat that would ferry them to the Statue of Liberty.

Buford had at first dreaded such a mundane duty as escorting the famous girls from Mexican Cap. While he was great with numbers and solving problems, he was also as shy as a garter snake. People made him extremely anxious and he was only rarely able to communicate effectively with more than one at a time. He had gotten stuck with this when Macy's favorite escort called in sick. He was definitely the last draw after other interns could not step in for other reasons. It was a frantic time at Macy's, these days before the parade, and everyone was engaged with something more important than the next. Buford was stuck. And then he saw Walli.

For the girls, the moment of arrival at the base of the statue was magical. This is what some of their forefathers had sailed by legally, not snuck in under cover of darkness to be used and abused by immoral men and women, not stolen from their home village to be bought and sold like chattel or cattle.

The girls knew that their kind was accused of all manner of deceit and illegal entry into America. It was true for some. Some risked it all for a better life. Some were forced to do it, like they had been. But some had passed under this icon of freedom the way others of all races, creeds, and religions had over the ages.

Uvi pulled the girls aside as best she could and officially declared them part of the latter category in honor of the dangerous, circuitous, tortured journey that had brought them to this official point of entry. She called them as American as herself and home-grown Pomp Peters, and urged them to believe in themselves and their new country, despite its many challenges. She called them citizens of Hardlyville and the US of A, regardless of how they got here and the innocence they had sacrificed along the way. They had earned access to the footprints they now stood in and could revel in the moment. This fiery call to celebration brought tears to eyes, lumps to throats, and applause from total strangers standing close enough to hear or understand.

WELLSPRING OF EVIL

Buford stared even more intently at Walli. He did not want to frighten her or make her feel uncomfortable, but she simply was the most beautiful human being he had ever seen. He was more than smitten. Buford was obsessed. He reacted in a manner he could not explain or foresee.

They ascended to the "Crown" for the penultimate view from whence most immigrants had come back then. Meanwhile Buford backed Walli into a hidden corner. She knew his name from perfunctory introductions but not much else. Just that he kept staring at and through her.

"I love you," quickly got her attention.

Walli wasn't sure what that meant, given her experiences in life. She had heard it whispered by despicable characters as they had their way with her. It had meant nothing to them. Nothing to her. That is what being a sex slave was all about. Nothing meant anything. She got subsistence. Everybody else got her. Until Pomp and Uvi broke the cycle and she got freedom.

And now she was free to do what she wanted.

"I love you," he repeated.

Walli only knew to tell the truth, as Pomp Peters had lectured her.

"I have been with many men," she responded with a sheepish look.

"Doesn't matter," Buford almost spit out. "You are the most beautiful woman I have ever seen and I need to be with you." Buford softly leaned into Walli and kissed her.

She tingled as she never could have imagined, after all of the other countless violent and heartless other times. Buford lit a fire that had never been sparked, let alone stoked, in Walli's young lifetime. She didn't know what lay ahead but her every sense was tingling and alive.

Finally, after all the trials and tribulations, the challenges and the obstacles, their time had arrived. The kids from Hardlyville stepped aboard the Macy's sponsored-and-constructed Mexican Cap Holiday Float. All were outfitted in traditional rural Mexican garb, again supplied by Macy's. They looked authentic and, with the exception of those few much beloved gringos in their party, were the real thing.

The day was bright and crisp, and the crowds were generous with their appreciation of the girls and their talents. Pre-float publicity was purposely vague about the girls' background to avoid embarrassing them, but it was clear to most onlookers that these young ladies of Mexican Cap, Inc. had come a long way from wherever it was they had begun.

Buford, clad in a brightly colored serape and straw sombrero, accompanied them as he had every step of the way since their arrival. He positioned himself as close as he could get to Walli, lightly brushing her small hand at every opportunity. She stared at him with glazed-over eyes. Though no one on board had the slightest idea of what had transpired between them the prior evening, it was hard to miss the sparks that were emanating from each subtle touch.

And then Rosie's water broke. Just like that. During the Macy's Holiday Parade? On the honorary Macy's Mexican Cap float? Half way down 6th Avenue? Almost to the televised area? Say what? Rosetta Flawed's water broke on the float. Followed closely thereafter by a baby. A little boy.

Pinky hoisted his new baby boy to the sky, wrapped in Buford's serape, umbilical still attached. Manhattan loved it. Must be one of those promotions for the re-release of that old Lion King movie, a bystander hollered. Some with gray hair even broke into "Circle of Life," a pleasant memory buried deep within.

Others offered a different take. It was the Christmas Story. Baby Jesus no less. This version rolled like a wave down 6th Avenue, past 38th street. They were now on live television. Startled TV anchors could only mutter that they wished the script had given them a heads-up. They then rushed to report the frenzied crowd's reaction.

It all seemed so real. Blood. Mucus. Afterbirth. Umbilical cord. Baby's cries. The special effects are stupendous, crowed the anchors.

Hallelujahs and Glorias soared heavenward from all corners of the viewing area. Some fell to their knees in wonder. Others thrust their hands skyward in praise. Television programming from other networks was interrupted as commentators broke in to provide their own coverage. It was a profound and emotional New York minute, unlike any in these anchors' memory.

Aboard the Macy's float all was chaos. Rosie's sisters were huddled about her to provide warmth and encouragement. Their cries to "keep pushing" were drowned out by crowd noise. Most were totally confused by the scene around them, wondering what all the hubbub was about. Their "sister" was having a baby, actually two of them, but staging a "Revival" all around was not providing much help. What they actually needed was a doctor. Pomp jumped from the moving float, landing awkwardly and breaking his ankle, then crawling into the crazed crowd screaming for a doctor. One older lady handed him a $20 bill adding the words "bless you." "I'm not a beggar," barked Pomp. "I just need a doctor, and need one now."

Just then Pinky hoisted the second baby up, this one a girl, wrapped tightly in his own undershirt. Twins. One in each hand now.

So much for the baby Jesus theory. It was if the giant Snoopy Balloon had been pricked by a pitchfork. All of the air was sucked out of the crowd.

Someone screamed "terrorist attack." "They are desecrating the baby Jesus," moaned another. *Where was Pastor Pat when you really needed him*, laughed Uvi.

In actual fact, Pastor Pat was where he needed to be. He sat doubled over in laughter, looking on from a heavenly perch, surrounded by a bevy of vestal virgins, marveling at the foibles of the human race he knew, understood, and loved so well.

At least that was the snapshot vision Pomp concocted in his own mind as he lay on the concrete amongst the crazed throng asking the same question. Uvi couldn't stop laughing when he shared it with her days later.

Pomp finally limped back to the float with a real live doc. "Both babies need you now," he shouted into the old fellow's ear. As they hoisted the doctor aboard he saw what he was getting into and quickly took over, cutting umbilical cords, swaddling both babies with any soft materials he could find, and cell-phoning the police to get an ambulance to the finish line. The babies would be okay, he assured Rosie and Pinky, but they needed to be cared for in a proper hospital for several days before they could be released. As did Rosie. As did the guy with the broken ankle who had hunted him down.

The crowd outside had taken on a surly mood, many thinking they had been duped into a humiliating display of irrational fervor. Some were embarrassed. Some were angry. Thankfully the terrorist accusations died down before anyone got hurt. As police gradually cleared the streets, the Hardlyville contingent was left shaking their heads at what they had witnessed and with a pretty strong urge to head home as soon as Rosie and the babies were able.

All except one. Walli went to Uvi and confided in her. She had never met a man like Buford before. He adored her despite her prior circumstance and had asked her to stay with him in NYC. She did not want to appear ungrateful to Uvi and Pomp, and all the Hardlyvillains who had embraced her as family, but she felt she owed it to herself to see if Buford was the real thing.

Uvi suggested that maybe Buford could go back to Hardlyville with them.

Walli had tried that line of reasoning but Buford could not afford to leave his parents who were old and in failing health at this time. He promised to revisit the idea at some point, but not now.

So Walli had only two choices. Stay with Buford or go home to Hardlyville without him. She was seeking Uvi's blessing on staying.

Uvi had never been a mother before. The sex slaves that first Pinky Flawed and then she and Pomp had rescued from the Bo Bevel nightmare were as close as she had come to mothering. She had nurtured, loved, and protected each of them as her own with a ferocity and determination befitting motherhood. She had never been required to face such dilemmas or support or deny their decisions. Until now.

She feared for Walli alone in the big city. She didn't know enough about Buford to fully trust his intentions. Her inclination was to say no. And then the pleading in Walli's eyes triggered the memory of her own reckless addiction to Pomp Peters, and her abandoning all she knew and loved in her native country of Lebanon to follow him to Hardlyville without reservation.

She simply nodded yes, bringing tears to Walli's eyes, followed by a hug from the heart. Uvi prayed that she had done the right thing. And she hoped with all her heart that Buford and Walli would return to Hardlyville at some point. Her own eyes began to tear up and she sobbed as only a mother could.

The remaining time in the big apple passed relatively uneventfully, except for when Walli shared her plans to stay with Buford with her "sisters." They kind of knew something was up when Walli didn't join them for dinner that night or slip into her bed in the hotel late as she had been doing.

Ethel flat out panicked. With "sister" Rosie and Pinky at neonatal in a large NYC hospital, Pomp in post-op for his broken ankle at another large NYC hospital, she had no one to turn to but Uvi, who had slipped out to comfort Pomp at the hospital believing all girls were asleep in their rooms. Uvi hadn't counted on Walli being unable to wait two days to be alone with Buford. Ethel banged on her door and, receiving no response, began to scream, rousing calls to security. She shared in broken English and tearful gasps her concerns about the disappearance of her sister, suspecting that she had been kidnapped.

By the time Uvi returned to her room, NYPD officers were everywhere. The girls were hysterical, trying to explain what even Uvi couldn't grasp. Then in walked Walli.

After the hugs and tears of relief had settled in, Walli explained where she had been and what she was going to do. Her time with Buford had been priceless and she was convinced she finally knew what it was to know love for a man. After so many who had abused and hurt her, she had found a quiet, gentle, caring one in Buford, who treated her with respect and dignity. And with great affection, she confirmed as well with a grin. She could not leave him and would move in with him this very day. She would remain with him for as long as she felt this way.

This elicited another round of shrieks and cries of dismay. She could not leave her "sisters," her network of love and support. She could not trade Hardlyville for the craziness of the Big Apple.

Yes she could, Walli quietly confirmed.

Opal, always the practical one who cut to the bottom line, asked if Buford had used a condom. Walli blushed while shaking her head in the negative. She smiled that she was ready for whatever came of that as well. Uvi could only nod her approval and hark back to the impulsiveness that had landed her in such a happy life in Hardlyville.

And so it was that the Hardlyville girls of Mexican Cap, Inc. and their chaperones set out for home with one less than they arrived. Walli promised to stay in touch and come see them, but all recognized that as a long shot. In the end, they were happy that lonely Walli had found her man. They prayed he was the right one.

The bus only broke down three times on the return trip with no substantial delays or consequences.

After the grand adventure in the Macy's Day Parade, the term "let's go floatin'" took on a whole new dimension in tiny Hardlyville.

CHAPTER 45: DOUBLE DOWN

"How did it happen?" Vixen asked.

"I don't know. I took the little pill every day. But then we did it every day too. Sometimes more than once. Maybe my man overwhelmed the defense with his persistence!" Robin said.

"So you made love with a complete stranger twelve days in a row."

"He wasn't a stranger after day one."

"You little tart!"

"What's a tart?"

"Someone who converts casual sex into a love affair."

"Believe me, there was nothing casual about our exertions."

"Twins, no less?"

"Yep."

"What's with all the twins in Hardlyville?"

"Maybe it's the water?"

"I'm worried."

"Why?"

"What if the evil presence that consumed our mother is lurking in one of us just looking for an escape route?"

"What if the goodness and love that we've been blessed with wants to share our good fortune?"

"How can you be sure?"
"I can't."

— THE END —

Until book Two in the Children of the Creek Series, coming in 2019!

Don't miss the Ozarkian Folk Tales Trilogy!

SKUNK CREEK
~ BOOK I ~

Who knows what lurks in the deep, dark corners of the Ozarks?

A gruesome murder on the banks of adventure story. Populated by the crusading editor of a small-town newspaper, an oversized Sheriff, a lovable band of merry misfits, and an evil cult, an Ozarks village is steeped in beauty, tragedy, love, and lust.

Hardlyville and her colorful, unforgettable Hardlyvillains bring laughter, tears, and celebration of life at every turn as they seek to prevail over natural and unnatural threats to their way of life.

Warning: Do not read if you blush or tire easily. Skunk Creek grabs readers from page one and rushes on through each disaster and fi asco. In the end, love of place and people carry the day to an unlikely conclusion.

Skunk Creek is rowdy, ribald, insightful, and grounded in Ozarks waters and history. It confronts and entertains amidst the vexing questions of our times.

Available in print and ebooks.
Read a free chapter now at
WWW.PEN-L.COM/SKUNKCREEK.HTML

SWINE BRANCH
~ BOOK II ~

The residents of Hardlyville! And what do a local environmental disaster of unprecedented proportions, a series of ghastly murders, corrupt state politics, a Bedouin shivaree, crooked investment bankers, and Noodler's Anonymous have in common? Skunk Creek!

For Sheriff Sephus Adonis, congressman Pierce Arrow, and his true love Lettie Jones, justice is no longer an intellectual concept, it's a matter of life and death. From Hardlyville city hall to Washington, DC's halls of government, to the international stage, resilient Hardlyvillains wage a fierce battle to protect their precious waters and way of life. Hilarity abounds in their madcap and unorthodox rush to remain alive—and relevant.

Swine Branch is rowdy, irreverent, insightful, and grounded in Ozarks waters and history. It confronts and entertains amidst some of the most vexing questions of our times. A worthy follow-up to Skunk Creek.

Get your print or ebook copy now at
WWW.PEN-L.COM/SWINEBRANCH.HTML

Donny Brook
~ Book III ~

The colorful characters of tiny Hardlyville are thrown into a panic when brutal murders, environmental disasters, corruption, and threats to their beloved and pristine Skunk Creek arise and upend their bucolic lives. Larger-than-life Sheriff Sephus Adonis, devoted newspaper editor Pierce Arrow, libidinous librarian Billious Bloom, and Hardlyville's most influential citizens are forced to contend with a community divided by greed and self-interest to solve the riddle of a mother's love vs. inherent evil.

Will the Hardlyvillains stop the murders and save their indispensable water?

Get your print or ebook copy now at
www.Pen-L.com/DonnyBrook.html

ABOUT TODD PARNELL

Todd Parnell began writing nonfiction during his years as a banker and educator, including published books The Buffalo, Ben, and Me, Mom at War, and Postcards from Branson. He is an awardwinning author inducted into the Missouri Writers Hall of Fame in 2012. He tried his hand at fiction upon retiring as president of Drury University and hasn't stopped writing since, completing the Ozarkian Folk Tales Trilogy, published by Pen-L Publishing, and is hard at work on a second trilogy, Children of the Creek.

In his own words, "I've had great fun writing about the Ozarks and tackling important contemporary issues in that rich and captivating context!"

Parnell is a civic leader, environmental advocate, co-founder of the Upper White River Basin Foundation, and retired CEO of THE BANK in Springfield. He recently completed his term as Chairman of the Missouri Clean Water Commission. He holds Masters degrees in Business from Dartmouth University and History from Missouri State University, and is a graduate of Drury University.

Born in Branson, Missouri, Todd is a sixth-generation Ozarker. He resides with Betty, his wife of forty years, in Springfield and is blessed with four children and five grandchildren, so far.

CONNECT WITH TODD AT:
www.ToddParnell.com
Facebook: Todd.Parnell.7

Dear Readers,
If you enjoyed this book enough to review it for Amazon.com or Pen-L.com, I would appreciate it!
Thanks, Todd

More great reads at Pen-L.com

Made in the USA
Middletown, DE
22 May 2019